Holy Water

Also by James P. Othmer

The Futurist
Adland

Holy Water

A Novel

James P. Othmer

Doubleday

New York   London   Toronto

Sydney   Auckland

DOUBLEDAY

Copyright © 2010 by James P. Othmer

All rights reserved. Published in the United States by Doubleday, a division of Random House, Inc., New York, and in Canada by Random House of Canada Limited, Toronto.

www.doubleday.com

DOUBLEDAY and the DD colophon are registered trademarks of Random House, Inc.

Book design by Michael Collica

Library of Congress Cataloging-in-Publication Data
Othmer, James P.
Holy water : a novel / James P. Othmer. — 1st ed.
p. cm.
1. Self-realization—Fiction. 2. Imaginary places—Fiction. I. Title.
PS3615.T48H65 2010
813'.6—dc22
2009027169

ISBN 978-0-385-52513-8

PRINTED IN THE UNITED STATES OF AMERICA

1 3 5 7 9 10 8 6 4 2

First Edition

For Judy

Contents

Riverfire 1

I Here Lies 7
Not a Station 10
The Land of EEEE 15
Nanoabsorbers™ 19
NPB 28
Reverse Outsourcing 34
Test Strip 40
Conceive Now! 45
The Ministry of Meat 50
The Permanent Snip 57
Come on Down 62
I Am the Ghost 66
Poolside 71
Analysis of the Self and the Semen 75
Non-motile 85
Motel Three 89
Snipped 92

II The New Oil 103
His Royal Smallness 111
One Man's Spa 122
Cue the Motivational Video 128

Double Blind   135

Continuous Partial Attention   143

Buddha Clause   151

Suburban Shambhala   155

For Tonight's Performance, Playing the Role of the Disgruntled
    Caller Is the Man Playing the Role of Henry Tuhoe   159

USAVille   164

iVoid   171

There Are No Bonus Rooms in the Ruins of an Imagined Future   175

III   Uninvited Guests   185

"The Lake That Fell Through a Hole in the World   189

Divining Purpose   198

Endorsed (or at Least, to the Best of Our Knowledge,
    Not Yet Officially Condemned) by the Gods   204

Same Cliff, Different Menu   211

Mister Henry   221

Royal Playdate   227

I Say Tomato   238

Home-Cooked   240

Bedfellows   243

Angle of Deterioration   247

IV   Rehearsing the Lie   259

If Sex Is Involved, Altruism Is Not   264

Bullet Points   269

Make-Believe Water   274

Terminated   276

Fahrenheit 212   279

Last Drop   287

Acknowledgments   291

Holy Water

Riverfire

The river is burning down.

Or is it up? The river is burning up. More than a hundred feet up. And since his boat is upwind from the night-burning pit furnaces to the south and stars are shining defiantly in a sky that rarely allows them to and the white-tipped lesser Himalayas loom on either side of the valley to the east and west, he thinks that this is a disturbingly beautiful thing. This riverfire.

They didn't tell him about this phenomenon at the executive briefing in Manhattan. The exit interview at the home office. Nowhere in the Winning Business Abroad Six Sigma PowerPoint presentation does he recall hearing anything about a body of water consumed by flame.

All they told him was, In this economy, be thankful you have a freakin' job.

His groin aches. The epicenter of phantom pains. The karmic vortex. The fleshy receptacle of damaged memories. Formerly known as his testicles.

The fire is highest where debris collects in the crooked river's bend.

He is a big believer in the symbolic weight of what song is playing at a particular moment. And if a song isn't playing, he will assign a song to the moment and force the symbolism, revel in the false epiphany. His suggested sound track for this moment would be Spoon's "The Beast and the Dragon Adored."

"That's beautiful. Is it some kind of welcome ceremony organized by the villagers?" he asks, even though he knows that this isn't some kind of

welcome ceremony organized by the villagers. He knows that the river up here was coated with a black skin of waste that was waiting to burn. Daring someone to light the match.

Like what? The Cuyahoga. Near Cleveland in 1969. He is too young to remember the actual fire but not too young to get his history from R.E.M.'s "Cuyahoga."

This is where we walked, this is where we swam . . .

"It is not a ceremony," explains his corporate liaison/host/executioner. "It is toxic, this river." The man waves at the flaming water as if it is a hyper-kinetic child. "Sometimes it does that."

Henry and the corporate liaison exchange a glance that signals a transition in their relationship. The end of bullshit. Previously the liaison had told him that a pro-democracy demonstration in the capital city was a birthday celebration for the king, that the black ash that fell like nightmare snow on Shangri-La Square was volcanic, and that his country was a human rights champion despite the fact that it still hasn't abolished slavery.

Let's put our heads together, start a new country up . . .

He sees this as a bad thing, this sudden telling of the truth. He decides that the end of bullshit means they no longer care what he thinks. His hosts. His corporate partners. The diminished bureaucrats of a fading monarchy. Because someone to whom they have decided to tell the truth is obviously someone who no longer matters. Out of the corner of his eye he sees the Madison Avenue PR exec brought in to work the same spin magic her firm did for the Beijing Games staring at her out-of-service iPhone and quietly weeping.

He decides to give the corporate liaison another chance to lie. To help matters, he even spells out the premise of the lie for him. "Maybe there was, you know, an accident. A tanker spill or a factory mishap. Perhaps the Chinese . . ."

The liaison shakes his head, lights an American cigarette. "No," he answers. "Even rivers burn. This one . . . toxic, twenty-four seven."

Cuyahoga, gone . . .

No one told him about any of this. No one told him about the corruption, the poverty, the malaprop billboard in the half-built "Free Zone" touting "Quality Manufactured Gods." No one told him that the nonparty constitutional democracy to which he was being extra-sourced was actually an unhinged monarchy which is, when the UN and Amnesty International aren't looking, a dictatorship. No one told him about the delusional, profit- and Bollywood-obsessed despot in waiting. And no one told him that his five-star "spiritual eco-lodge" with a private bathing garden, infinity pool, and extensive spa menu was also a whorehouse that sat on a hilltop less than a mile from a water-challenged village with one occasionally working pump that tapped into an aquifer of the most polluted and, as it turns out, flammable river on the planet.

Which would have been nice, since he works for a recently purchased subsidiary of an American-held bottled water company whose mission statement, printed on the cover of its lavishly produced annual report, is "Bringing fresh water to a thirsty world."

No one told him. But then again, it's not like he'd asked a whole lot of questions.

"What do you put it out with?" Henry asks. The liaison doesn't answer. He just watches the flames.

But the front man from the yet-to-be-dispatched U.S. congressional delegation, a young Republican who vomited over the side of the boat less than ten minutes ago, does have an answer. "You put it out with truth," he says. "And courage."

This elicits laughter from the in-country deal-maker for the biggest brand at the gates, the Walmart delegation, which is just waiting for the proverbial green light. The wink and nod from the palace. He removes from his lips the stem of a silver hashish pipe that had been passed to him by an Australian corporate mercenary. "Courage? My God, son. Don't start going all John McCain on us now."

Randy Newman had a Cuyahoga song too. "Burn on, Big River."

He squirts a glob of Purell into his left palm and rubs as if it can kill nightmares and coups d'état as well as 99.9 percent of most common germs.

Before he left New York he did the most perfunctory of searches. Google. Lonely Planet. An old atlas. It's all he had time for, considering what he left, how fast everything happened. His boss called Galado a chance to start over, an opportunity to lose his inherent wussiness. His boss's boss called it, via e-mail, history waiting to happen, the next Bangalore. Wikipedia called it "a secret and mysterious kingdom, long isolated from international politics and commerce."

"Wow, what a shit-hole," he hears the Walmart guy say as they skirt east of the fire and drift past a shoreline village. Women with buckets are wading into those sections of the water that are not burning. Children are running along the river's edge, keeping pace with the slow-moving boat.

He's not sure where they're taking him. Either to a party in his honor, he thinks, or to kill him, to preserve what's left of theirs.

His soon-to-be ex-wife called it the perfect place for him to suffer the slow and painful death he deserves.

The woman with whom he thought he was falling in love called it something too, but he can't be sure, because she said it in a language he doesn't understand.

He doesn't know and no one told him anything.

Yet here he is. A newly made VP of global water, investor relations, for a company whose headquarters he's never seen, whose founders he just met, and one of them is huddled somewhere in the hold of this boat, on a burning river in a country he didn't know existed three months ago.

As they reverse engines and slow alongside a floating dock at the far end of the village that his suspiciously beaming colleague has just called a shit-hole, he looks at the people gathering to meet them, to throw them a line, their faces aglow with hope and reflected riverfire.

Or is that hate instead of hope?

He listens for the symbolic song to accompany the moment. Perhaps a chant supplied by the locals or faint notes from a far-off boom box. Then, hearing only the wailing of strangers, he attempts to assign one. But this moment needs more than one song, he decides. It needs a sound track. A playlist.

A mix tape for the apocalypse.

I

Here Lies

Depending on where he wakes up, Henry Tuhoe's train ride is either a life-affirming journey through a pastoral wonderland of lakes, woods, and river palisades or an oppressive death trek through the biggest cemetery ghetto in the world.

Today it's all cemeteries. Gravestones of all shapes, denominations, and price tags, a mile-long stretch of a half-million granite guillotines on either side of the tracks, pinching in.

Lately, even on those less frequent occasions when he does happen to awaken and look out upon a glorious stretch of river, the tacking sailboats and tug-drawn barges, he sees nothing. He doesn't see or feel the beauty of any of it. Instead he sees only the slack tide of the river inside him, separating anxiety from despair, and the only thing that he feels is regret. Regret for not having even the smallest urge to take some kind of meaningful action, to pursue something even remotely honest or admirable regarding . . . well, anything.

Which is to be expected when one is living a middle-manager, commuter life at the age of thirty-two, when one's wife, who of late has taken an interest in the occult, recently insisted that one get a vasectomy and then rarely lets one touch her anyway.

This morning, awakening to the gravestones, Henry sits up in his window seat and sees everything. Every plot, every marker, every mass-molded ornament in all of its excessive, maudlin detail. From the crudest unpolished stones, for which even the word *slab* would be an overstatement, to the condominium-sized mausoleums of those who felt obligated to say *fuck you* to their neighbors, even in death.

The song in his headphones is "Fleeing the Valley of Whirling Knives," by Lightning Bolt.

In these first waking moments, as the train jerks and shudders toward Grand Central and the sleeping businessman next to him leaks drool on the keyboard of his laptop, oblivious of the soft-core love scene from a Hong Kong action flick playing on his screen, Henry thinks of how his life to this point has been so precisely planned and ordered, the conscientious fulfillment of limited expectations. So much so that he decides if he were to write down how the next fifty years of his time on earth will play out, he is certain that he would get a troubling amount of it right.

Last week on the 6:18 into Manhattan the train slowed to a stop just below Tarrytown. After ten minutes the engineer announced over the PA that because of police activity on the southbound track they would be backing up and switching to the northbound. Henry sat up and looked out at a gathering of forlorn police and MTA officials contained in a ring of yellow tape, stooping over a body bag just beyond the shelf of the Tarrytown platform. Later that day he read on Twitter that it was a suicide. Not the first track-jumper he'd heard of, but seeing the body bag as dawn broke over suburbia had affected him.

On the way home that night, passing the scene, he thought, If you do it in the morning, you hate your job. If you do it in the evening, you hate whatever it is you're going home to.

Looking back out the window this morning, he can't help but feel that these graves are all his, and that he lies rotting beneath every last piece of stone, every cross, every Star of David, every pedestal-mounted archangel twisting skyward. He lies beneath the faded miniature military flags, the wreaths of white carnations, the single red roses, and the tilted vases of flowers plastic and dead. He lies beneath the rain-smeared Polaroids, crayon notes from children and grandchildren, yearbooks signed by teenagers who weren't in the car that night. Beneath the Barbie dolls and baseball gloves and dog biscuits, the footprints of grave dancers and the stains of grave pissers. Beneath the paperback copies of Wordsworth and Whitman and Danielle Steel, the half-drunk bottles of fine champagne and small-batch bourbon, twenty-five-year-old tawny port and brand-stinking-new Mad Dog 20/20.

He lies beneath all of it, staring into the wet press of earth above.

Henry Tuhoe, all of thirty-two, without the slightest inclination to rise.

Yet he does.

Not a Station

The world is sweating. Billions of gallons a day oozing, dripping, puddling, staining. Beading on foreheads, glistening on backs, trickling down anxious underarms. Sixty percent water, with traces of sodium chloride, ammonia, calcium chloride, copper, lactic acid, phosphorous, and potassium. The universal metaphor for hard work. It's sexy. It's disgusting. And if you happen to be the vice president of underarm research for the world's largest maker of antiperspirants, it's gold.

The world is sweating and it's Henry Tuhoe's job to stop it. Or at least make it smell better.

The rush-hour walk through Grand Central. Madness or beauty, entertaining or terrifying, depending on who you are, where you're going, which path you choose to spit you out onto the concrete of the city, the ambiguity of career.

Not long ago, even before his unfortunate move to the suburbs, Henry would consciously alter his route to avoid the main concourse because he was certain that it would be attacked. Smartbombed or dirty-bombed or lit up with the rush-hour gunfire of a martyr. He used to try to arrive extra early or a little late to avoid the prime-time crush of people, because only an amateur would bring down a landmark off-hours. He used to walk up the ramp from the lower level by the Oyster Bar or take one of the side halls to the east or west. They wouldn't attack there, would they? Could the Oyster Bar ramp have been in their recon photos, their crude schematics? But now he just walks the shortest distance, not because he's suddenly become courageous or defiant or because he feels invincible or the least bit safer. He does it because he's been trying to convince himself that he no longer gives a shit.

The brush of shopping bags against his wilting quadriceps. The smell of fresh bagels and overpriced coffee from the market on the Lex side. A blur of suits. A swirl of skirts. Hints subtle and nauseatingly acute of every imaginable varietal of sweat. Once in a workshop they asked him smell it. They passed around beakers.

He obliged.

At the base of the mezzanine stairs a crew is trying to film stop-motion footage of the crowd for a TV commercial, but in a subconscious expression of what they think about the cinematic cliché, commuters keep bumping into, getting too close to, the camera. Bustling, time-lapsed Grand Central? Show us something we haven't seen. The director, his powers useless in the real world, throws up his hands.

Some days Henry glides through the crowds in perfect sync. Sometimes he plays a game in which he tries to avoid physical contact for the entire workday. On the train he'll sit near the window on a three-seater without fear of being bothered, because on good days people would rather stand than take the middle seat between two other humans. He will dodge bodies walking through Grand Central, and on the sidewalks leading to his office he will slip and slide, juke and glide, eluding contact like a tailback, a Formula One driver, a xenophobic, germ-phobic, paranoid freak.

However, on other days he'll find himself jammed three across on the train and slamming into everyone off of it. He'll attempt to bob and weave, to synchronize movement, to change speeds and anticipate footsteps, but nothing will work.

Today is one of those days. Gathering himself after blindsiding an angry businesswoman while sideswiping a SWAT cop with a bomb-sniffing dog, he wonders if there is any kind of correlation between the cemetery-waking days and the awkward-passage days, or how about between the level of difficulty of the walk to work and the level of difficulty of the day that follows? He decides to make a note of it, which means he'll never think of it again.

He's listening to "Subbacultcha" by the Pixies.

A trade show in the old waiting room, Vanderbilt Hall. Well-scrubbed, blond white girls in old-fashioned Dutch dresses and kerchiefs handing out tulips and four-color travel brochures. Henry thinks Grand Central is so much better now than when he first came through it with his father in the eighties. Transvestites beating off in the men's room then. Foul-smelling squatters in the waiting room. The stars overhead in the main concourse buried beneath generations of diesel soot and cigarette smoke, decades away from restoration.

It's a terminal, not a station, his father had corrected him back then. Stations connect to other places. Terminals terminate. They end.

He accepts a complimentary tulip from a blue-eyed, pink-cheeked girl and asks how the weather is in Holland this time of year, hot and muggy or cool and dry. Armpits of the world want to know. The girl hesitates a moment, looks at the bunched tulips in her hand as if they are a bouquet of roadkill, then looks over her shoulder for help from her team leader. Of course she's not from Holland, Henry realizes. She's just some college kid part-timing for a travel bureau, wearing a costume like a Disney character.

His father was forty-six when he died at a corporate teamwork off-site. Massive heart attack. Jostling among junior execs eager to be the first team member to administer CPR, to catch the eye of the boss. Then a dozen white-collar workers in matching T-shirts that say *No Limits!* carrying his stretcher in a synchronized sprint to the ambulance, the medi-chopper, all thinking, or at least attempting to demonstrate, *Together we can do anything* while the paddles fail and the tiny monitor flatlines.

That's how Henry imagines it, anyway.

He puts up his hand to retract the question, to wave off the not quite Dutch girl, but before he can speak he's jolted by the vibrating phone in his pants. Rachel. He recently told her it has become illegal to use the phone on the train, so now she calls him within minutes after his scheduled arrival.

"Yes?"

"Did you check . . ."

"Yes."

"And the pool?"

"Yes?"

"It's green. Again. Like a fluorescent radioactive green. What did you do?"

"I used the tester. I added the stuff."

"Did you?"

"No. I'm lying. I'm lying about the pool, Rachel."

"When?"

"Last night."

"In the dark?"

"I could do it in the day, but that would mean I'd have to quit my job to be a full-time pool boy."

"I just didn't notice."

"I did it at three a.m. when I woke up downstairs in front of the TV."

"All I know is our pool is disgusting."

He takes a breath. He doesn't want to fight. Doesn't want to feel this way toward her. "You don't even like to swim, Rachel."

"It's an embarrassment. Every other pool on this block is a perfect shade of blue, but ours looks like a Superfund waste site."

"Every pool except at the houses that have been foreclosed. Look, I'll check it again when I get home." He moves to hang up, but reconsiders. "Listen, did you, you know, think about going back to talk to that guy? Philip?" Her shrink.

This time she clicks off. He puts the phone in his briefcase rather than his pocket. She's not a bitch, he reminds himself. She's afraid.

"Actually, I'm not from Holland," the young woman tells him.

At first he has no recollection of speaking to her, no idea what she's talking about. Rachel's calls have a way of doing this to him, detaching him from the present, clouding reality, making him breathless with what he hopes is anxiety, because he's far too young for a heart attack. "But," she says, "I hear it's real sunny this time of year."

He scrolls to Scissor Sisters' cover of Pink Floyd's "Comfortably Numb," taps Play.

The Land of EEEE

Four years ago they transferred him from Oral Care to Non-headache-related Pain Relief. Three years ago they transferred him from Pain Relief to Laxatives. Two years ago he was fast-tracked to Silicon-based Sprays and Coatings and was making quite a name for himself, but when lawsuits not of his making led to the rightsizing of the division (because discontinuing it would send the wrong signal to class-action lawyers), they transferred him to Armpits.

He has a nine-thirty focus group, which leaves just enough time to drop off his briefcase and check his messages. Outside his office sits Meredith, his administrative assistant. "Morning, Meredith."

"You are a sought-after man." Meredith is reading the *National Review*. On her desk, already devoured, are the *Financial Times*, the *Wall Street Journal,* and the *Daily Racing Form*. Meredith's auburn hair is pulled back, as it is every day, in a bun. A 1950s librarian's bun. Her loose-fitting skirt suit makes her look short and, if not exactly fat, then chunky. But Henry knows better.

"Who's doing the sought-aftering?"

"The emperor of eccrine glands."

"The armpit czar."

"Aka Doctor Sweat."

"Aka Giffler." He loves this machine-gun give-and-take. He loves the way it makes him feel as if they really know each other, as if he's one of the regular guys, nice to coworkers above and below, even though Meredith, a five-year employee of the firm, looks up to no man.

Meredith thinks the give-and-take is banal. "You got it. Giffler."

"His mood?"

"Bloodcurdlingly chipper. He said he'll stop in on your nine-thirty."

Henry rolls his eyes. Poor me. Poor us. Meredith looks away, turns the page. The ironic rolling of eyes, the office politics of Henry Tuhoe and Giffler and the rest of them: beneath her.

His office has a decent view of Park Avenue facing east, but he doesn't bother to look anymore, unless there's a demonstration in the street or an aerial view of a tragedy. Like the runaway cab that killed three on the sidewalk last month. They gathered in his office, Giffler, Meredith, the rest of Armpits, not because Henry is the one they all run to for calm and assurance in a crisis, but because his office has the best view. That's the type of thing that seems to bond them now. Fatalities on the street below. Rumored and unexpected layoffs. So-and-so's cancer scare. The collapse of a market, an industry, a way of life.

On those occasions they'll gather and talk. They'll inquire about non-underarm-related, occasionally personal topics. They'll linger and joke, briefly revealing intimate aspects of their lives while chalk lines are drawn on the sidewalk below, gurneys loaded and lifted.

By contrast, the supposedly happy occasions—the baby showers in the seventh-floor conference room, the champagne toast for a job well done, and the soon-to-be-extinct ritual of after-work drinks—have the opposite effect on their relationships, their morale. Those rituals bore them, crystallize their sources of anger, and are breeding grounds for future resentment. She's making how much? They had sex where? The nerve, taking the corporate jet with more cuts to come. It's gotten to the point where even the people being honored can't finish their Carvel cake and warm Korbel and get out of there fast enough. Or maybe this is just how Henry has begun to see it.

He closes the door, hangs up his jacket, and turns on his laptop. Standing, he bends over the keyboard. He has twenty-nine e-mails, but he's not interested in them. E-mail now has all the urgency of snail mail, yet nothing, not Facebook or Tumblr or Twitter, has risen to replace it. He opens his Web browser and peeks up to look through the frosted glass of his interior windows. Meredith is standing, talking to someone. Through the lens of frosted glass she's relegated to a vaguely defined shadow, but on his desktop screen Meredith is about to become something altogether different.

On a heart-shaped ruby red splash page with an adult content disclaimer, Henry clicks EEEEnter. He begins to ease himself into his seat, ready to enjoy the opening montage—which consists of Meredith's alter ego, tanned, heavily made up, topless on a Harley, topless as a cheerleader, a dominatrix, schoolteacher, nurse, commando, construction worker, trial judge; Meredith poolside, oceanside, in the rain forest, in the cab of a bulldozer, on a mansion roof, beside the broken white passing line of Route 66—when, to his surprise, "Steady as She Goes" by the Raconteurs begins playing on his speakers, loud enough to cause the shadow blobs outside his office to react. He quickly mutes her audio intro, looks at the window to make sure he hasn't blown his cover. When the blobs outside seem to have stabilized, he slouches into his multi-adjustable, lumbar-supporting swivel chair, for which he feigned to Office Services a chronically bad back, and begins reading the wit and wisdom of the home page.

Welcome to the Land of EEEE. Home of EEEEVA EEEENOR-MOUS and her 46EEEE Twins. And there she is, Meredith who is not at all short or fat, or even chunky—unless you're talking about her breasts, still topless—straddling some kind of missile, smiling more brightly than she or anyone else has ever smiled in this building.

Henry clicks to the What's New VIP page, but there's nothing new, really. At least, not since end of day yesterday. Just some additional, never-before-seen shots from a months-old naughty accountant layout. No new message for her loyal subscribers. No breaking career news or video updates. Maybe if she'd stop reading the damned financial pages, Henry thinks. He shuts the machine down and stands up.

Back outside, Meredith doesn't acknowledge him as he walks

by. She continues talking to Giffler's admin, a gay temp named Brad who could probably run the whole division if he were more interested in making a living and less interested in full-time clubbing. *If you only knew what I know about the young woman to whom you're talking, Bradley.* Indeed, if anyone knew. *But your secret is safe with me, EEEEva.*

"I'm off to the Oven," he says over his shoulder.

Meredith briefly considers Henry before turning back toward clueless Brad.

Nanoabsorbers™

The Oven is the 101-degree-Fahrenheit observation room in which focus group participants are paid in the area of $75 to spend approximately two hours applying product and having their armpit sweat measured. An insensitive nickname, especially at a New York–headquartered company with more than 11,000 Jewish employees worldwide, but it is accurate.

On Henry's side of the glass it's a comfortable seventy-two degrees. He grabs a Snapple from the mini-fridge on the back wall and picks up the spec sheet on the participants. Women, aged twenty-four to thirty-four, median income of $30,000. As they file in, he tries to match the specifics of their lives to their nametags. Hobbies, jobs, marital status, children. Stick, roll-on, or aerosol. Hygienic rituals. Brand affinities.

He's disappointed that none seem particularly attractive, although it's hard to tell, since most of them are wearing sweatshirts and who looks good in a sweatshirt in 101-degree fluorescent light? That will soon change, when the heat begins to register and they have to apply the product, which in this case features an innovation called Nanoabsorbers™, which isn't really an innovation as much as a new name for an old technology, which isn't really a technology as much as it is a bunch of loosely regulated, decades-old, sweat-blocking chemicals or ingredients, one of which is active.

Typically they'll apply product, overheat the humans, and micromeasure how much sweat is released, but today the test is more about the word *Nanoabsorbers*™ and the perceived increase in dryness that hearing the actual word and watching three short computer-generated Nanoabsorbers™ demo films (variations on swirling, swarming molecules sopping up waterborne evil from free-floating, disembodied armpits) bestows upon the subjects. Someone in name generation came up with the word, and everyone creamed all over it. Moniker testing was through the roof, and now it's just a matter of finding the right ingredients, the right product, to invent around the word.

When he first started in Armpits, Henry found sessions like this degrading for parties on both sides of the glass. He felt dirty when the participants, especially the women in the twenty-four-to-thirty-four demo, would glance his way through the two-way mirror. That first glance, or glare, really, before they became desensitized to the environment and caught up in the throes of ego and opinion, always made him feel ashamed. They looked angry, as if they knew they were about to be violated and dehumanized, all for $75 and as many soft drinks and salty, trans-fat-based snacks as they could consume. The stifling heat didn't help their moods, either. He used to look away when they made that initial stroll by the mirror. He used to think about what their lives must be like outside of the Oven, beyond the spec sheet. What music did they listen to, how many brothers and sisters did they have, had they ever had an affair, where were they on 9/11? But now he just tries to predict which of them will have the most active eccrine and apocrine glands. Which will sweat more profusely than all the others.

Sometimes they bet on it. Five bucks a head. Draw numbers to determine who goes first. Sometimes they do the over/under version, but usually it's sheer volume that makes for the most interesting competition. Winner takes all in the sweat pool. But this morning he's alone in the dark room as the subjects do the stroll and sulk. And even as they reluctantly start removing their sweatshirts (with one more obligatory glare for the perv on the other side), he's not interested in any of it.

He just wants to get it over with.

The door in back of the room swings open. As yellow hall light seeps in, Henry averts his face from the group on the other side, because anything less than total darkness on his side will expose him as the solitary underarm voyeur he is. He sees Giffler's face for an instant before his boss shuts the door, depriving the room of light.

At first he's just a voice. "How do they look? Anyone bangable?"

Henry laughs, then regrets it, then feels disgusted with himself because he knows that while Giffler's words are offensive, particularly when spoken in the hallowed workplace, he thought the same thing moments earlier.

Giffler reaches for the volume. "Mind if I turn this shit down?"

"Sure. If I miss something, I can check the tape."

"They tape everything now, eh? Or record, because I doubt anyone tapes much of any fucking thing anymore. What they ought to do if they want to learn anything is tape-slash-record what goes on *this* side of the mirror. I heard Dworik did a moderator against the glass last week while a baby-wipes group was in progress on the other side."

"Wonderful. Quite the role model."

On the other side women are removing their outer garments, revealing the sleeveless T-shirts and tank tops they were requested to wear. "Look at the cans on her. Jesus."

Henry turns and looks with lust. Doesn't look. Then looks without lust. He goes through the whole outrage/guilt/self-loathing ritual again.

"I wonder if there's a link between tata size and volume of underarm sweat. Or type of odor. For instance, do chicks with fake tits smell different? That's a piece of research I'd like to oversee."

"I'm sure Dworik would green-light it."

"So why am I here, you ask."

"All the time," Henry replies, watching the women apply the generic stick product with the Nanoabsorber™ logo.

"Tell me that's not erotic? Even the ugly ones. Were you here back in the day when we did the hairy group? Four weeks' armpit bush minimum to get in. Even that you can't help but find—"

"So you've told me." Henry thinks if the DVDs from the hairy armpit sessions just happen to come up missing from the archives, he'll know where to look first.

"Anyway, I'm here to tell you that you owe me a great old big one. A huge fucking one."

"Okay."

"Because . . ."

"Because . . ."

"Because I saved your ay-yass, Tuhoe. As we have this conversation that never happened, your whole level, most of this division, is being outsourced to fucking Bangalore, India."

"They can't do that."

"Or Hungary. I forget. Some are going to Budapest and Prague and some to India. Anyway, I know. It's an outrage. Makes one sick. Blah-blah-blah."

"India? What do they know about what we do here?"

"They have armpits too. Besides, most of R & D is going to be humanely put down. Should have done it long ago. They're going to stick with basically repackaging and repositioning what we've got. I mean, you're only allowed to stop thirty percent of the sweat by law, and we can do that in our sleep, so what other mountain is there to climb in the world of sweaty pits?"

"They can't outsource my job. I deal with clients and customers every day. I innovate. Some kid in India can't do that over the phone."

"Oh yes he can. And for one tenth the price."

"That's bullshit. I'm a knowledge worker. A right-brainer. Even in this economy, Dan Pink and Thomas Friedman say knowledge workers are untouchable."

"We've already outsourced the entire Eye Care Division."

"That's not true. I just spoke to Warren last night. We had lunch yesterday. He's all excited about—"

Giffler puts his hand to his mouth. "Whoopsy. I forgot that pit-sniffers and eyeballers occasionally cross-pollinate. Forgot he was your friend. So I misspoke. Let's forget I said that. Actually, I never did say it, you lying bastard. Eye Care is rock-solid. Warren is golden. Safe as ever."

"He's in his office. I passed it this morning. He's not out-sourced."

"Oh yes he—or the hypothetical employee whom we'll call *Warren*—is. Off the record, someone in Bangalore or Mumbai or perhaps Prague is doing his job right now for pennies on the dollar. We're just being redundant for a little while to make sure it doesn't bite us in the ass with some kind of cultural glitch, or typhoon, or Pakistani warhead. So don't tell him."

"He's one of my closest friends in the company. And you should know that unlike everyone else in this place, Warren loves his job."

"Right. Real American tragedy. This goddamn outsourcing. Soon we will outsource ourselves to death as a nation. Anyway, tell him and you're fired too."

"What about Nanoabsorbers™?"

Giffler looks at the ceiling for cameras, mics. He bends down, cuts his flat hand across his throat. "Already causing problems in white mice."

"Too much sweat?"

"No. Massification."

"What?"

"Growths."

"Tumors?"

"Your word. I'm sticking with massifications."

"Which technically is not a word."

"Which technically is why I have a particular affinity for it."

"But it's the same ingredients as always, reconstituted."

"All I know is something went kaflooey and they're pulling the plug. Your entire division is being rightsized."

"Layed off. Fired. Wrongsized."

"Think up a better word for it, a more employee- and economy-sensitive phrase that big business and cable hosts will embrace, and we'll make millions. We'll write a book."

"Pillow-fucked, redundafired, gangBangalored."

"Should have seen it coming. Asia rising. China. India. Shit, I've already got our nanny making our two-year-old watch every Chinese-language and Bollywood piece of shit she can get her hands on. *Bend It Like My Big Fat Crouching Hindu Wedding*. To understand those cultures is to be eternally wealthy."

"So why not me?" Henry speculates about the package the others have been given, wonders if maybe being an outsourcing victim is just the fashionable kick in the ass his life needs right now. A chance at a fresh start. Away from focus groups, team meetings, armpits, or worse: Giffler.

"Because you were right is why. You *are* a bit of a knowledge worker. Your previous job, the one you were doing five minutes ago, was not a knowledge job per se. Anyone can stand here and whack off while chicks apply things to their naked sweaty pits. I did it for years. But your supplementary skills, they can't be replicated."

Henry stares through the glass. He thinks one of the participants is saying she feels dizzy, but because she's saying it while looking into her armpit it's hard to read her lips. "You know," he says, "there are probably employees who would volunteer to be, you know, rightsized, if the package were enticing enough."

"Indeed there are. And those are precisely the ones we cannot afford to lose. Those who want to leave us of their own volition but lack the courage or bank account to do so are indispensable. Beloved."

"For instance, I know someone who would love that, um, opportunity."

"Not gonna happen, Tuhoe."

"So where am I being transferred to? Dental? Bath and Body? Chemical Weapons?"

"Here's a hint: two thirds of the earth is covered with it."

"Bullshit?"

"Hint number two: two thirds of the people on this great planet can't get enough of it."

"I'm being transferred to the Department of Bacon? Please, rightsize me, Giffler. Downsize me. GangBangalore me. Offer me a package. Make me a victim of whatever euphemism for shit-canned Human Resources can come up with."

Giffler laughs, but shakes his head.

"Water?"

"Yes, sir."

"We don't even have a water division."

"Do now. Like . . ." Giffler counts on his fingers. "Like six. They're buying up companies like there's no tomorrow. Like when they had to play catch-up with the whole trans-fat scare. Twentygrain this. Organic that. Some number-crunching muckety-muck must have told the C-suiters between lap dances at their favorite upscale gentleman's sports cabaret that water was the future. A tremendous quote-unquote long-term growth driver. So they've been on a tear."

"Water? I'm not—"

Giffler waves him off. "We're talking the sustenance of billions. It's over my head, but they told me that by 2025, five billion of the world's nine billion people will be facing a scarcity of clean water. So there's big money to be made. Every time you take a shower, a drink, or a shit, someone somewhere's going, *Ca-ching!*"

"I have no background in water."

"Not true. Did you not minor in geology at Northeastern?"

"Christ, Giffler."

"If Americans continue to use their current average of one hundred gallons per day, thirty-six states will have significant shortages by 2013."

"So I'd be focusing on what, the Southwest? Arizona, California?"

Giffler shakes his head. "There'd be some traveling."

"I hate traveling. You know that. I hate flying. I hate leaving New York. Where, then?"

"I'm not at liberty to say. But you might want to gain some proficiency with chopsticks."

"Japan?"

"And get your malaria, your bird, your swine flu shot. Your Ebola booster, if there is such a thing."

"I will not go to China."

"Not China or India per se. From what I hear. Wonderful cultures, though. On the rise. My guess is that someplace that is impoverished, polluted, riddled with disease, and even more economically flawed than we are would be your quote-unquote territory. But what do I know?"

"I have no knowledge of the industry, the languages. I know nothing about those cultures. I hate travel. Plus you know that I have a huge problem with germs."

"These are some of the most fertile economies in the world

we're talking about. It is the Asian century, Tuhoe. You'll probably just be a relationship placeholder until they figure out what they're really gonna need, but think of how you can exploit that on your résumé."

"Placeholder?"

"Let's call it investor relations. VP of global water, investor relations, let's call it. Talk about fulfilling. You could actually be doing something that makes a difference."

"So it's what—desalinization? Ultra-filtration? Some new way to help people in the third world have access to fresh water?"

"Bottled, actually."

"We're going to give them bottled—"

"No. Not them. You're going to help them learn customer relations and set up a customer call center for a U.S.-based bottled water company. More back-office stuff than anything. But still, terribly important."

"Which company?"

"Oh, you know. The one that fucking hippie lesbian couple started in Vermont."

"Happy Mountain Springs? They're privately held."

"Were. Apparently even save-the-planet hippie lesbians have their price. Of course, they're contractually obligated to stay on as the face of the company for three years and let us use their likenesses."

"Why do you need me if you're outsourcing it?"

"Someone's got to *set up* the outsourcing. Teach the locals how to perform as cluelessly as our customer service people in Lincoln, Nebraska—for a quarter the salary, of course."

"Jesus, Giffler."

"Let's call it presourcing. Much more 2010, much more marketable than outsourcing."

"I'm not gonna do it."

"Fine. Just remember that refusal to accept a plum assignment like the one that has just been hypothetically proposed to you would constitute a breach of contract that would result not in a rightsizing, or laying-off, or the gift of a package or parachute, golden or otherwise, but in a good old-fashioned 'You're fired and Luther here from Security is giving you six minutes to clean your sorry personals out of your desk and get your ass out of the building.' Hypothetically, of course."

"What about you? What are they doing with you?"

"Me? I'm firing people, mostly. But until the day comes when I must outsource my despicable self, I'll be your U.S.-based boss and life coach."

"I'm not gonna do this, Roger. I've got so much shit going on at home. I can't . . . My wife and I aren't even . . ."

Giffler puts up his hands. "Here's what I'm gonna do. Take the rest of the day off. Go home and talk it over with Raquel."

"Rachel."

"Take tomorrow too if you'd like. I'll give you two days to come to a decision. And you know why?"

"Because you love me like a son."

"Bingo!" A blade of light slices the darkness, then vanishes as Giffler closes the door.

Henry stares at his reflection, his face ghosted over the scene on the other side. On the far right a body wobbles, crumples to the ground. As two other participants grab the woman under her arms and try to lift her off the Oven floor, the moderator flails with both hands up at the projection booth. At first Henry thinks it's to call for an ambulance or to tell someone to lower the heat. But when he sees the moderator draw her fingers across her neck, he realizes that she's telling them to kill the camera.

NPB

Henry's phone is vibrating in his pants. Rachel, making her presence felt.

She knows that he had the focus group and that, according to Henry, the cell phone is off-limits in focus groups, so he doesn't pick up, even though he's no longer in the focus group, even though he's no longer at work. He doesn't know how the phone got back into his pants. He remembers stashing it in his briefcase but has no recollection of taking it back out, returning it to his pocket. Does it have a homing device? Some kind of boomerang function?

Walking down Park toward Thirty-third, he checks his watch and figures he's got an hour, maybe two, before he absolutely has to get back to her, and by his calculations, if he gets it right, he can call when she'll be unavailable in a videoconference with clients.

Not long ago he'd have been the one calling Rachel. Seeking her counsel, telling her everything. Not long ago, if he'd gotten a chance to scoot home early, regardless of the reason—promotion, transfer, early dismissal—he'd have pounced on it. He'd have picked up a bottle of cab and some Jarlsberg and Amy's Bread and told Rachel to finish up early to meet him. But now going home early is the last thing that he wants to do, because Rachel, a respected independent Internet security consultant, very much in demand, works out of the house, and rare is the day, no matter what the hour, that she's not home when Henry walks through the door. Before they moved out of the city he used to say he'd go crazy if he had to spend so much time in the suburbs, no matter how interesting the work. But now she assures him that she's living a dream, telecommuting, videoconferencing with Kuala Lumpur in her slippers and cloud pj's, doing every preposterous thing the tech commercials promised, all the dreams they assigned us to live. And now, of course, the irony or coincidence is that she's the one who's going crazy and living a lie, not a dream.

One option would be to go to a bar and drink himself silly, but he isn't much of a drinker, and when he's stressed alcohol hits him in the worst way. So, with his phone again vibrating in his pocket, he's heading toward the gym, and he is listening to "Novocaine for the Soul" by the Eels.

The clientele in the gym at eleven a.m. is quite different from what you'd see at, say, six a.m., or six p.m. These aren't the sweat-soaked type As grinding out Thing One on the day's to-do list before heading to work. These aren't the lean and jovial early risers, with notebooks and heart monitors and bottles filled with secret concoctions. At eleven a.m. the gym is almost empty.

The young woman at the front desk doesn't look up when he swipes his membership card, or when he waves or says good morning. Eighties monster rock is the sound track for those who dare exercise without iPods. Journey, Henry thinks, but he can't be sure. En route to the locker room he checks out the free-weight area. Two unemployed bodybuilders are doing dead lifts in the far corner. Near the dumbbell rack a Jack LaLanne–like seventy-five-year-old man in a purple-and-white-striped unitard is doing preacher curls, ogling his blood-engorged biceps at the peak of each four-count rep, mocking age, gravity, and the spirit of all things weak and flabby. In the empty yoga studio a Botoxed, liposucked, and tummy-tucked fifty-year-old woman is practicing spin kicks targeted at, Henry thinks, the testicles of imaginary men. The ghosts of husbands past, present, and yet to come.

He stands naked before the mirror in the empty locker room, appraising his enigmatic body. Arms and shoulders still defined, still strong at thirty-two, despite some seven years at a desk job, ten since he last played third base, in college. Legs lean and muscled, but less so since he stopped mountain biking. But his abs, or more specifically the belly that covers them, are something in which he can take less pride. Not fat, but loose, settling in a roll on his hips, rounding out beneath his navel.

On other days, when he looked at his belly he thought of defibrillators and fat-clogged arteries in waiting, of corpulent bodies sprouting tubes in ICUs. He felt a certain age creeping in and another slipping away.

But today his wistfulness is focused on his testicles. Almost six weeks since they were shaved in preparation for surgery, three since the last of the prescribed icings. They're once again covered with fine brown hair, once again looking very much like Henry Tuhoe's testicles of old. Yet despite this superficial return to testicular form, Henry feels a rumbling churn in his lower abdomen just thinking about them, a knifing pain in the top of his skull just looking at them. And when he lets his left hand drop to touch them, to gently tumble them like Queeg's steel balls, he feels as if he's holding not a surgically altered reproductive organ but two tiny bombs planted by terrorists of the self, waiting to blow his life apart.

Not Journey. Foreigner: "I Want to Know What Love Is."

When he looks back up, balls still in hand, Henry sees the reflection of the old muscle man in the purple-and-white unitard staring at him with a disgusted look on his face.

"Five, six, seven, eight."

Henry is on his back on the bench press, listening to the voice of Norman, his personal trainer. But he's not lifting anything. Hasn't since the count of two. The bar sits racked above his head; his breaths are silent and regular, not the breaths of someone working hard.

"Nice job, Henry. Really excellent," says Norman, who agreed to see Henry on short notice because he had nothing better to do.

"Really?"

"Yeah. You're making real progress."

"What if I told you I didn't do a rep after two?"

"I'd be shocked and offended, Henry. I'd consider it a breach of an understood trust. One more set, then we'll do some, what? Some incline." Henry pumps out a set of twelve reps. When he sits up, he sees that Norman is staring across the gym at an unoccupied hack squat machine, and that he is crying.

At first he tries to ignore it, to pretend he hasn't noticed that his personal trainer, the man he pays $30 an hour to get him energized, motivated, and physically transformed, is crying. Again. He's also trying to ignore the fact that Norman is wearing street clothes: black polyester slacks, an untucked black button-down shirt covered with yellow daisies, and flip-flops that have a bottle opener built into the sole. But Norman's sobbing now, and Henry's afraid if he doesn't at least acknowledge this, things may escalate to a genuine scene, a spectacle, and the last thing he wants is to attract the attention of the disgusted old musclehead and the kickboxing man-hater.

"Norm?"

"Yeah. Give me a second. You did great. That an NPB?"

"Norm?"

"A new personal best?"

"Christ, Norman. I don't know. Why are you crying?"

"Just some tough times, Henry, man. I just feel sometimes kind of down, you know?"

"Is it because you're, you know, taking downers again?"

Norman scratches the dry, thinning hair of his scalp, which looks like it needs a good scratching. "Painkillers. Not downers. Percocet. Mostly they help a lot, but sometimes even though the physical pain subsides the mental anguish lingers, and sometimes, I guess, comes up and devastates my ass, mentally."

"Uh-huh."

"Hey, did you see my latest film?" Norman is talking about the latest of many short films he has shot and posted on YouTube and several of other aggregate, viral video sites.

Henry has seen it—a four-minute, genre-defying video featuring an inferno of spider monkeys, icebergs calving in reverse, the poetry of Billy Collins, and a mock German techno track that he couldn't get out of his head for days—but he tells Norman no, he has not had the chance.

"Well, check it out when you get home and vote, vote, vote! If I want to get a development deal, I need to show I have a following. I told you I talked to that ex-client of mine with the friend who knows that documentary guy, the child prostitute guy?"

"Yeah. You've been taking these, um, painkillers for what? Six months at least, right?"

"This time around? Sure. About that. Okay. Let's keep it moving while we talk, Henry. Let's keep the energy positive."

While they set up the incline bar, Henry stops and turns to Norman. He's holding a forty-five-pound plate. "I don't know what to tell you, Norman. I mean, you know you can't do this. You know you have to quit. And Percocet, you can't just do cold turkey. You need some kind of help."

"How are you set for protein powder these days?"

"All set. What do your other clients think when you start sobbing in the middle of their workout?"

"Well, that's the thing . . ."

"What do they think when you neglect to give them a spot? Or don't pay attention to their set while they're lifting? And your personal trainer–slash–Colombian drug dealer outfit—what do they think of that?"

Norman tugs at the bottom of his shirt, shrugs.

"When we first started two years ago, you were built, Norman, you had this whole sleek-white-Adidas-warmup-suit thing going. You were motivating. You shaved."

"I actually thought of something cool for you. Involves tossing a sort of medicine ball and tying your ankles together with a piece of string."

"I saw *Rocky* too, Norman. You can do better than that."

Norman watches Henry slip clamps onto the bar. He sits on a nearby bench and puts his head in his hands. The old guy is coming out of the locker room again, unshowered and in street clothes, and he is looking their way.

"What, Norm?"

"That's the thing. I don't have any other clients right now. You're pretty much it. The owner lets me do a spinning class on Tuesdays, but since I kind of spit up in my mouth during the warm-up last month, I don't even ride anymore. I just spin good music and talk all kinds of smack while I walk around the room with one of those Britney Spears headsets on."

Henry wonders if he should tell Norman that his only remaining client is about to be fired, or at the very least transferred to the bottom half of the third world. He leans back and does a set on the incline bench. The same weight as usual, but it rises and lowers with ease. After his twelfth rep he glances at Norman, who is looking somewhere far away, so he decides to keep going and bangs out another five reps. When he's done he looks to Norman for recognition, a glimmer of positive reinforcement, but now he's text-messaging someone. After thirty seconds Henry grinds out another set and feels even stronger. This time he doesn't look to Norman or anyone for approval, and when he guides the weights down he feels a warm, uncomplicated, guilt-free rush of endorphins, all of his own making.

"Where do you get them?"

"The painkillers? Clients. Ex-clients, actually. Why? You want?"

He thinks. Not so much about the painkillers but about his own situation at work, at home, and with his balls, and how he doesn't know what to do, how to feel about any of it. Of course he won't mention any of this to Norman. But if not Norman, then who?

"I'm just kidding," Norman says. Then: "Hey. How's work, Henry? Still the absolute pits?"

Norman laughs so enthusiastically at his joke that this time the old man and angry kickboxing woman both turn to stare at them. "You're a funny man, Henry. I mean it. Without fail, after our sessions, I always feel so much better."

Reverse Outsourcing

Only when an office is consumed by the maudlin does it become remotely interesting.

He'd tried to come up with a reason for returning, such as claiming to have forgotten a valuable document or needing to complete a mission-critical task. But unless a cruel joke has been played on him, there are no more valuable documents in his portfolio, there is no mission-critical anything to be done in the soon-to-be-extinct Underarm Research Division.

He's returning because he doesn't have anywhere better to go.

Dworik, the CEO, and three executive handlers are on the up elevator. Henry wonders if Dworik knows that one of the men he's in the process of firing or shipping around the world for no apparent reason is standing alongside him. Then again, he wonders if Dworik even knows who he is. It's only been seven years, after all.

Just before the door opens on the executive floor, Dworik looks at Henry. He turns his right thumb and forefinger into a pistol. "Underarms, right?"

"Yes, sir. At least for the moment."

Dworik blinks and tilts his head like a dog listening to a harmonica. He doesn't quite understand and doesn't do a very good job of hiding it. Has this young man been fired? Is he quitting? Or something else? This is why he usually shies away from spontaneous downward-directed small talk. Always ends up with the big guy being made to look bad, one way or the other.

As Dworik steps off the elevator he looks to his handlers, one of whom whispers into his ear, presumably about the impending fate of the employees of the aforementioned Underarm Research Division. As he's hustled away Secret Service–style from a potentially ugly employee-CEO confrontation, Dworik glances back one last time, and his face contorts into the most artificial smile Henry has ever seen, a smile that somehow manages to convey every type of emotion but sincerity—fear, loathing, disgust, hate, and contempt—all punctuated with a double thumbs-up gesture.

Meredith looks up as Henry rounds the corner.

"I had to come back," he says, then adds with what he wants her to think of as his trademark sarcasm, "Can't stay away from this place."

Her look tells him that his trademark sarcasm, always weak at best, barely qualifies as sarcasm under the circumstances. She knows, sadly, that it is true. He can't stay away from this place. And something that is so thoroughly true cannot be considered sarcastic. She also knows that his job is not that difficult and that lately he's been staying in his office much more than necessary because he does not want to go home. She knows that his most recent personal days were for a vasectomy and that his wife calls him with obsessive frequency and varying degrees of hysteria on his work and cell phones and that he is a paid subscriber who regularly checks in on her Web site, sometimes up to ten times a day. Her Web traffic reports tracked them right back to the corporate server and his hometown cable provider.

"Anyone call? Anything going on?"

Meredith also knows that he's been given an ultimatum between China or India or wherever the hell they're sending him and unemployment. She knows the Underarm and Eye Care Divisions are being outsourced to India. She knows that Henry knows that Dworik banged a demographer in the focus group room during a baby-wipes session last week. And she knows that Henry knew that their friend Warren in Eye Care was going to get the ax this morning yet waved at him as if everything were wonderful when he walked past his office. "Nope," Meredith says. "No calls. And do you really want me to tell you what's going on in this place?"

Henry thinks about this for a second. Looks into her eyes. He's trained himself to do this, because he's paranoid about getting busted for staring at her breasts. "No," he says. "I guess that's the last thing I want to know."

He closes his door and stares out his window onto Park Avenue. There's a mentally ill man standing on the median at Forty-sixth, his regular station for this time of day, waving a dog-eared Bible and screaming doomsday prophesies that Henry cannot hear. To the south, cars slide toward the traffic arch under the New York Central building and slip into its dark portal as if, he thinks, into some kind of urban genocide machine.

When he turns around, Warren from Eye Care is standing in the doorway with Meredith. "If the windows weren't hermetically sealed, would you?"

Henry smiles. "The old ones in the conference room on eight open just fine. So if you don't mind landing in an alley . . ."

"You waved at me when you walked by this morning. Twice."

"The first time I didn't know."

"The second?"

"Giffler slipped. He told me to pretend I didn't hear it and then denied that it was going to happen at all."

"Which you knew was a lie."

"When did he tell you?" Henry asks.

"Two minutes after he left the focus group. Right after he told you not to tell anyone."

Meredith backs up a step. "I guess I'll be leaving."

"No," Warren says. "Stay, Meredith. Don't you want to know who else is getting axed?"

"Well, for starters," Henry replies, "I am. Or at least I've been given an ultimatum. But don't worry, Meredith. I imagine you'll be moving somewhere else once I'm gone."

Warren looks at Meredith, who pretends that all of this is news to her. "I feel like a jackass, Henry."

Henry waves him off. "They're overhauling this division too.

The deal is I can either take a call-center job in some kind of newly acquired bottled water division in a third world nation, or refuse and be fired."

Meredith says, "You hate to travel, Henry, and aren't you a bit of a germphobe?"

He smiles. Even now, all he can think of is her boobs. Boobs, boobs, boobs.

"What will you do?" she asks.

"One week severance per year." Boobs. "Right, Warren?"

"Correct. I know how I'm spending mine."

"Really? Giffler's giving me two days to think about it. But I've already made up my mind. Beside the fact that Rachel and I are already ass-deep in debt and our house is worth half what we paid for it and I have no discernible skill beyond being guardian of the psychological secrets of parity hygiene products, I'm kind of looking forward to getting out there and maybe, you know, actually stumbling upon something that doesn't make me feel completely ashamed of myself."

Warren closes the door and walks closer to Henry. "So you're saying you didn't like your job here?"

"Don't. Didn't. Never will. You knew that, Warren."

Warren looks at his hands and shakes his head. "You always said it, but I thought that was just white-collar bravado."

"The work we do here gives white collars a bad name. We're like bureaucratic clerks in a Kafka novel."

"Then why have you stayed here so long?"

"Because I'm an asshole. Because I didn't know what else to do. And not just with the job, with everything. You say you like it, but you're telling me you truly enjoy what you do, Warren?"

"*Enjoy* does not do justice to how I feel about my job. I love the mission statement, the product mix, the day-to-day responsibilities. I love the research, the customer interaction, the *Eureka!* moment that comes with a genuine insight. I never wanted a promotion or a transfer. I wanted to do this, customer insights, Eye Care, for the rest of my life. And that's what I intend to do."

"But that job, if I'm not mistaken, has been assumed by a twenty-two-year-old man-child in Bangalore, India."

Warren nods. "Exactly."

"So you know of a similar job at a similar company?"

"Not really."

Meredith and Henry exchange glances.

"I'm going to get my job back, people. This *exact* job."

"Okay," says Henry, the way he'd say it to a crazy person.

"I've already done some research. I'm pretty sure I found the company in India they're subcontracting to."

Meredith sits down on Henry's black leather couch. "And you're going to try to convince them to bring it back here?"

"Oh, no," Warren says, walking over to the window. "Not that. I'm going to go over there."

"To India?" Henry asks.

"Uh-huh. To Bangalore. Or Mumbai. Could be Mumbai."

Henry looks at Meredith again, but she is staring at Warren, transfixed.

"Listen," Warren says. "I'm thirty. Single. Divorced. Childless. My parents are dead. My friends have all moved on with kids and spouses and midlife crises of their own. What I have . . . what I had was a job that I loved. It gave me pleasure. Fulfillment. I found it challenging. I felt as if I was helping people. Christ, Henry, listen to what you just said. And Meredith, you've as much as told me that if it weren't for the medical benefits and the profit-sharing, you'd be long gone, trying to become a new media millionaire. What's so wrong with me deciding that I want to travel halfway around the world to keep the job that I love?"

"Warren," Henry says. "They've outsourced it because it's an unskilled job and they're probably paying someone one tenth of what they're paying you. You couldn't live on that."

"I could in Bangalore. Besides, I've got one point three million dollars in the bank. One point three. With no kids and no alimony."

Henry does the math. The son of a bitch was here for the takeover eight years ago that he'd just missed, but still. "One point three after the crash?"

Warren nods. "I yanked it all out way before and put half in gold, which I sold at the high."

"But you don't speak the language."

"I'll learn. Besides, most of the people I'll work with speak English."

"I think it's crazy, Warren," Henry says.

Meredith disagrees. "I think it's adorable."

"I think it's better than your plan, Henry," Warren answers.

Meredith nods. "Whatever that is."

"When Giffler told me this morning," Warren continues, "I was devastated. But now I feel liberated, because I absolutely know what I want to do. I may not be able to do it, but knowing what that is, and being on a mission to achieve it, to make it a part of an adventure, feels incredible. What is it that you want to do, Henry?"

Henry considers the millionaire, Bangalore-bound, reverse-outsourcing customer-service-rep pioneer and then the all-knowing, multimillionaire (probably), big-boob new-media porn star/administrative assistant in front of him and then looks back out the window. The preacher man on the median below has gone wherever he goes when this part of his shift is up. The soup line? The gym? He's probably rich and fulfilled too. Taillights continue to flash into the black mouth of the traffic arch down the avenue before vanishing, never to be seen again. He feels the dull throbbing in his scrotal sac that the doctors said might occur for several weeks after the procedure, and in some instances for several years. As he slips his hand into his pocket to make a discreet adjustment, his phone buzzes, and the jolt of it almost causes him to leap through the supposedly unopenable window.

Test Strip

In the first days following your vasectomy, elevate your legs and apply ice packs liberally to the scrotal area. Lasting or significant pain is uncommon, but you should not have, and probably won't feel like having, intercourse for several days to several weeks. Your doctor will tell you when to bring in your first semen sample for examination.

—Snipped.com

The pool is indeed green. A different green from the last time he'd seen it in daylight, on Sunday. Now it's more of an Amazon jungle river green than an electric Kool-Aid, Chernobyl green, but green nonetheless.

Henry squats and takes a test strip out of a small blue plastic bottle. He dips it in and out of the deep end of the pool and compares its small multicolored panels to their idealized version on the back label. At first he thinks he's holding the strip upside-down, because none of the colors come close to corresponding with those on the label. But he's wrong, it's right. Which is sort of a relief, he thinks, because if it all lined up perfectly and the pool was still green, he'd really be screwed.

Still, what a mess. And why does it have to be so difficult? And not just the pool but the entire, thanks to the real estate mess, drastically devalued house. So much breaking down, so much to maintain, even though it's relatively new. Gutters to be cleaned. HVAC filters to be replaced. Furnace needing servicing, toilets clogging, water-treatment systems failing, minerals building up in a $2,000 dishwasher. Cracks in the driveway, water in the foundation. Always depreciating, never easy. And no matter how well stocked his basement workbench becomes, he never seems to have the right tool for the job. And parts. The part that he'll dedicate a Saturday morning to finding in the Home Depot's endless aisles is always, for reasons he never finds out, wrong. Wrong length, wrong width. Wrong model, color, pattern, gauge, grit, grade, viscosity, voltage. Wrong.

Right now, the entire house, even the parts that work, he thinks, is wrong. Four thousand state-of-the-McMansion-art square feet of wrong. Or maybe, it occurs to him, he is what's wrong with the house. He's the one fouling up the works, the one in need of maintenance, the one depreciating at a greater than anticipated rate. Maybe he's the one who should be foreclosed upon.

He thinks, if the house had to shop for parts for Henry and Rachel Tuhoe at the *Human* Depot, it would get it all wrong too. Wrong age. Wrong attitude. Wrong ambitions. And absolutely the wrong model. As he looks up at the towering clapboard wall of the back of the house, the screened-in porch, the rear windows of the three-car garage, the matching pool house, it's all he can think. Wrong place, wrong time, wrong life.

Yet less than two years earlier it had seemed, or at least Rachel had convinced him to believe it was, kind of right. They had lived together on the Upper West Side for three years, two as a married couple, and had enjoyed it immensely. The laughable commute, the late-as-you-want dinners at the most eclectic places. They enjoyed watching friends' bad indie bands in Brooklyn and not understanding the art they kept going back to see in Chelsea. Waiting on line for midnight cupcakes at Billy's. Sunday brunch with childless friends at Café Luxembourg. They enjoyed having the gym and the dive bar and the bookstore next door, the megatheaters two blocks south, and the art-house theater a few blocks beyond that.

And then they (Rachel first, he's certain) decided that they had outgrown it. Their friends' escapades with love and drugs, real careers and fantasy vocations no longer seemed original or terribly important. Tedious patterns began to emerge. Ill-considered behaviors were repeated. What had seemed outrageous began to register as immature. What had once passed as interesting had become banal. Melodramatic. It had rained three weekends in a row at the end of that summer, canceling the last August visits of the season to their Amagansett beach rental, which, after three years with the same people, had also become tedious, tiresome, banal. Melodramatic.

They'd both been working social-life-killing hours at jobs at which their entry-level, young-professional-on-the-rise energy and optimism had already been replaced by increased responsibility and, yes, money, as well as questions of a deeper philosophical nature. Also, Rachel was in the middle of a feud with her best friend, which added to her already bored state of mind.

So the early October invitation to a fall harvest festival at the northern Westchester County home of one of Rachel's married co-workers seemed like something worth trying. Something new. On the Hudson Line train heading north, coming out of the first tunnel and seeing the sun-blasted leaves against a cloudless sky, they both felt it—that they were no longer mired in the expected but on the verge of something new and fresh and altogether different. Even the sky seemed of another place, much cleaner than the sky they'd just left.

And even though her friend's fall harvest festival was tedious and corny, apple this and pumpkin that—"They're acting like they grew and harvested everything down to the last gourd and are sharing them with the original *Mayflower* pilgrims," Rachel had whispered to him—they had to admit they did enjoy themselves, and the children running through the leaf piles were kind of fun.

On the train ride back to Manhattan that evening in a slight drizzle, during which some leaves had already begun to fall, they sipped takeout cups of green tea with lemon and leaned against each other, talking about the river and hiking trails and adjustable-rate mortgages. By the time they slipped back underground and their day in the country had come to a close, they had already made up their minds. It was time to leave the city, cash in their options, and buy a big-ass house in the country like her kind-of-friend's, and maybe, at some point, start a family.

For a second Henry looks directly into the sun hanging over the magnolia on the southwest side of the pool and is so blinded by its afternoon rays that he becomes disoriented. He loses his balance and slowly tips over sideways. Scrambling back to his knees, he glances toward the kitchen window to see if Rachel was looking. Hard to tell for sure, but he doesn't think she's in there. Probably in the office, still on her conference call. And even if she was looking, he wonders if it would have registered that he had fallen. Because looking at something and seeing it are completely different things, and he knows that she hasn't seen him in a long time. He gathers himself with several deep breaths and realizes that he has not eaten since breakfast. Not during the focus group or even after the psychiatrist/workout session with Norman. So it's no wonder he stumbled, especially in this heat.

He knows there's one thing you're supposed to balance first, and once you get that right, you move on to the others. He thinks it's the alkalinity, but he can't be sure. The back label of the alkalinity increaser jug offers no help. Neither does the label on the pH increaser. He has an entire milk crate filled with chemicals: increasers, decreasers, clarifiers, shocks, algicides, balancers. He has liquid chlorine, powdered chlorine, one-inch tabs and three-inch hockey pucks of chlorine. In addition to the test strips, he has more elaborate testing kits, small chemistry sets with tubes and droppers and their own color charts.

Everything he needs to get it right is here. All he needs is to figure out the prescribed sequence, the proper balance, and they'll be swimming in no time. Because it needs both, he decides to dump in half a gallon of alkalinity increaser and then four or five—how many gallons of water does the pool hold again? Twenty thousand? Thirty? What the hell, make it an even six scoops of soda ash. Standing back up, brushing off his pants, he figures he'll give it a few hours and see how this all takes before reappraising.

———

Inside, he finds Rachel standing in her office with her back to him, dressed for a casual night out. Fitted jeans and riding boots, a green embroidered silk shirt. She is tall and athletic and in many ways, he thinks, still beautiful. But in other ways she isn't. Her long, dark brown, shampoo-commercial-worthy hair is now dry and frayed (stress? age? meds?), and for the past three months an unnatural Marilyn Monroe blond. Her once perfect Mediterranean skin has deep creases around her eyes and mouth, a condition he attributes to her increased propensity for frowning, twitching, and furrowing her brow. And her eyes, her wide dark gorgeous clean-edged eyes, which had an energy that coursed through him when she was happy or angry or horny, now seem a half-shade lighter, ten watts duller, and, up close, softer, milkier, murkier. Of all the things they have been through in the past year, it's the change in Rachel's eyes that saddens him most.

"Hey," he says, but she turns and gives him a *shush* wave. She's wearing a wireless Skype headset and is holding some kind of spreadsheet. In a way, he's relieved that she's busy. Soon she'll be leaving for a dinner date with one of her new girlfriends from her most recently organized social group, and he'll be off to the latest iteration of what has become a tedious monthly male ritual: Meat Night, with five neighbors, five other men he barely knows, at a house a few blocks away. Not enough time to sit her down to talk about water for the third world or outsourcing, the chemistry of their pool and their marriage.

Maybe later. Maybe tomorrow.

He leans over her desk to wave good-bye. He mouths the words *Meat Night* and she looks at him as if he is insane. As he straightens up to leave, he notices a paperback on her desk called *The Postmodern Cauldron: Diary of a 21st-Century Witch*.

Before he can pick it up, Rachel snaps it away and glares at him again, as if he is the crazy one.

Conceive Now!

It's too late for the butcher shop, and that's too bad, because it would have been a nice manly touch, a butcher-shop-procured prime cut of an exotic species wrapped in a sheet of coarse white paper, a hint of blood beginning to soak through. The only thing better, Henry imagines, would be to have killed and butchered the species in question himself. Maybe next time. This time, however, the A&P meat counter will have to suffice.

He takes special care to avoid aisle four, personal hygiene, because the last thing he wants right now is to start thinking about the quantity and quality of deodorant shelf space. Instead he takes the long way along the far edge of the store, where the aisles are lined exclusively with frozen and refrigerated goods. At the butcher's counter in the back of the store there is a small line. An overweight young mother in camouflage stretch pants is yelling at her two-year-old son, telling him he'd better start adjusting his attitude right quick. Directly in front of him a middle-aged couple in matching Dale Earnhardt, Jr. number 8 NASCAR shirts and hats are having a heated debate over whether they should go with the sweet or the spicy Italian sausage. When Henry looks back at the mother and child, he sees that the little boy has stopped crying and is contentedly gnawing on the cap of a six-ounce Redwood Honeysuckle Spice stick, the best-selling version of the brand he worked on until eight hours ago.

———

As soon as they closed on the house, having a child went from something they might want to do to something they would try to do to—for Rachel—an obsession.

On the train back and forth to Manhattan (while they still commuted together), Rachel no longer read literary fiction; she began to read books on fertility. She no longer drank coffee or diet soda; she drank herbal teas and tinctures and potions from the health-food store that had names like Fertile Harvest, Women's Blend, Leaves of Splendor, and, to Henry's amazement, the disclaimer-free, citrus-flavored powdered supplement Conceive Now!

While their lovemaking in their Manhattan apartment had sometimes involved items such as vanilla-scented candles, massage oil, or one of Rachel's Mazzy Star albums, those accessories had been replaced for their suburban sessions by menstrual calendars, alarm clocks, and digital thermometers.

Several times he had to leave work early, or not go in at all, because like it or not, it was time. This was around the same time that he began to notice that she was missing from the bed late at night. Sometimes he'd find her outside in her nightgown, staring at the glow patches of clustered houses in the suburban sky. Sometimes he'd find her smoking in the empty upstairs bedroom.

After three months without success, Rachel began to question the heartiness of his sperm, the character of her eggs. They went to doctors, who essentially told them that they were fine. That they should calm down. Henry suggested that she might want to talk to another doctor, to, you know, help calm down. But Rachel responded by telling him he was crazy and didn't speak with him for a week.

After six months Rachel blamed their inability to conceive on her job, the stress of her commute, so she quit and found less demanding, lower-paying work as a freelance, work-at-home (mostly) Internet security consultant. In the meantime, she bought more books, took up yoga, and had Henry ingesting up to twenty different vitamin and mineral supplements a day. Beyond C, E, and A, he didn't know what most of them were. He knew only that his urine looked radioactive and at nine every morning his bowels would erupt with Old Faithful–like regularity.

After nine months of trying to conceive, Rachel slipped into a mild depression. Even though she was only twenty-five, she began to play the role of a hopeless, barren, childless spinster out of the pages of a Victorian novel. She watched a lot of daytime TV and read a lot of Victorian novels, several about childless spinsters. She began, without prompting, to tell her friends and family and random strangers about their tragic predicament. She envied her neighbors' fertile wombs, coveted their chemical-free cedar swing sets, and resented their $700-stroller-pushing nannies and baby-formula-stained minivan floor mats.

Then, after almost a year of this, when prime conception opportunities presented themselves, she began to ignore them. When Henry reminded her, mostly because he realized it was his last best chance to have any kind of sex with her, she ignored him too.

Eventually the thermometer went back into the medicine cabinet, the tinctures were shelved, and the vitamins sat untaken long past their expiration date.

"Can I help you?"

Henry looks blankly at the butcher, then at the unimpressive display of meats behind the counter. No grass-fed organic New Zealand lamb racks or sides of free-range bison hanging from chains in the back room. Just your basic chucks and chops, T-bones and pork loins.

"Yes," he says. "I'm looking for a special kind of meat to barbecue for me and five, um, friends." Five men so desperate to validate their manhood they dedicate an entire night to the burning and consuming of large quantities of animal flesh. "Any suggestions?"

He told Rachel to snap out of it and stop feeling sorry for herself. He said there was nothing wrong with her eggs or his sperm and she still had another twenty childbearing years in front of her, if she'd only stop obsessing. He even showed her an article he'd downloaded on the effects of self-imposed pressure on a couple's ability to conceive.

Then, that September, he took her to Block Island, to a two-hundred-year-old bed-and-breakfast on a hill overlooking the Atlantic.

And it worked.

Getting away from the house prompted some kind of psychic release, and they made anxiety-free love twice a day for three days. On the ferry back to Point Judith, a transformed Rachel said that she was sorry, and that maybe they should wait to have children anyway. After all, they were still kids, and maybe it would be for the best if they sold the house and moved back to Manhattan. Henry felt as if the four-thousand-square-foot weight of that house had been lifted off him. He promptly contacted their Realtor in the country, a new Realtor to help them find a place back in Manhattan. He booked a return trip to Block Island.

Two weeks later, when he got home late one night from work, Rachel told him that she was pregnant.

"How do you know?"

"I missed. I never miss."

"Holy—"

"It's a miracle. Why are you not ecstatic? Where is the beaming face of the proud father-to-be?"

"I . . . It's . . . Considering what we've . . . it certainly is . . ."

"What? Don't say shock. Our first child will not be considered a shock."

"How about ironic?"

"We wanted this, Henry. We desperately wanted this, and now our prayers have been answered."

"Yeah. Great, Rachel. My God, but . . ."

"Well, if you're not ecstatic, your mother certainly is. Maybe she'll stop pitying my barren womb now."

"She never . . . You told my mother?"

"And my parents. I knew you'd be home late and I didn't want to tell you over the phone and I couldn't sit on this all by myself."

"Did you see a doctor?"

"No. Tomorrow. I used a strip. Then I got another test at the drugstore. Positive-positive. Isn't it amazing?"

"Yes," he said, and as he hugged her his gaze drifted out the kitchen window and over to the murky surface of their pool.

The next day her ob-gyn confirmed that Rachel was two, maybe three weeks pregnant. They took the house off the market and told the Manhattan broker they were no longer interested in moving. She went back to the health-food store with a vengeance, loading up on products with names like Fetal Fortifier, Mother's Essentials, and Living Womb. At night after dinner he painted constellations on the ceiling of the baby's room.

Rachel still wasn't herself, still wasn't the carefree woman he had fallen in love with and married, but she was happy, and that was an improvement. Regarding having a baby just then, he wasn't sure what he wanted beyond wanting Rachel to be happy. For the first time he thought of his approach to their relationship in terms of saving her. And him, and them, of course. But he was convinced it had to begin with her.

At eleven weeks her mother and sister began plans for an extravagant surprise baby shower.

At fourteen weeks she began to spot blood.

At sixteen weeks she was put on bed rest and given medication, a special foam wedge to put between her legs.

At nineteen weeks they made their first trip to the emergency room.

The fourth time they went, at twenty-one weeks, they lost the baby.

That night they cried together on their living room couch. Later, in bed, he promised her they would try again. They would have another child. He was still crying, but Rachel wasn't. She rolled over without answering.

The Ministry of Meat

"Gentlemen!" proclaims host Gerard Fundle. "Honorable members of the Ministry of Meat, behold the bounty and the spectacle, the revolting beauty that is . . . Meat Night!"

He raises the platter of assorted meat over his head as if it is the Stanley Cup, the Holy Grail, something more than dead flesh.

"The carne-val of carne!" shouts Victor Chan.

Marcus LeBlanc raises a glass. "The fusillade of flesh!"

"Meat! Meat! Meat!" The Osborne brothers are pounding on the glass-topped table, fists clenched around knives and forks.

Henry would laugh if he hadn't first been exposed to each of these "spontaneous" outbursts via an embarrassing string of e-mails, messages bearing subject headings such as "A Meat-eater's Manifesto" to "Man Rules for Meat" (number three: "Gristle is our friend").

He would laugh if it weren't for his own sad contribution to the spectacle: Kobe beef hot dogs.

Besides Henry there are five of them gathered in the bluing twilight, all fathers at least eight years older than Henry. They all live within a half-mile of Gerard's house, and all except for the Osborne brothers, who grew up in the first iteration of this subdivision, have landed here through the randomness of corporate migration.

Gerard is working three separate cooking stations: a coal-filled Weber kettle for the indirect heat purists, a massive stainless-steel

Weber gas cooker for bulk, and a smoker that for the past sixteen hours has been working its magic on Gerard's self-proclaimed (yet never before attempted) world-famous brisket. There's a red plastic tub filled with an eclectic variety of international beers—Belgian ale, India pale ale, German Hefeweizen, Slovakian pilsner, and, in a nod to Gerard's less exotic college years in upstate New York, Genesee Cream Ale. Henry randomly selects a bottle of Blue Point Toasted Lager (Long Island), which, as he fumbles with the opener, Gerard is quick to point out recently won a gold medal in Munich. Henry hears himself saying "Wow!" even though, except on nights like this, he doesn't drink, especially beer, and he could give a shit about Munich or lager or medals. But after his first sip he has to admit that while nothing about this beer tastes particularly toasted or medal-worthy, it is good. He says as much to the group, because saying no to beer on manly Meat Night or poker night is much more of a lightning rod for sarcasm than nursing one or two until it's time to go home.

He takes another swig, laterals his bag of exotic hot dogs over to Gerard, and begins shaking hands with his geographically mandated friends. Forty-something WASP Gerard; the forty-something Irish American brothers Osborne, John and Eric; forty-two-year-old Chinese American Victor Chan, who has a yet-to-be-explained purple and black shiner around his left eye; and forty-one-year-old African American Marcus LeBlanc.

They're all employed in some form of corporate middle management. Financial services. New media. Apps. Digital widgets. They're all wearing cargo shorts with cell phones clipped on the waistband, sport sandals, and colored cotton T-shirts stamped with the logos of places and things that might be cool if any of them actually existed. *Freddie's Bait and Tackle. Death Valley Road Rally. Chattanooga Charlie's Chile Sauce.*

They've been gathering like this, once a month or so, since they recruited Henry two years ago. Not only for Meat Night, but for everything from Lawn Jarts and horseshoes to bocce and Wiffle ball. Last fall they even had a brief beer pong season, which concluded on an ugly note, with that night's champion and subsequent former group member Louis Bell getting a DUI from a state trooper on Route 9.

The games themselves don't matter. What supposedly matters is the ritual of talking them up for days and sometimes weeks prior to the event. At first Henry wasn't interested in any of it. The drinking, the "I'm a Jarts *God*!" e-mail shit, and especially the company of men much older than he.

At first he went out of politeness and because Rachel encouraged him. She said it would be good for him. Then later, during her obsession with getting pregnant, her obsession with staying pregnant, and her prolonged depression after she lost the baby, he found himself wanting to go, looking forward to it. Anything to get out of the house.

But now he's unsure of where he'd rather not be: in his giant empty home with Rachel, ignoring each other or, worse, talking about his vasectomy; or here, feigning camaraderie in the universal epicenter of displaced manliness.

Before settling down, he announces to the others that he has to take a piss. That's what you do on Meat Night, you announce it— *I'm pissing in your house whether you like it or not, perhaps with the seat down*—because excusing oneself is a sign of weakness, is for pussies. He stops in the kitchen to look at the corkboard near the phone. Besides the preponderance of takeout menus, which reinforce his theory that Gerard's wife and kids may be "vacationing" in Long Beach Island longer than Gerard wants to admit, there are two calendars, both turned to the month of June, even though it is now mid-August.

The first calendar is for Gerard's soon-to-be fourth grader, Gerard Jr., and every day is meticulously inked in, from morning until bedtime, with appointments for everything from soccer practices to karate and alto saxophone lessons to three-times-a-week SAT prep tutoring with a woman who, Gerard has told Henry, virtually guarantees that Gerard Jr. will be accepted into an Ivy League school if he sticks to their long-term, increasingly expensive plan. The second calendar is for Gerard's other son, Phillip, who is in preschool. There are no written words on it, only hand-drawn smiles for the days on which young Phillip hasn't bitten anyone. Of June's thirty days, there are only three smiles.

Back on the patio, while the meats sizzle and sputter on clean-brushed, recently oiled grates, Henry takes the only remaining seat at the glass-topped patio table, in between the Osborne brothers. The seat is empty for a reason. The brothers are notorious for their passionate discussions, with one taking the opposing view of everything the other believes in, from sports to how to light coals to, of course, politics. Henry's never seen it, but several times the Osbornes' arguments have escalated to the physical, the most famous of which was a 2004 St. Patrick's Day dance that left the basement of the Catholic church in ruins and Eric cupping his hands over his bleeding, shattered septum.

Henry's not even sure which one is Eric and which is John. He's known them long enough that he should (it's not as if they're twins), but to ask for clarification this late in the game would be counter-productive. They give him the slightest of nods before resuming their debate on immigration. One wants to close the borders and build an electrified wall and the other, he wants to . . . Henry stops listening. Lately he's been doing this a lot. As soon as someone starts in on health care or taxes, playgroups or some neighborhood committee, he glazes over, shuts down. Same goes for stories about Facebook or Twitter or the social network du jour. Sports too, especially golf. And office crap. Lately, even the parts that involve him. Sometimes he daydreams and others, such as now, he wonders how he ever got himself living this doomed existence, at his age.

Rachel became convinced that their troubles were some kind of sign, that their having children just wasn't meant to be. As soon as he agreed to at least consider having a vasectomy, she threw herself into the research. She downloaded articles and printed diagrams for him that were intended to allay his fears about loss of libido and the pain of recovery. What he was most concerned about, beyond the mental state of his wife, was having someone take a scalpel to his testicles, and no chart or penis-friendly phrasing could make it go away.

Whenever he tried to tell Rachel that perhaps they should wait just a little longer, because one day they might want to try to have a child again, she told him that she couldn't handle the emotions of expectation and loss, that if it happened again it would break her completely. Whenever he mentioned therapy or counseling, she responded with anger, accusations, and prolonged periods of silence. Pushing harder, he thought, would be the end for them. So, while not assenting, he let her run with it, with the hope that things would change, she'd get better, or at least find a replacement obsession.

But she didn't. Soon Rachel knew enough about the vicissitudes of vasectomies to do a dissertation for the *New England Journal of Medicine*.

Henry accepts another beer. "A Slovakian—not Czech, there's a huge difference—pilsner," Gerard explains. One of the Osbornes, deep into a criticism of the latest government bailout, stops pointing his index finger at his brother long enough to say, "That's what we want to see, Junior. Pounding some fine eastern European swill. We'll make a man out of you yet."

Henry raises the bottle in a toast. They have taken to calling him Junior, or Kid, or H. After two years he is still the plebe, the pledging frat boy. He has remained the disciple and they the wise elders, the savvy veterans of the mysteries of suburbia, marriage, fatherhood, and the sub-prime lending fiasco. They played every aspect of their hazing, mentoring roles to perfection, he thought, except the part about the actual dispensing of wisdom, the leading by example, or the solving of even the smallest problem.

LeBlanc asks Victor Chan for more details about his swollen and blackened left eye. "Happened at Kenny's T-ball game." Chan looks away from LeBlanc, hoping that this is description enough.

"What," shouts Gerard, "did you get clipped with a line drive by a toddler on steroids?"

"Or did one of the parents clock you?" Henry offers with a laugh.

Chan turns and stares at Henry. "Well, actually, yes," he says, as if Henry is the one who did the sucker punching.

"What happened, V-Chan?" asks Marcus. "This is T-ball, correct?"

"Yeah. There was this little kid, this little prick, actually, who started mouthing off to the first baseman, a nice kid twice the size of the other kid. The first baseman didn't do anything, except catch the throw that sealed the other kid's fate. I thought they were playing, but the little brat began throwing punches. Soon the big kid had him on the ground. I ran over and started pulling them apart and the next thing I know this other father, the little kid's father, grabs my shoulder, spins me around, and clocks me."

Gerard approaches from the grills, brandishing tongs and a long grease-slick fork from which dangles a piece of charred grizzle. "Holy shit, Victor, what'd you do?"

"What I did is fall down, Gerard. You think I know kung fu or something just because I'm Chinese?"

"You didn't hit him?" Gerard is shocked. "I would've—"

"I would've sued him," says Osborne the First.

"Further destroying our overly litigious society," counters Osborne the Second.

"I did nothing. It wasn't even my son in the fight. My son, who, by the way, won't even talk to me because I walked away."

"You have to redeem yourself," Gerard insists. "You must bust that dude right in the nose, Victor Chan, for your dignity, your son's future, and the integrity of our national pastime."

"Did he at least apologize?" Henry asks. "Have you seen him since?"

"No. We have a game tomorrow. I feel sick just thinking about it."

They grimace as one as the testosterone is sucked out of their manspace. No one speaks for a while. Clearly this tale of passive nonviolence at, of all things, a sporting event has been a level-one Meat Night buzz kill.

"Well," Gerard finally declares. "That's just weak, V-Chan. Effin' pathetic."

Victor doesn't respond as Gerard heads back inside. A few moments later Green Day's "American Idiot" comes through the exterior wall-mounted speakers. Marcus LeBlanc starts jerking his head to the music. The Osborne brothers finger-jab to the beat. Henry is fairly sure that none of them know what's playing, what it's saying. What's important to them is that even though it was released more than six years ago, it sounds younger than they are and that, at least among themselves, they are getting away with co-opting it.

Gerard reappears and turns to Henry. "Too loud?" he asks, but what he means is, "Too much of a reach?"

Henry shakes his head and gives Gerard two rocking thumbs up. Meanwhile, Victor Chan seems to have collected himself after his tale of T-ball terror and is proudly removing the contents of the traveling martini kit he received for his fortieth birthday. Not especially macho, Henry thinks, as Victor reassembles, then begins to measure and pour and shake. But there is hard liquor involved, in this case a Polish vodka distilled from a particular type of wheat or something (Henry lost interest after the words *distilled from*), and it does provide the others with the opportunity to point out Chan's numerous tactical errors. Henry takes a long drink of a beer (English Porter) that he doesn't remember opening and closes his eyes.

"That rude son of a bitch."

Henry opens his eyes. It's Victor Chan. "Who?"

"Gerard. The man's man. If you only knew."

Henry knows he's supposed to follow up Chan's tease, but he doesn't. Doesn't care.

The Permanent Snip

Rachel wasn't the only one doing research.

He told her about the man who'd gotten one, yet his wife got pregnant anyway a month later. Then he told her about the guy at work whose wife had him get one even though she'd secretly had her tubes tied after a C-section. When the man found out, after it was too late, his wife said she didn't want him to go running off and having kids with some bimbo and watering down her children's estate. "But can't I still get it reversed?" the soon-to-be-cuckolded man had asked her. "Nope," his wife said. "Yours is irreversible. We got you the permanent snip."

At the end of the story, Henry asked Rachel, "Do you want mine to be permanent?"

"No," she said. "I just want it to work."

Six weeks after the procedure date he's still haunted by dreams of phallic mutilation, is still reminded of it in the quotidian images of his daily routines. So it's understandable that watching Gerard take a Ginsu knife to a heat-plumped kielbasa and his own sizzling Kobe beef dog is something his eyes cannot abide. Instead he looks away, drinks his martini, and manages to listen to the Osbornes argue long enough to discern that they've changed their topic from the auto industry bailout to waterboarding.

Soon after Victor gets up to make another batch of sub-par martinis, Marcus pulls a chair alongside Henry. Marcus is drinking
seltzer. He says it is because he is on antibiotics for Lyme disease, but
they all know it's because Marcus is on antidepressants. Marcus's
wife, who is white, had told the other men's wives, including Rachel,
after their firefighter's workout class that Marcus is depressed over
his diminished blackness in white suburbia. But Henry and the men
at the round table of meat know that the real cause of Marcus's
depression is that his wife has been cheating on him with a man who
has significantly more ghetto in him than Marcus. They know
because Marcus confessed to them two months ago, after being over-
served on small-batch bourbon and Raw Bar Night.

Marcus tried to win her back. He gave up golf, khakis, and, for
a while, the Protestant church. He tried cooking soul food, watching BET and Samuel L. Jackson films, and listening to old-school
hip-hop. He tried to alter his diction and even attempted to cultivate
a genuine resentment of the Man. But none of it worked, he told
them, because he was the Man. Born and raised in white suburbia.
Soccer coach. Churchgoer. Occasional cardigan-wearer. What he
realized, or what couples counseling helped him realize, just before
his wife abandoned him and his two daughters and moved in with a
man in the Brownsville section of Brooklyn for five weeks, is that
she had a thing for *dangerous* black men and Marcus, in retrospect,
was way too white.

The Brooklyn experiment was a failure, and they are currently
living under the same roof, trying to make a go of it for the sake,
they say, of the children.

"Mister Tuhoe."

"Monsieur LeBlanc." Henry smiles. He likes Marcus LeBlanc.
On occasion they've actually had some decent conversations.

"How goes it at work?"

But apparently not today. And yet, though he hates talking
about work while he's away from work—primarily because talking
about what he does for a living (which in itself is a depressingly
accurate phrase) angers, humiliates, and frustrates him—here he is
finishing up Polish specialty wheat martini number two and beginning to tell Marcus LeBlanc about his day.

About how goes it. How went it. About working hard or hardly working. About everything.

At first he doesn't notice, but soon he sees that they've all stopped what they were doing—Gerard (cooking), the Osbornes (ranting: presidential citizenship), Victor Chan (fretting)—and, smelling the blood of genuine emotion, the scent of angst other than their own, have gathered closer to revel in his tale. He tells them about the morning gravestones, the fainting woman, and Giffler's ambiguous ultimatum. He tells them about Norman from the gym, the lurker in the locker room, and Warren's Bangalorian reverse-outsourcing ambitions. He even tells them about Meredith, though he refuses to reveal her name, real or porno.

Midtale, Victor refills Henry's martini glass and Gerard gets him another beer (Hefeweisen, Germany). Moving back and forth through time, pausing for dramatic effect, and occasionally standing to pantomime an event, Henry tells them that after two miserable entry-level jobs in sales he fell into a job at his current company. And though it was better than sales, he never did like it. He tells them that he probably would have left the job long ago if he had had the slightest clue about what he'd like to do, about what gives him satisfaction or pleasure. He tells them that he's probably being transferred, or expatrio-sourced, the name he invents on the spot, to what he's being told is a customer-service satellite for the newly acquired Water Division, even though he has little call-center knowledge and none of the bottled water industry, and that he'll probably have to travel quite a bit, probably to a third-world-type place—India, China, South America—and that it troubles him deeply, because, as they know, he hates flying and has a bit of a germ phobia.

When he's done he feels spent, but in some ways better for having told them, for having told anyone, and they certainly seemed to be eating it up, to be moved by his story, the tale of a man with whom they are sort of familiar, in actual conflict. Indeed, here is a chance for all of them to know Henry better—to know any human being better—and it seems, Henry thinks, to have registered with them on some deeper, more visceral and purely emotional level, to have transformed the banal dynamic, to have brought all of them a little closer to having more meaningful, truer relationships. To signal to them that his tale is now done, that he's ready for a little Q&A session if they're interested, Henry pushes aside the martini and takes a long drink of the Hefeweisen.

Gerard (of course it would be Gerard, Henry thinks—Gerard the wise, Gerard the caring) steps forward. He has a dripping piece of ostrich meat on a barbecue fork in one hand, a Trappist ale in the other. Gerard the shaman. "Tell me," Gerard says with the warmth of an uncle, the gravitas of a trusted adviser. "Tell me more about this porn-whore secretary of yours."

"Yeah," says Marcus. "Exactly how big are that chick's fun-bags?"

There is a condition that occurs among a small number of men known as post-vasectomy pain syndrome (PVPS). Symptoms include a dull ache in the testicles beginning immediately or months or even years after the procedure. It may resolve on its own or require another surgery. In some cases the patient experiences psychological depression seemingly unrelated to the vasectomy.

—*Snipped.com*

The meat is paraded across the patio like May Day missiles past a Kremlin reviewing stand. Kielbasa, Italian sausage, veal chops, ostrich strips, T-bone steak, Gerard's tender brisket, and Henry's Kobe beef hot dogs. Henry takes some of everything and a second helping of the ostrich—not because he likes the way it tastes, but because it's giving him a rarely experienced sort of primal pleasure, eating ostrich. "I never liked ostriches anyway," he announces, spearing another piece off the main platter.

"Better get used to eating weirdness, the places you're going," says Osborne the Second, and his brother laughs for a moment before catching himself.

"That's the thing, and I told you guys this," Henry says, gesturing with his martini glass, which is impossible to do sober, let alone buzzed, without spillage. "I am not going to goddamn China, India, anywhere that requires the administering of shots or the crossing of an ocean, dateline, or border."

"So you're not ruling out Mexico, then," says conservative Osborne, winking at his soft-on-immigration brother.

"No way. I'd rather take a job in the mailroom of another soulless mega-conglomerate. I like my life right here, in quiet, vanilla American suburbia with easy access to New York City restaurants and the occasional Disneyfied theatrical production, just fine."

"So what does Rachel make of all this?" asks Marcus, but the way they all lean forward to hear the answer, it's clearly a group question. "What does she think of the ultimatum, of them wanting you to drop everything and relocate to the other side of the world?"

Henry rubs his face and drags his fingers through his hair. "Well, that's the thing. When I got home this afternoon she was on the phone, a conference call, and I had to get the meat, the beef— *vive le boeuf!*—no, le veal! So, you know, it had to wait."

"You're gonna tell her when you get home, then?" Gerard asks on behalf of the group. Gerard the snoop. Gerard the girly man. Gerard the cuckold.

Henry raises his glass, finishes the final half of his third martini. Or is it his fourth? Something buzzes in his head and he feels a little sick. The dull ache in his groin has spread up into his abdomen, his chest, his brain. "Tonight? I think not," he says, before unleashing a magnificent belch. "For a light-drinking semi-vegetarian, I'm not doing bad tonight, eh, fellas?"

Victor Chan leans back and shakes his head. Marcus LeBlanc folds his arms. One Osborne gives him a thumbs-up, the other a thumbs-down. Gerard Fundle stands and whistles the universal melody of "Oh boy, are you in some deep shit."

Come on Down

As directed by his urologist, he stopped taking aspirin two weeks prior to the procedure date because it thins the blood, increases the risk of bleeding. For three nights before the date he thoroughly scrubbed his scrotum with an antibacterial wash to reduce the probability of infection. Although not essential, it was recommended that he shave from the base of the penis down to the front of the scrotum. Just to be sure, Henry shaved everything from his navel to his inner thighs. In those final weeks he made a point of keeping Rachel apprised of everything, to demonstrate that he was on board with the idea, that he had embraced it.

In those final weeks he also started to masturbate more often. Much more often. With urgency. With abandon. Indiscriminately. At first maybe once a day in the shower, or in bed during a middle-of-the-night anxiety attack fused with an erotic dream. Sometimes he'd do it to downloaded porn on his home computer or retro-style with a discreetly archived *Playboy* or Victoria's Secret catalog. But with each passing day he stepped up the intensity and frequency of his self-pleasuring, while conversely broadening the standards of what he found arousing enough to make him reach for the Nivea.

In the final days this included not just the conjuring of fantasies traditional and kinky or the watching of porn downloaded or purchased, but also the absorption of whatever sexual nutrients he could extract from sources as diverse as late-night basic cable erotica to a Scarlett Johannson appearance on *Conan* to a scantily clad cartoon heroine in a graphic novel to, disturbingly, on more than one occasion, the late-morning giggles and cleavage of the prize girls on Game Show Network reruns of *The Price Is Right.*

Come on down.

The way Henry had begun to see it, he and his penis had been given six weeks to live, and short of committing adultery, having sex with his wife, or fantasizing about Meredith, aka EEEEva EEEEnormous (which for some reason he had always declared off-limits), they were going to make the most of every remaining sperm-laden salvo.

Henry thinks he hears children, but he's still sober enough to remember that Gerard's children are not home. Now he hears a splash, followed by more youthful laughter. Must be the neighbor's kids in their crystal-clear, perfectly balanced pool, he thinks, and not a malevolent hallucination. A few months ago he might have let himself slip into sentimentality about children, or his and Rachel's lack of them, but as he listens he feels nothing of the kind. Rather than coveting children, or resenting them, or, if Rachel had been around, trying to pretend they're not there, he feels only happiness for them, and instead of wishing they'd be quiet, he finds himself wishing that he was one of them again, splashing about in midweek, midsummer, preadolescent twilight with nothing on the agenda for tomorrow except a lot more of the same. Of course, he realizes, the primary reason that he feels this way is that he's drunk, his formerly pure system churning with the chemicals of four or more 100-proof vodka martinis, five different kinds of imported beer, and the flesh of six different animals.

The tiki torches are lighted. Gerard is in the kitchen Saran-wrapping the undevoured meat. Victor, Marcus, and Henry are talking music, but though he recognizes the names—Springsteen, Clapton, even Kiss, for Christ's sake—the others' taste seems to Henry as if it comes from not just another generation but another galaxy. As they continue to talk his mind wanders again, this time to the Upper West Side. To images of people his age doing the exact opposite of what he's doing now. People who would rather be on the menu at Meat Night than attend it. It's gotten to the point where even the sorriest New Yorkers with whom he works seem to have more exciting lives than his. They tell him about the Hal Hartley movie they saw the night before at the Angelika, the installation at Emergency Arts in Chelsea, or the next killer band he's never heard of in Williamsburg. Up here the cineplexes are filled with talking animals and incendiary spectacle. White-haired women in museums that close at five champion the arts. And the music scene is a guy with a guitar named Joey doing covers for the after-dinner crowd at the Lakeside Bar & Grill.

In the city, even people with kids seem to lead much more interesting lives. Henry lowers his face and rubs his eyes, as if his fingertips are erasers. But before the scene around him can be wiped away he hears one Osborne tell the other that he's "an effin' A-hole." Then Henry hears the antiwar, pacifist Osborne's martini splash against the prowar Osborne's face. By the time Henry opens his eyes they're lunging out of their chairs, bull-rushing each other. Henry is knocked back against the table. A beer bottle (Magic Hat #9, Vermont) smashes on the bluestone. The others quickly descend on them and begin prying the pacifist's hands from his brother's neck.

Everyone except Henry. Still seated, all that he can manage is to say, "Hey. Guys. Not cool. Not effing"—when did I start saying *effing*?—"cool." Which he does not say with a great deal of emphasis, because part of him wouldn't mind seeing the brothers fight to the death with steak knives and shish kebab spears. Once separated, they quickly give up the fight, and within seconds they start feeling foolish. They apologize to Gerard and the group, and then to each other. After they clean up the broken glass together, the fighting Osborne brothers apologize all over again and then say their goodbyes and leave together, because they have to. Tonight is John's turn to be Eric's designated driver.

After the Osbornes leave, the remaining four make a game of trying to remember what topic sent the brothers over the edge. Marcus thinks it was executive bonuses for government bailouts, combined with the more disturbing aspects of Henry's just-told bombshell. Victor thinks it was gay marriage. But Gerard and Marcus eventually determine that the topic that drove the brothers to violence, the last of their many subjects, was, appropriately, the obscure House Bill 5991, a resolution to prohibit the injection of carbon monoxide in meat products.

"Whatever that is," says Marcus.

"I think," Henry offers, "that House Bill 5991 has to do with protecting the individual's, or group of individuals', inalienable right to completely fuck up an otherwise tedious social gathering." The other three almost begin to laugh and then realize they shouldn't.

Gerard lowers his head and wipes his hand on his apron. For a few moments the men on the patio are silent, and it looks like the night might be coming to a close. A ridiculous near fistfight between brothers and an increasingly obnoxious young maverick who can't handle his liquor seem like good enough reasons, but Gerard decides to let Henry's comment pass. Gerard the patient. Gerard the lonely. Screw the housewives, Gerard's the one who's desperate for companionship, likely to remain alone at his house until his family comes home at the end of the summer. If they decide to come back at all. One of Victor's compilation CDs—"Chick stuff this hot tech person I work with burned for me"—has taken over as the sound track of their lives.

"So, Henry," Gerard prompts. "What's with you tonight? What's on your mind?"

Never taking his gaze off Gerard, Henry rises and walks to the cooler. Henry opens them all a fresh beer, whether they are ready or not. When Victor starts to wave him off, he tells him to sit back down, the night is still young, and then he proceeds to tell each of them what he really thinks, what's really on his mind.

I Am the Ghost

"I think if you apologize everyone will be cool with it."

Marcus LeBlanc and Henry are parked in Henry's recently sealed driveway. Marcus is at the wheel of Henry's Audi A4. Behind them, Victor Chan has just gotten out of Marcus's Audi A4 and without a word to the others has begun walking the three blocks to his house with his fortieth-birthday traveling martini kit tucked under his arm. Henry laughs.

"I called Victor an embarrassment to his race. The anti–Bruce Lee. Whatever I say to him he should absolutely not be cool with."

Turning to his surroundings, he stares at the dimming solar lights that line the driveway edges, the curved path to his front door. Two helix-shaped topiaries at the end of the path twist into the darkness like flawed DNA. Runaway chromosomes. He doesn't know what he hates most, the topiaries, the solar lights, or the new-tar smell of his flawless driveway.

"This is the problem. An apology should not fix this. Words were said: *Cuckold. Douchebag. Beard. Stepford Husbands.* Even if I were truly sorry that I said them, which I can't in good faith say I am—and the fact that I've been drinking is no excuse—they were thought and they were said. The words. Anyone with a backbone would not and should not accept my apology. Which is why I won't do it. It would be embarrassing for all of us. Henry Tuhoe is not an apologist. At least, not anymore. Do you realize how many times I've said I'm sorry to Rachel in the last twelve months? In the last twelve hours? Sickening. I don't even know what I'm saying I'm sorry for anymore. I'm thinking, basically, if this will shut her up for five minutes, then I am truly, genuinely, forever sorry. For a long time I was one sorry bastard. But no more."

Marcus takes the keys out of the ignition. "You know, Henry, I had the procedure too. After our second. It's not easy, mentally or physically. And mine was relatively side-effect-free."

Henry either doesn't hear Marcus or doesn't want to. Inside, the house is dark, but through the living room window he can see two red dots, from the sound system or the TiVo, or from Satan, he thinks, staring out at him, more of a presence in his house than he himself will ever be.

"They know," Marcus says. "They all know. The Osbornes have even debated it. In case you're wondering, Rachel told Viv, who told everyone."

One night just before the procedure date, Rachel had over a bunch of friends whom he'd never met. For kicks, they had booked a psychic. To stay out of their way, Henry made plans to work late and have dinner with Warren. Warren ended up canceling, something big had come up in the Eye Care Division that would soon lay him off, leaving Henry with nothing to do. He browsed the aisles of Posman Books in Grand Central. He stopped at the Blazer, a roadhouse near the train stop, and had a cheeseburger at the bar. That killed another hour. It was too dark to take a walk. Too late to drop in unannounced on a neighbor, friend, or relative, not that there were any candidates. So he slowly cruised the streets of his hometown by default, like a stranger, an alien, a pedophile on the prowl.

He headed up Route 9 as far as the quaint river town of Cold Spring, but all the quaint river town shops were closed. He parked at the gazebo and looked across at the Hudson Highlands, the lights of West Point. For ten minutes. Then he went home. The driveway was still full and cars were lined up at the curb, so he pulled in behind the last car on the road and dimmed the lights. For a while he stared at the house as if it were a trig problem. A metaphysical equation. The only light that he could see was the flickering of a candle in the great room.

Finally he got out and walked across the lawn, eschewing the path. Rather than going inside, he continued on to the edge of the great room window and, leaning over the boxwoods, peeked in on the gathering. There were more than a dozen of them sitting around the candlelit table, women holding hands with their eyes closed, some talking, some smiling, every face fixed with an expression that said, even though they couldn't see him, that he was not welcome here.

Rachel had given him an ultimatum: Do it or we're through. He didn't want them to be through, but he didn't want to be neutered and married to the unfamiliar woman chanting in his living room either. When he suggested that if she was uncomfortable going to an office, he could arrange to have a psychologist come to the house, she said that if he did, she would have both of them arrested.

The next day he asked her about the gathering.

"We had a ladies' night."

"What was that smell? What was burning?"

Rachel laughed. "Alicia, who did the readings . . . sometimes she burns some things—sage, myrrh—beforehand to sort of cleanse the house."

"I never heard of psychics burning things for readings."

"She's a witch, actually. And it wasn't just readings. It was a séance."

"Sounds like fun. Was it a hoot?"

"No, it was not a hoot, Henry. It was fascinating."

"Really? Did you . . . I mean, did she . . ."

Rachel put her hands up. "Sorry. We promised not to discuss it outside the group."

"After a while," he finally says, as much to himself as to Marcus, "it's accompanied by a certain loss of dignity, the apologizing. A diminishing self-respect."

"You got that right," Marcus replies. "After I had it, I did lose some of that. Some dignity. A little respect. Eventually I could get it up just fine and all, but there's that ego thing that your boys—your swimmers—they're no longer a part of the event. Disqualified before the medal round. So I'd get wistful. But none of that mattered, because within two months of the procedure, which was her idea, she took her little adventure, which you were kind enough to allude to during your diatribe."

"Do you know," Henry says, half out the window, half to Marcus, "how some people who are troubled, in a certain kind of emotional turmoil, how they claim to see ghosts? To be visited by the ghosts of dead family members or famous people?"

No, Marcus does not know, but he nods anyway.

"Well, lately in my dreams, waking visions, hallucinations, whatever you want to call them, I am the ghost. The one visiting these people, these now-dead people back when *they* were alive, before I knew them, sometimes before I was born. And get this: I'm the one scaring the shit out of *them*, haunting them, and ultimately I'm the one pissing them off, because you know, after I do my thing, they realize that unlike most visitors from the great or not-so-great beyond, I've got absolutely zero wisdom for them. Nothing. They know that I'm talking to them from Tomorrowland, a place from where I should be able to tell them all sorts of helpful things. Key dates. Critical events. Potentially life-saving things to avoid. Other things or people to seek out. To embrace. But I have zilch. I have nothing to give them except that which makes the dead absolutely terrified of the living."

Marcus has no comment. He has to get home, for no reason, really. And even though this talk is making him feel uncomfortable, it is compelling. But the pull of the habitual is stronger. Certain digitally recorded shows. Certain slippers. Half a pint of Cherry Garcia still in the freezer, if he's not mistaken. "I've really got to get going, dude."

Henry ignores him. Takes a deep breath. Even this late at night, the air smells of just-mowed grass. Some nut whose house hasn't been foreclosed came home from work and got on the John Deere in the dark. Before lawn care became a competitive sport, a neighborhood obsession, before he lived here, he used to like that smell too. "Do you have any friends, Marcus?"

Marcus shifts in his seat. Where to put the keys? He doesn't want to insult Henry, but he doesn't want him to go out for a joyride in the condition he's in either. Plus there's the liability issue. "Sure, H. I've got friends."

"Really? You have someone you can totally trust? Someone you can absolutely count on to make you laugh, to help you out, to let you know when you're messing up? Someone you've known a long time who looks forward to your company and whose company you look forward to?"

"Yeah. Sure. I guess. Sure I do, Henry. I consider you my friend."

Henry turns and looks at both Marcus LeBlancs. He shakes his head and closes his eyes for a second, but that makes him dizzy, makes his stomach turn. When he opens them again he sees a singular Marcus, and he decides that he won't reveal the harsh truth to him about their supposed friendship. About all friendships. He decides that tonight Marcus has earned the right to go home wrapped in the comfort of the lie. "You want to know the most disturbing part about my marriage, about my vasectomy, Marcus?"

Marcus LeBlanc sits upright. Maybe the Cherry Garcia can wait. He smiles and nods at his very good friend Henry Tuhoe. Yes. Yes, he certainly does.

Poolside

The first week after the vasectomy procedure:
- Stay off your feet as much as possible.
- Ice the scrotum for 20 minutes every hour (except when sleeping). You can make your own ice pack by using a bag of frozen peas.
- Do not have sex or lift anything heavier than 10 pounds.

—Snipped.com

Henry sits poolside on the end of a chaise lounge, staring at the cloud-scrimmed moon, listening to the wet hum of circulating water. He wants to lie back and close his eyes, but the sour swirling in his stomach will not allow it.

Rachel may or may not be inside. If she's home she's surely asleep, the sound machine on her nightstand soothing her into REM with "Ocean Waves" or "Rain Forest" or the urethra-taunting "Trickling Stream." Speaking of which. Henry rises and crab-walks to the bed of impatiens near the pool house and releases a long, scattershot piss.

Two days before the procedure, Rachel went away for her annual weeklong Internet Security Convention in Vegas. If things had been better between them, Henry would have accompanied her, as he had in previous years, and they would have made the most

of it, gambled, tried to see Prince's show, maybe piggybacked a trip
to Tahoe onto it. But he told her that this was the first available date
and he wanted to get it over with. Even though he could tell that
Rachel was relieved, she had offered to cancel the trip, to stay home
to help him, but Henry would not hear of it. It wasn't a big deal;
plus she generated most of her new business leads for the year at the
Vegas convention.

"There's really nothing you can do," he said. "Most people have
it on a Thursday or Friday and if all goes well are back to work on
Monday. I've already got the peas in the freezer. A vegetable medley
too, for variety. So you see, you're not the only one capable of icing
my balls."

He shakes, zips, and sits back on the edge of the chaise lounge.
The night that they closed on the house, they had a poolside candle-
light dinner with a $200 bottle of red Bordeaux that one of Rachel's
clients had given them. Afterward they swam naked in the clear
heated water and began making love in the deep end, then moved to
the shallows, the pool stairs, and finally the carpeted floor of their
otherwise empty family room. Once last May they'd had a poolside
party, just over three months after the miscarriage. At the end of the
day, while he was barbecuing and Gnarls Barcley's "Crazy" played
on their outdoor speakers, he heard a woman shriek and looked up
to see Rachel pulling their neighbor's two-year-old girl out of the
bottom of the deep end. The parents had not been paying attention.
No one except Rachel had even heard the tiny splash. She jumped in
wearing a beautiful white sundress and with a red hyacinth in her
hand. He'd brought a dozen home from the city the day before.
When they came up, the wet flower was pressed against the little
girl's blond hair. Staring at the very spot where it had happened,
Henry remembers thinking that maybe saving the girl would change
Rachel. Maybe she would interpret the event as a life-altering moment and she would revert to the way she had been, or mutate into
something altogether new, rather than what she'd become. Yet the
only change that came from what Henry would later refer to as the
Hyacinth Incident was Rachel telling him that she was now certain
that she wanted him to get a vasectomy. A bomb had gone off somewhere in the world that morning. A jetliner had mysteriously

dropped out of the sky the day before. The markets were in free fall, and in the past week another house on their block had been abandoned by its owners in the middle of the night. Did any of that inform her decision? Or something else?

Or had she made up her mind long before that?

"Why?" he finally asked her. "Why are you so certain?"

"The world feasts on evil and random tragedy," she said. "And I will not bring another innocent child into it."

After the Hyacinth Incident, after the vasectomy request, Henry fell into a funk of his own. At work, in addition to researching all things vasectomy, he Googled the word *hyacinth* and clicked on its mythological origin. Hyacinth, he read, was a beautiful youth killed by his jealous friend Apollo. Rather than allowing Hades to claim the boy, the supposedly distraught Apollo kept him and made a flower, the hyacinth, from his spilled blood. Other versions have Apollo accidentally killing Hyacinth or someone orchestrating diabolical events, but the spilled-blood-into-a-flower bit remained the same. Henry didn't believe in mythology, and the fact that there were two entirely different takes with different villains and heroes of the same story didn't help. But even though the parallels to his life were vague at best, the story freaked him out, and the image of his lost wife and the red flower pressed against the saved girl's dripping hair troubles him still.

For a few moments there is a gap in the clouds, revealing the half-formed patterns of constellations whose names he'll never know. The light of the moon spreads across the motionless pool like a coroner's sheet. Henry gets up and turns on the switch for the underwater lights near the pool house. Illuminated from above and below, the water comes back to life. To his amazement, it is as clean and blue as he has ever seen it. As clean as it looked the day they moved in. Did he see this in her then? The quirkiness? The instability? Over the past year he has tried to help her, but now the word isn't *help,* it's *save.* Still, she wants none of it. Counseling, getaways, walking, talking, and absolutely no counseling or psychiatric help. She fought it all. Insulted him. She wanted none of it, and less and less of him. He'd be lying if he said he'd never considered leaving her. Kids wouldn't be a problem. But she wasn't well. And leaving someone who isn't well is different from leaving someone who is, for instance, a bitch. So it's not that simple, especially since lately she has been more than a bit of both, not well and a bitch. Regardless, he determines to work harder at everything.

It starts with telling her everything—he really has to, and she will have to understand. They will talk deep into the night again, every night, and make a series of plans. They will keep the house or sell the house. They will stay put or drop it all. Move back to Manhattan. Start over in San Francisco. Go off the grid. Whatever it takes. They will rediscover each other. The woman she was. The man he ought to be. And she will promise to make a commitment to get well.

Or what?

At water's edge he kneels and lets his fingers brush the smooth surface. Just to be sure, he undoes the cap of the test strip bottle. As he bends to dip the strip into the water, to confirm what he already knows, his throat constricts, his stomach seizes and heaves. Before he can stand, remnants of six cuts of fire-cooked meat, five specialty martinis, and a comprehensive selection of the world's finest beers shoot from his mouth and arc through the bone-white moonlight before splashing down into the pool, botching its chemistry all over again.

Analysis of the Self
and the Semen

At your physician's discretion, you can collect your intitial seminal specimen at home and bring it directly to the doctor's office or lab.

—Snipped.com

Rachel is gone when he wakes up. Pilates. Spinning. Group walk on the bike path. Broomstick-making. Who knows? They never saw each other last night. She didn't say good-bye this morning, but that's nothing new. He slept on the living room couch, but that too is nothing new. He's taken to sleeping on the couch more and more to see if it will bother her, but she hasn't even pretended to notice. He's still not sure whether Rachel got home first or sometime after he did. He doubts that she knows that he was drunk, or that he puked in the pool, in part because that would have required her to pay attention to him, and also because he hasn't gotten drunk in years, hasn't vomited from alcohol since college. Not that she'd be upset with him. In fact, before she changed, Rachel used to urge him to let loose more, get out with the proverbial boys, even if in this instance the boys were more likely to be addicted to Viagra than, say, adrenaline.

But rather than brightening his disposition, the outings would trigger fits of morbid self-reflection, scenarios that always played out to the ultimate endgame. After men's nights, even the most innocent reverie about, say, fishing, or granite countertops, or honey Dijon potato chips, would invariably end for Henry with a lurid contemplation of death.

Yet he kept going back.

Tossing Jarts and Wiffle balls, talking bourbon and brisket and bocce. Saying things like *Man up* and *Dude.* For all of his complaining, for all of his regrets, he still maintained a perfect attendance record. But no more.

Last night, before the Osbornes blew up, before he became drunk and obnoxiously forthcoming in his opinions, someone—was it Victor, perhaps to help him get over post-vasectomy anxiety?—suggested having next month's men's night at a strip club. *They serve a surprisingly good buffet there,* he remembers someone saying. He imagines himself standing in line, the PA announcer calling Dynastee to the main stage, strobe lights flashing off sterno-warmed aluminum banquet trays, passing the chicken cordon bleu spoon without making eye contact to a stranger with a post-lap-dance erection. No, sir.

Shuffling into the kitchen, scanning the cereal cabinet, he figures he has an hour, maybe an hour and a half before Rachel returns home. Just to be sure, he determines to be gone within the hour, before nine. Now is certainly not the time to have the most important conversation of your marriage. Indeed, right now his mind is incapable of forming fully developed concepts and sentences. Just staccato thoughts of disjointed anguish.

He mixes health-food-store raisin bran with supermarket Cocoa Crisps. The benefits of the former, he figures, cancel the consequences of the latter. But life is a series of trade-offs, right? Compromises and concessions. Bending but not breaking. Treading water. Sinking. Avoiding. Lying. Feigning impotence, then jerking off.

On the kitchen table he notices the witchcraft book again and assumes that's where she was last night, bitching about men, conjuring and executing pagan rituals. Coming up with new ways to rid them of their sanity, their dignity, their semen. Last week, after he'd had an especially trying day, only to come home as she was walking out the door, he asked what she did at the witches' group.

"It's a women's group," she answered.

"One person's women's group is another's coven."

"We discuss womanly things."

"Like how to use black magic to destroy men."

"Only the ones who deserve it, Henry," she said, smiling. "So you really have nothing to worry about, right?"

The night returns in crude flashes. The Osbornes tumbling onto the bluestone, locked in mortal ideological combat. The piles of bloody meat. The embarrassing chick music. Telling Gerard he has no soul and Victor he has no guts, or was it the other way around?

And of course everyone knowing about his vasectomy.

And then babbling in the driveway to Marcus. How much did I say? he wonders. Who should get the first letter of apology? Whom should I call? Or how about an e-mail? The same e-mail to the entire group—apologetic, contrite but not without a bit of humor. Maybe something like *It was the ostrich talking*, or *Who did I think I was, the third Osborne brother?* Would that suffice? Or how about this, he thinks, finishing the final bit of soggy cereal, lifting the bowl to drink the last of the brown, sugary soy milk substitute. How about cc-ing every adult male in the United States on a memo with this for the subject heading: *We are an embarrassment.*

The calendar on the wall next to the refrigerator has a large red asterisk Sharpied across today's date. Beneath it, in Rachel's bold red handwriting, is written:

Sperm Day! Sample #3 Due! No cheating!

Hispanic men at the train station, waiting for contractors to put them behind a wheelbarrow, a lawn mower, a toxic spray gun. Insourcing. The 9:02 is gliding away from the platform while he is still looking for a parking space. He can wait an hour for a local, or he can drive in, or what?

He puts the shift in park and decides to think about it. A

politician handing out fliers for an upcoming primary is talking
with an aide, wondering if it's worth it to stick around for the next
train. A mason's dump truck pulls up to the curb, and after a brief
negotiation, three day laborers climb onto the back. Henry wonders what the politician thinks of this. Shit, what does *he* think of
it? As the truck passes, he sees that one of the laborers is wearing
an FDNY hat and a *Vote for Pedro* T-shirt.

He fiddles with the radio. Hate rhetoric, liberal and conservative. Contemporary Christian death metal. Doodoo jokes from the
wacky morning crew. Lionel Richie on the best of the old and the
hottest of the new. "Truly." Should've charged the iPod. Suddenly it
becomes extremely important that he find NPR.

Henry locates it just in time to hear the newswoman finishing
up the national segment announce that today is the day that the
world has used up its allotted resources for the year and it is operat-
ing at an environmental deficit. From now on it will be borrowing
against next year, when the deficit day will arrive even earlier. And
so on, earlier and earlier, every year of the foreseeable future, until
there's nothing left to borrow.

He decides that he doesn't want to go to work, or to the city, but
he can't go home and can't think of anything to do here. Lost in the
suburbs and lost in the city, and it's funny how residents of each
place assume that he's distinctly of the other.

A train that he didn't know about comes and goes. His phone
buzzes on the empty passenger's seat. Rachel. "How'd it go?"

"Splendidly. I just hope they don't check for alcohol content."

"You got drunk with the boys last night! I thought I heard you
banging around by the pool."

Her happiness jars him. What's the motive for that? He considers telling her that he insulted every one of "the boys," that he vomited into said pool, destroying its briefly perfect balance, and that
he's done with Meat Night forever, but it's too complicated. He's
afraid he'll start babbling and tell her everything the wrong way.

"So did the doctor say anything?"

"No. This was strictly a drop-off. Splash and dash."

"Where are you?"

"In the parking lot at the train station. I just missed two trains."

"How is it possible to just miss two trains?"

"It's an acquired skill, Rachel."

"So you're still going in?"

He thinks. What the hell. "Unless you'd like a little company."

Nervous laughter. "I'm . . ."

What? He thinks. Swamped? Crazy? Trying to make me crazy too? Anything but interested.

". . . sorry. But today's bad, Henry."

"Sure. Actually, it's not looking so good on my end either."

He clicks End and stares at the phone.

He thinks, I can go to the beach. I can go for a hike. I can go to the library. I can go bowling.

During his research he came across several stories of homosexual men who had vasectomies.

He calls Meredith. "What's the good word?"

"Who is this?"

"Your soon-to-be former coworker."

"Giffler came by. Tried to peek through the smoked glass to see where you were."

"Did you have the Henry Tuhoe life-sized action figure placed in the hard-at-work position?"

"He didn't buy it. Lingered for a minute, spraying just enough executive pee to let you sense he was here."

"Did he say anything?"

"He had me put you down for an eleven o'clock with him tomorrow morning."

"La fin du monde."

"Only to the self-absorbed and melodramatic among us."

"Easy for the self-absorbed and still employed to say."

"I know too much to be fired. So are you not going to accept the transfer?"

"Not a chance. This is the best thing to happen to me, Meredith. I had a drunken epiphany last night, actually a series of them, and I'm going to do something with my life that matters."

"The other line's flashing. Anything else?"

"How's Warren?"

"Still pissed at you, but very excited about India. He's already tracked down his Bangalorian doppelgänger job."

"You know what? I would like to take you and Warren out to lunch tomorrow. No, how about drinks after work? A sort of going-away party in my honor, given by me."

"Wow. Drinks with two recently laid-off middle-aged men. Can't get any better than that."

"How about Ginger Man at five?"

"Will you be in today?"

"No. I don't want to see Giffler yet. Plus I have a doctor's appointment."

He thinks he hears Meredith cluck her tongue, her audio equivalent of the skeptical eye roll. "I see," she says.

Two black vans claim the last of the day laborers. The politician is long gone. No votes left to court. Off to record telemarketing messages, Henry thinks, about immigration, or the tangible evil his opponent stands for. Such as telemarketing, campaign finance reform, and mudslinging. He shuts off Lionel Ritchie and lowers the windows to better soak in the late-morning commuter rail station silence. At 10:37 a northbound train stops and more than a dozen black women in white nurse's outfits get off. A small bus pulls in seconds later, ready to drive them to hospitals and nursing homes, the lonely residences of the affluent and infirm. Insourcing for the soon-to-be permanently outsourced.

Before his grandmother died six years ago, while she lived alone in an apartment in White Plains, he tried to convince her to let a nurse come in to visit once a day. But she wanted no part of a stranger in her house, and sometimes he felt that included him. The day before she died, he called to say he was coming by on the weekend and asked if she needed anything. She said yes. "Get me the vitamin drink where the old couple on the rowboat in the middle of the lake are laughing and drinking and saluting the feeble, no-vitamin-drinking couple languishing onshore."

He thinks, I can get a Swedish massage. I can get the car washed. I can text-message every person whose text messages I've ignored in the last three months.

More buzzing in the passenger's seat. Norman from the gym. Henry watches the screen signal that a message is being left, probably confirming tomorrow's workout, which he most likely will have to cancel. How to break it to Norman?

Next to the message icon is a small movie camera icon. Norman has left a video message as well. He opens the file and hits Play. Soon his small screen fills with the title "Jump" in white letters on a black background. As Van Halen's song of the same name begins to play, Henry watches a series of vignettes presumably filmed by Norman. Nursery school children jumping in a classroom. Kids on blow-up castles. Trampolines. High schoolers dancing. Sweet, sappy, happy stuff. Boring, clichéd stuff. Then it changes with the chorus. The happy kids give way to grainy long-range footage of a man standing midspan on a great American bridge—yes, it's the Golden Gate—poised to jump. Then jumping. Before the man hits the water and presumably dies, the piece cuts to footage of another jumper on another bridge, leaping. Then another. Might as well jump. A half-dozen suicidal jumpers on a half-dozen bridges, each falling with his own morbid choreography, arms windmilling, arms spread like a bird, torso locked straight, tucked, tumbling, spinning, hands at sides, over head. All plummeting. Go ahead and jump. When the chorus ends it match dissolves from bridge jumper back to happy jumper footage—a small girl and a dog on a playground, a chubby old man on a pogo stick, a yellow lab grabbing a Frisbee—and it has a profoundly different effect on Henry.

He shuts it off in the middle of the second chorus, after the third of three new jumpers, a teenage girl, appears poised at the rail. This is less than halfway through the film, still several minutes away from Norman's printed signoff urging people to vote for his film at this address, to make it a daily favorite on his preferred aggregate video channel.

Closing his eyes, listening to another train pulling into the station—northbound or southbound, he can't be sure—Henry decides that it's a good idea to cancel tomorrow's workout.

I can go for a jog. I can go clothes shopping. I can talk with a certified financial planner. I can take a short trip to the middle of the Tappan Zee Bridge.

Today's women want a real man fucking them in the bedroom, someone had said at some point last night. But outside the bedroom it's the other way around. They are the ones doing the fucking, the ones in charge, making us do the most emasculating things, subjecting us to the most humiliating shit. Shit that a real man would not do. Making the whole bedroom thing a sort of doomed construct.

Did Marcus say that? Did I? Do I really believe that?

He hears a chain saw in the distance and thinks of the months after they first moved up here. Whenever he would fire up his new chain saw, Rachel would throw a fit. She'd shout things like "Hire someone else to do that!" and "Please don't hurt yourself, Henry."

And then she didn't. And he's certain it had nothing to do with his improved cutting skills.

He sleeps.

For how long? How many hours? How many trains?

The phone's vibrations bring him back, spur the Pavlovian act of clicking Talk without checking caller ID.

"Henry Tuhoe."

"Tick, tick, tick. How goes the desperate searching of the soul?" Giffler.

"The search has been called off. No survivors."

"Where are you? We're worried to death."

"Who?"

"No one, actually. But I was curious. Your wife too."

"Oh."

"Called the casa and she said you were on your way into work, which is a big stinky lie. But I didn't say a thing. I played along with whatever it is you're up to. Figured you were considering the possibilities. Unless you *are* on your way into work at what, one o'clock?"

"I'm not on my way into work. I had a doctor's appointment. Now I'm heading home."

"We're on for ten tomorrow?"

"Eleven."

"Before we meet, and the reason I'm calling, because of our undeniable father-son-like bond, I wanted to give you some more information to run up the flagpole of your conscience. I wanted to tell you what else I've learned."

"Okay, Dad. Lay it on me."

"Where they're sending you. It's a tiny kingdom on the India-China border called . . . shit. Should have written it down."

"Bhutan?"

"No. Not Bhutan. Bhutan is like the Land of Oz compared to this place. Anyway, the government there is really making a play to open its once closed gates to, if not democracy, then capitalism. You're to be part of a historic corporate delegation that will turn their wretched history around."

"By setting up a call center for an American bottled water company?"

"Exactly. Hugely important, because this mind-bogglingly impoverished nation, whose name still eludes my memory, is like the water industry, bottled and otherwise, on the rise. You'll be helping their economy, albeit not their thirst. Still quite admirable, the whole mission."

"Nepal?"

"Not Nepal. Some place considerably less developed. Less known. But I'll have all the facts by tomorrow."

"Don't bother. Doesn't matter. All that matters is what kind of termination package you can pull together for your favorite son, because I'm not going anywhere."

"Didn't hear that. Click."

Click.

Non-motile

If the second test shows non-motile (also known as dead) sperm, then a third test will be necessary. If the follow-up test shows moving or active sperm, the patient will be declared to have had a vasectomy failure, and it should be redone.

—Snipped.com

He thinks, I can be a research consultant. I can work for the competition. I can teach. Go back to school. I can work for a not-for-profit. I can work with my hands, building houses or honestly constructed pieces of furniture. I can become a personal trainer, a webmaster for a big-boob porn star, a day trader, an online five-card-hold-'em poker legend.

I can do whatever I want.

When I tell Rachel, she will understand. The job part, at least.

Pulling into the cursed driveway, turning off the incongruous car.

In fact, she'll probably be happy, because she hates my job more than I do.

Stretching, staring at the unfortunate subdivision, the malevolent house, the thing that never should have happened. The window of the room where the recent orgasms were counterfeit, the funny faces forced.

He thinks, One thing I will absolutely do, first thing tomorrow, is call the doctor. Then a travel agent to book a trip. Nothing like an exotic trip to provide the perfect . . . what? The perfect sorbet for stagnant lives.

Walking up the foreign path, past the detestable topiaries, wondering how it will feel to be unemployed and watch a landscaper trim your hedges.

Nearing the door he never wanted to open, thinking, We'll take a trip and sort it all out. Like we did in Cabo. And Maui. And even in Block Island. She's always wanted to go to Belize. With enough tranquilizers I would be willing to fly to Belize.

Reaching for said door but getting hit in the cheekbone by it first. Sensing blood before it flows. "You son of a bitch."

Canceling Belize. Reaching for a possibly broken nose.

"You lying, duplicitous son of a . . . prick. We didn't have much left, but we had the truth."

Absorbing a two-handed push. Backtracking down the foreign path, brushing against a detestable topiary. "I just found out yesterday."

"Yesterday? That is an absolutely unconscionable lie."

Raising hands to block a series of roundhouse smacks.

"All you had to do was tell me. But you . . . this is deliberate, hateful, almost criminal."

"I was going to tell you right now. Tonight. There wasn't time last night. I just spoke to Giffler about it yesterday."

"You told Giffler before you told me?"

"It's his specialty. Besides, it's not even official. I assume he broke my confidence and told you when he called today."

"Your confidence? What? What are—"

"You're talking about the layoff, right?" Realizing that the horrified look on her face has nothing to do with his employment situation. Watching her look for something to throw. Watching her fingers and eyes point at his crotch.

"Layoff? I'm talking about *that*. I'm talking about a procedure that never happened, Henry."

"Operation, technically."

"The shaving, the follow-up tests. The frozen fucking vegetable ice packs. What a freak you are. My God. We were having unprotected sex when I thought you were testing negative!"

He holds up his right middle and forefingers. "Twice. And that's because you were drunk on witches' brew. And I never orgasmed, Rachel. I faked. I made the face, but both times I faked."

"I will not stay in a marriage built upon lies and fakes."

"I did lie and I did fake. But it's because I didn't believe I was talking to the real you. I thought that you were going through a phase, that you might change your mind."

"Well, I'm about to enter a new phase. It's called life after the lying faker."

"I want to work with you, Rachel. Get you some help. I mean, get us some help. I mean, what the hell happened to us up here? We were never meant to come here."

"Get *me* some help? I didn't pretend I had an operation!"

"Years of moping. Years of your refusing to get out of your own way. You stopped paying attention to me, Rachel. It was as if I never lived here."

"That's the first true thing you've said. You never did live here! And now you don't have to physically be here either. Now go."

"I was laid off yesterday. Take a job somewhere in Asia or be fired, was the ultimatum."

"This isn't about yesterday, Henry. This is about long-term dishonesty."

"I did it for us."

"Hah! Go, Henry. Go on unemployment, because God knows you're too boring and afraid to do the other thing." She raises her hands as if to hit him again, but she continues to raise them overhead, closes her eyes, and begins chanting something in a tongue not of this world.

"I don't want to leave you the way you are. I'd be willing to—"

"What, Henry? What have you ever been truly *willing* to do?"

He has no answer.

"That's right. Now get you and your lying penis out of here."

———

Stepping away from the malevolent house, onto the cursed drive-way. Reaching for the door of the incongruous car. Pulling away, thinking about sweat, and then sperm, and now water. Feeling a sharp phantom pain in the recently shaved but otherwise undis-turbed scrotal area.

Leaving.

Motel Three

A chain of hotels for wayward men. Displaced men. Men who have been given the boot. Men who have run away. There definitely is a market for it, Henry thinks, heading south on Route 9, in search of just such a place.

Within an hour after she kicked him out, Rachel called to say she was giving him two hours to come back and gather his belongings. When he asked if she'd be there, she told him no. She said she was going to her friend's house to learn how to put a spell on his lying ass.

While lurking around the house in which he had never wanted to live, he thought about his belongings. He thought about how they were different from his stuff, his shit, his necessities, and he decided that a belonging was a thing he valued, that he'd miss and possibly even fight for. And he was surprised at how few things fell into that category, and even those could hardly be considered belongings. Clothes and music, mostly. His passport. The big bottle of Purell.

Whether he'd be gone a day or forever, it didn't matter. These were all the belongings he had.

What amenities would his hypothetical hotel for wayward men have? Free legal and alcohol counseling for monthly guests? An on-call private investigator for the cuckolded? A nutritionist for the fast-food heart attack victim in the making? A concierge specializing in creative visitation outings and local strip clubs? How about a Barcalounger in every room? A maxibar?

Although he had no idea where he might go, the act of packing filled him with a sense of excitement he hadn't felt in many years, and the realization that he was actually leaving was a relief, at least when he wasn't thinking of the shame and disgust bubbling one layer down. When he wasn't dwelling on the death of love, the resurrection of guilt, the consequences of everything, and what the hell he was going to do with the rest of his life.

Just before he left, right after he locked the front door for perhaps the final time, out of curiosity, he took a final look at the pool, and even after the vomit episode it was perfect.

The Rabbit Angstrom Suite. The I-Told-You-So Post-Nup Business Center. Only men's rooms in the lobby.

The first motel he sees is a one-story cinder-block structure just south of Tarrytown, with none of the aforementioned amenities. "Just for the night," he tells the old man behind the Plexiglas.

"You can have it by the hour too," the old man offers.

He takes out an order of hot-and-sour soup and Szechuan chicken at a strip mall across the street and eats it looking out the window of Room 111 onto the parking lot. Already he's seen others like himself, unfolding out of the second-string family car, sulkily walking to their rooms, carrying their takeout, their brown paper bags, one with all his belongings in a gym bag, another with more luggage than anyone would ever take on a business trip.

Motel Three (because she's getting half of everything you have), you could call it. Or the Cleaners (because that's where you're about to be taken).

Or simply Asylum.

———

He spends the rest of the night oblivious of his surroundings, transfixed in front of his laptop, downloading songs and albums off the Internet and thinking of what to do next. Sometimes the music informs his thinking and sometimes it is the other way around. It has always been that way with Henry. He cannot carry a tune and has never shown any aptitude for playing an instrument, yet he believes that music has moved and taught him far more than any book or person. He's spoken to others who claimed to feel the same way, but they were different. They always seemed more obsessed with the facts and dates of when a group formed, when it changed drummers, when it broke up, when the import single became available in the States, but Henry never cared about any of that. What he cared about was the music and how it made him feel. His father often told him that he used music as an escape, a way to hide from the world, but Henry had always thought about it as a way to discover it.

Tonight he is ripping and sampling songs like a man who may never hear music again.

When he falls asleep, it is three a.m. and David Ford's "State of the Union" is playing, from the album *I Sincerely Apologize for All the Trouble I've Caused*.

Sometime in what's left of the night his cell phone rings. "One more thing," Rachel says. "In Vegas, I met an old friend. And the sex was outstanding."

Snipped

The song for the morning commute, by design, is "Rusty Cage" by Johnny Cash.

You wired me awake
And hit me with a hand of broken nails . . .

At nine a.m. he walks unannounced into Giffler's office and closes the door.

Giffler puts down a book he's pretending to read: *Beehive Management: How Life in the Honeycomb Translates to Winning in the Workplace.* "Dworik gave me this. What a bunch of hooey."

"I want a guaranteed contract, first-class accommodations, and a hell of a lot more money than these assholes are paying me now." Crazy he can put up with. Work with. Adultery? Not so much.

Giffler smiles, does a slow-motion slap of his hand upon the desk. "That's my boy."

"Is a typhoid shot a billable expense?"

Meredith nods. "Typhoid, hep A, hep B, Japanese encephalitis, malaria, rabies, swine, avian, and a tetanus-diphtheria booster. All billable if not universally recommended."

"The perks never stop," Henry says.

"Who says this is not a compassionate multinational conglomerate?" adds Warren.

Henry smiles. They are in a side booth at the Ginger Man in Midtown, a long, narrow beer hall filled with young, end-of-the-workday drinkers. The morning and most of the afternoon were spent decompressing with one Human Resources group and introducing himself to another. Accelerated orientations, a crash course in international business protocol, were scheduled. Background packets were expedited his way. He was green-lighted, fast-tracked, and shown the door. And this is his party: Meredith and Warren, who is wearing a vintage Indian Nehru shirt that Henry decides not to acknowledge. Norman from the gym said he'd try to make it and Giffler swore to God he'd show, but Henry knows better than to count on that.

He could have invited others—the rest of the Underarm Research Division, whoever's left from his days in Oral Care or Non-headache-related Pain Relief or Laxatives, or the ill-fated Silicon-based Sprays and Coatings team—but that would have been just a clusterfuck of negativism that would have had a *This Is Your Life* vibe that would have cast an all-too-revelatory light on an extended period of said life that Henry, in retrospect, would rather forget.

This degree of negativism is much more manageable. And because this is his going-away party, and his wife has just evicted him from his house and her life, and he'll be taking a very long plane ride to a very strange place, very soon Henry has decided that it is absolutely okay to drink again. Just a beer or two. As long as he's not chasing it with ostrich.

Meredith and Warren want to know how it went with Giffler and company this morning, so he gives them a best-of version of the wit and wisdom dispensed by his delusional life mentor and soon-to-be long-distance supervisor. Such as:

"The more efficient we get as consultants, the less money we make, so . . . By. All. Means. Take. Your. Bloody . . . Time."

And, "I've outsourced hundreds of jobs these last few weeks, but you, Henry—your whole miserable *life* is being outsourced."

And, "Our clients want to hear that we're outsourcing people assigned to their business, not because it's the strategically right thing to do but because it covers their trembling asses and says, 'I am a fiscally responsible manager and a passive-aggressive advocate of the corporate trend du jour.' Which is why we're diversifying beyond India and Prague. It's the newness of this place, not the practicalities of it, that makes us seem enlightened."

And, "Don't ever say the word *millennium* again. It will be nine hundred and eighty years before that word will be in the least bit cool."

And, "Teach your children engineering and Mandarin or else in ten years they'll be mowing lawns and cleaning toilets for someone with the last name of Hung."

And this: "Be careful over there, because I swear to God, Hank, if anything ever happened to you . . ."

Meredith shakes her head. "Hank?"

"Confucius-like in his wisdom," Warren says. "Most people go to the East to absorb its ancient truths, but you're going with a whole suitcase full of your own, courtesy of a white-collar sociopath."

"Are you excited?" Meredith asks.

Henry stares at her. Is he? Simple enough question, but he is stumped. He tries to guess what's playing on the sound system. Fergie? Duffy? Pink? Doesn't matter. No meaning, ironic or symbolic, to be gleaned there. "Actually, I don't know enough about where I'm going to be excited. I'm excited to be leaving, but I should be equally excited about my destination. But the truth is . . . Truth is, I haven't given it a whole lot of thought."

Meredith pretends to sip her seltzer as she maintains eye contact with Henry. Warren looks around. Coughs into his fist. "I've got to take a leak."

After Warren leaves, Henry says, "Rachel threw me out yesterday."

Meredith nods. "I know. She called."

"Did she tell you why?"

"No. I already knew."

He starts to ask how she knew, then decides it doesn't matter. Just assume she knows everything.

"She's been studying witchcraft, you know."

Meredith nods. "She said she put a virility-sapping spell on you."

Henry opens and closes his legs under the table, sips his Hoegaarden. "She said she knows how to make my penis dry up and fall off."

"So you're going to leave the country to work in a place you never heard of because your wife threw you out?"

Henry nods.

"Because you falsified a vasectomy?"

Of course she'd know. "Pretty much. Yeah."

Neither speaks for a while. Henry decides that anything he says to Meredith will be redundant, something already known. It *is* Fergie on the sound system. Fergie with the Black Eyed Peas, anyway. "Boom Boom Pow."

"I chickened out. She didn't seem all that . . . all that stable. She'd already changed her mind about kids, our house, her job, several times, and I just thought that this was something that you don't want to mess with unless you're certain."

"What about saying no, Henry? Did that ever occur to you?"

"She's studying to be a bloody witch."

"Probably because she's looking for what is lacking in her life."

"She could have joined a reading group."

"Again, all you had to do is tell her you don't want a vasectomy and you are not interested in being the soul mate of a child of Artemis."

"We had no sex life. I'm thirty-two, and even after I was supposed to have had it, she barely let me near her anyway."

"But—"

"And she cheated on me. In Vegas."

Meredith straightens up. "I see. This is more info than even I need to know. Listen, you're a great person on the inside, Henry. With all the right principles and convictions. The problem is you lack the balls to act on them."

"So I should go?"

She sighs.

And indeed there will be time
To wonder, "Do I dare?" and, "Do I dare?"

. . . *"Do I dare*
Disturb the universe?"

He looks at Meredith and feels ashamed. Few people have this effect on him, but often without prompting, condescending, or saying a word, she has the ability, in her mere presence, to make him fully aware of his deficiencies as a human. Boom Boom Pow.

"Shakespeare?"

She shakes her head dismissively. "Eliot."

"I guess you know I've visited your Web site."

She nods. "Several times a day. Every day. I can track the hits right back to our server, your office, your home PC."

"Right. Well, it's very well done, you know. The graphics and the . . ."

Warren comes back and slides into the booth. "Miss anything?"

They order sandwiches and another round as Warren begins to lay out his plans for his forthcoming trip to India. Flights, inoculations, accommodations. Lots of talk about *Slumdog Millionaire*. Henry appears to be listening, but he isn't. Maybe 50 percent of the time the words register, but the other 50 percent he is thinking about the course of his life so far and he realizes that Meredith is right, that he is the problem. Not suburbia or Metro-North or overdosing on armpit sweat focus groups or a cheating, mentally unstable wife who wants to be a witch. Well, maybe all that is part of the problem, but what has he ever done to change it? To prevent it?

"I got a two-bedroom place in one of the most exclusive condominiums in Bangalore for next to nothing," he doesn't hear Warren say.

But he does see two construction workers at the bar looking at Meredith, then at him in a way that can be described only as disdainfully. As if he is half a man. Unworthy of the company of a woman like Meredith, let alone, if they only knew, none other than EEEEva EEEEnormous. And he has to admit, they might be half right.

"I'm not just gonna be in Bangalore, though. All over their

region. Mumbai. Delhi. Shit, I may even make it up to your neck of the Himalayas, Henry."

Henry doubts that his father ever dwelled on his role as a man. His vocation. His direction. He went to Vietnam against his will and never spoke about it again. He got married to a woman his brother fixed him up with, got a job in sales because his father-in-law set it up, and to this day it remains a mystery to Henry whether or not he enjoyed any of it. He just kept his mouth shut and soldiered on. Like a man. Right up until the off-site. The coronary.

After his father died Henry wanted to ask his mother if she was satisfied with the path of her life. Marriage. Kids. Suburbs. Taking a backseat to Dad's supposed career when he's certain she would have been a star at whatever career she'd chosen if she'd been born in a different family, or ten years later. But he never asked, and sixteen months after his father died she was married to a real estate man named Alexi who made her—to Henry's . . . what? *Dismay* is the only word for it—so happy that he no longer had the desire to ask the question or the stomach to handle its reply, because who enjoys seeing his mother more in love with a man than she was when she was with his father?

Norman arrives and slides in alongside Henry. After introductions Henry asks if he can get him anything. "No thanks. Got really wasted last night."

"Wow. Where was the party?" Meredith asks.

"Actually, I was alone in my apartment, doing a marathon viewing of season one of *Gossip Girl* on DVD."

Within minutes Norman has given up on abstinence ("Oookaaay . . . Bourbon, rocks") and may or may not have slipped something into his mouth, Henry can't be sure, and has his laptop open and is showing them his latest film, a four-minute documentary on a day in the life of a Gulf War I reenactor. It's hard to hear what the reenactor is saying over the tiny laptop speakers because the music in the bar is so loud, so they can only watch as a man in full U.S. Army Desert Storm fatigues goes through SCUD gas-mask application, entrenching, and weapons drills in what looks, at least initially, like a desert environment.

"So he's the only one?" Meredith asks.

"Yeah. For now."

"And was he really there?"

"Oh, no. He's just a buff."

"I think I just saw the mast of a sailboat," Warren says. "Where'd you shoot this?"

Norman takes an exaggerated breath. "That's the thing. We had to do it at Robert Moses State Park. We started at Jones Beach, but it was too crowded, even on a weekday morning, and the park police kicked me out for not having a permit."

"I *thought* I heard waves crashing," Meredith adds. "Far off in the desert."

Henry watches the reenactor lumbering along the beach/desert and diving into the sand to get a better look at the invisible Republican Guard. The laptop screen is small and there's a glare from the outside window, but at one point a sand castle is clearly visible in the background, and now Henry is fairly sure that the protagonist's assault rifle is plastic.

"Are there many more like him?" Meredith continues. "Are there, like, Falklands reenactors? Sons of Grenada?"

Norman shakes his head. "He's the only one. Which is the appeal, you know. The uniqueness of his story."

Norman and Warren hit it off. They continue talking about film and vocation and life long after Meredith and Henry lose interest. They continue talking even after Norman realizes that Bangalore-bound Warren is not a potential personal-training client.

"Anyway, ultimately," Meredith tells him, "I think it can turn into a good thing, your taking this trip, this job. If only for a while."

"But you just mocked my lack of preparation, my going for all the wrong reasons."

"That doesn't mean something good won't come of it. I mean, were you really happy doing . . ."

He shakes his head. "No. I mean, what have I ever done? All I do is what someone else tells me. I mean, every day it made me feel less like—"

"Hence the poker night, cigar night."

"Meat Night."

"The reluctance to have your testicles sliced with a knife."

"Snipped."

"Snipped from the gang. From tradition. From a chance to prove yourself beyond a valuable conference report." She looks at Warren and Norman. "The definition of manhood is going through a major transition, Henry." Then she looks down at the top of her breasts. "Women, on the other hand, have never been more confident."

"Is it because we're not used to being so afraid? Because terror has marginalized us? The economy?"

Meredith shakes her head. "It's because we've gone from a manufacturing- to a technology-based economy. It's harder for a man to find a place to display physical strength now—it's no longer socially or professionally rewarded. And men haven't figured out how to deal with that. How to remasculate."

"I'm going to try."

"Good. I hope you really tear it up over there, Henry. Wherever it is. I really do."

Finally a song he recognizes. "How We Operate," by Gomez. He listens to the words, finishes his beer, and stares at Meredith. Meredith the wise. Meredith the compassionate. Meredith the enormously buxom. His eyes betray his thoughts.

"Not a chance, mister."

II

The New Oil

In the book *1000 Places to See Before You Die*, which Giffler had given Henry as a going-away present, the imperial palace in the Kingdom of Galado is listed as number 998.

And now, in-country less than eight hours, Henry is already inside the royal gates, smack in the middle of an after-party for a business conference he didn't attend, surrounded by people who seem much more important than him, even if he is a VP of global water, investor relations for Happy Mountain Springs.

"The world is parched," this brute of an Aussie named Madden is telling Henry, presumably because he noticed Henry's name-tag title. "Parched not like a bloke in a beer advertisement who's just played a homoerotic touch football game with a bunch of handsome, scruffy young lads. It's parched like a severely dehydrated, lost soul in the midday sun in some unforgiving desert. Deranged and naked, on trembling hands and knees, tongue wagging in the blistering heat, hallucinating, clutching its stomach, praying for something that can facilitate a more forgiving form of death before its organs shrivel and its heart explodes. That kind of parched. So congratulations—you're in the right bleedin' business then, mate."

Henry nods, and for a second he wonders, If the palace is listed as the nine hundred and ninety-eighth place to see before you die, could Madden's face be the nine hundred and ninety-ninth? The last? "Well, then," he finally replies, raising his mineral water without bacteria-laden ice, "I guess I'll drink to that."

He scans the room for possible asylum. Scores of white men in dark suits and locals in burnt-orange *ghos* with finely decorated sashes. In the opposite end of the great hall, small beings in what appear to be clown masks—children? dwarfs? robots?—are performing some kind of interpretive dance to the dull throb of indigenous drums. Shug, his official guide and interpreter, stands beside a giant golden urn against the near wall, watching Henry but not acknowledging him, disinclined to guide or interpret.

"So what do you reckon to accomplish here, Tuhoe?" asks Madden.

Henry considers this giant sunburned man who is what, his coworker? Competitor? Colleague? Employer? Mate? He hasn't a clue. Nor does he have a clue about what he wants to accomplish. Saying *First of all, I'd like to forget about the last five years of my life, with a heavy emphasis on the last twenty-four months*, seems a little too forthcoming under the circumstances. "Well, I guess it's our job," Henry hears himself saying and asking, "to somehow, not necessarily quench, I guess, but alleviate that thirst?"

"*Our* job?" Madden laughs and snorts at the suggestion. "*Ours?* Hardly *my* responsibility, Tuhoe. I will say this about your product, though: someday very soon nations will go to war not over oil but over water. And it will tear the planet asunder. So where do they have you staying, then?"

Henry removes a slip of paper from his pants pocket. "It's supposed to be a simple place near my office just outside the city. Something Djong. Didn't actually get to see it yet."

More laughter from Madden, who smells of sweet booze and a smoke residue not unlike marijuana. Hashish? Henry doesn't know what to make of any of this, but he is willing to blame it all on a monster case of jet lag. He was unable to sleep at all on his JFK-to-Bangkok flight (during which he watched three in-flight movies and read two Graham Greene novels) or, after a six-hour layover in the *Jetsons*-like Suvarnabhumi Airport, on the four-hour connecting flight to Galado. After landing soon after dawn and waiting almost three hours to clear customs and for the last piece of his luggage to be found, he was informed by his chaperone, Shug, that there had been a late change of plans: his presence had been requested at the Royal Palace by His Most Serene Majesty the prince of Galado.

Even though Henry was weak and exhausted to the point where he was having trouble standing, let alone keeping his eyes open, he thought, Why not? This was the new beginning you sought, right? The much-needed adventure. The first day of the rest of your up-until-now pathetic life.

"For your information," Madden begins, "the Ayurved Djong and Spa is a five-star, hilltop, multiculti eco-lodge perfect for the searching of the soul and its libidinous depths. Far from a simple place, it is a spiritual retreat of the highest order. That is, if you like your Eastern spirituality backed by Western money and served up alongside vintage wine tastings, seaweed wraps, and a mind-blowing selection of in-room . . . let's call them diversions."

Not knowing how to respond, Henry decides to pretend he didn't hear Madden. He looks to his surroundings for diversion. The palace is much as he had imagined a royal residence in this part of the world might be—high paneled walls and coffered ceilings lavishly decorated with intricate Chinese- and Indian-influenced scrollwork in vivid blues and reds and yellows. Ornately carved dark-wood chairs and servers. Pink marble floors. Twelve-foot windows looking out on terraced fields, a glimpse of a river. But what he hadn't expected were the movie posters, some from contemporary Hollywood, but most for lavish musicals from India, hanging where in past centuries there were surely gorgeous framed paintings or frescoes or tapestries.

"Nice, eh?" Madden again. "You can thank the prince for that. The bloody loon. Obsessed with the pictures, with Bollywood, he is, almost as much as he's obsessed with money, which plays into our hands quite conveniently, what with his father, the once saintly king, losing his own set of marbles in some faraway corner of the kingdom."

"How long have you been here?" Henry asks.

"Long enough to know that it's about to blow wide fucking open. This is a country that has just met its steroid dealer, Tuhoe. Hungry to grow, no matter how fast or unnaturally. They try to fill us all up with this magical-little-kingdom shit, but if anything, it's a corrupt, filthy, environmentally bankrupt fucking kleptocracy."

Henry fumbles with the minibottle of Purell in his pocket, thinking, as he tries to undo the cap, of Lady Macbeth's damned spot, Mary's typhoid, Dorothy's heels trying to click, the cocked hammer of a pistol.

"It's more like San Marino without the human rights," Madden continues. "Bhutan without the commitment to gross national happiness. So what exactly will you be doing in the water business here? Ultra-filtration membranes? Desalinization? Rural wells?"

"No," answers Henry. "None of that."

"The LifeStraw?"

Henry shakes his head, thinking of his original conversation on the subject with Giffler. "Bottled water, actually."

"Really? Distribution center? Treatment plant? Because while there is plenty of water here, most of it is—"

"Actually, it's more back-office stuff."

"Pardon?"

"Back-office. You know, like a call center. Customer relations for Happy Mountain Springs in Vermont."

Madden takes a step back and allows Henry's reply to register before laughter overtakes him. "You're going to run a goddamn call center for a water company *here*? In a country where for all intents and purposes the majority of the people are without potable water, you're going to have employees spend their day talking about crystal-clear water from the springs of . . . where did you say?"

"Vermont."

"From the lush mountains of bloody Vur-mont. They'll spend their days talking in Galado-tinged English about its crystalline purity and their nights fretting about where they can get a few clean drops for their own parched families. Did you know, Tuhoe, that every day diarrhea kills hundreds in this happy little country? Most under the age of five?"

"Actually, no."

"Or that one in three people here—and that's a conservative estimate—has no access to safe drinking water?"

Another shake of the head.

"Good Christ, this is so wrong it's almost beautiful."

"Well, then," Henry offers. "I'm sort of just getting up to speed, but perhaps I can bring this to the attention of management back in the States and figure out some way to help. A donation. Funding some wells. Distributing some . . . what did you say they were again?"

"LifeStraws. A three-dollar water purifier that lasts up to a month, with seven filters, a membrane basically with holes as fine as six microns, plus resin treated with iodine and activated carbon."

"Wow. The LifeStraw."

"Ninety-nine point nine percent effective for parasites and bacteria."

"For just three dollars. Are you involved with the inventors?"

Madden laughs again. "Shit, no."

"Are you with a human rights organization or a regional distributor?"

"Hah!"

"Do you mind if I ask what business you're in?"

"I'm in the business of business."

"For instance?"

"For instance, if someone wanted to get into the LifeStraw business here, I could facilitate that. Also, most recently, I've become quite the domainer."

Henry blinks, shakes his head.

"Internet domains. I hold the rights to Galado dot-com, dot-net, dot-org, plus every suffix variation on dot-Galado. Once this country opens its doors and officially embraces the Internet, these domains will be worth countless millions. A colleague of mine recently sold the domain rights to a Polynesian island nation for mid-seven figures. Right now I get money just from people typing anything Galadonian and getting the ads on the land pages. Wanna buy shares in it?"

"What else do you do?"

Madden raises his hand to his chin. "Here? Well, I'm also in the carbon-management business. Basically that means I can broker a deal that will let your company or country pollute more by paying other countries or companies to assume your carbon debt. Unlike a Realtor, I collect fees from buyers and sellers, and of course more often than not I'm the person who opens and owns those 'other,' environmentally aware companies."

Henry stares at Madden. "And I was letting you make *me* feel shitty about my corporate mission."

"I was just reveling in the irony of the situation. Truth is, the only problem I have with your mission, mate, is that it's for corporate rather than individual gain. I like to see individuals make a go of it."

"Even if it means exploiting a third world nation?"

"No one's breaking any laws that I'm aware of. Plus, screw the third world. It's in the *second* world, between extreme poverty and extreme excess, that the real heat is. The real opportunities. And this place is a royal heartbeat away from joining the second world."

Henry scans the room. People are bowing and shaking hands, heading for the way out. Not much longer, he thinks.

"So what's your plan for setting up the call centers?"

He stares at a pretty Galadonian woman in a Western business suit, jacket and slacks, wide-collared blue silk shirt, as he answers. "From what I understand, we have office space out near the spa, a small classroom building. While tech people are looking into the IT infrastructure, I'm to start training educated locals who can speak some English."

"The Bangalore model."

"Yeah. I guess that's right. In fact, an Indian consultant is to join me in a few days to show me how they did it."

Madden laughs.

"More irony?"

"An Indian teaching an American how to teach Galadonians to act like the Indians he taught to act like Americans."

Henry nods, allows a smile. "I guess that's right. Any pointers?"

On hearing the question, Madden stops smiling and rests a long, heavy arm upon Henry's shoulder. "Obviously you've been around the block a bit, Tuhoe, or they wouldn't have sent you to the likes of this place. Even so, I will give you two pieces of advice. One, do *not* get involved with the locals. The peasants' struggle and all that shit. Make your fortune and keep your conscience and your libido stowed in your briefcase, because it is fruitless to try to get in the way of the unstoppable momentum of money rolling downhill."

"And the second?" Henry asks.

"The second? Well, actually, in your capacity, you don't have to worry about the second. Oh, look. Here comes your man, Tuhoe. Your 'official translator.' And don't you believe a bloody word he tells you."

"That's the second?"

Madden sighs, then lowers his voice. "The second piece of advice—and this is mostly for heads of state, ambassadors, and C-suite execs, not blokes like you and me, whom he could care less about—is to avoid the prince. At all costs. Not only is he bonkers, he's a bloody sociopath."

Shug is alongside them now. He half bows at Madden, who responds with a heel click and a sort of hand-twirling salute. Henry suspects that each just told the other to fuck off without opening their mouths.

"I was just telling Mr. Tuhoe about the many pleasures of your magical little kingdom," Madden says.

Shug's brow crunches as if he's translating Madden's words for an unseen dignitary. "Yes," he says. "We have much to be thankful for in Galado, Mr. Madden. Now, if you'll please excuse us, we must be going."

Shug escorts Henry toward the doors to the great hall. "Interesting man, that Mr. Madden," Henry says.

Shug considers Henry as he attempts to proffer a reply, then decides not to respond at all.

In the vestibule outside the great hall they stop by another large set of windows. Shug wanders away and begins an animated conversation with a Galadonian official. Henry pulls out his small container of hand sanitizer and gives himself an unobstructed squirt. It is not raining outside, but the sky is dark for two p.m., the sun obscured by a low-hanging, unnatural blue haze. To his right, across the dull surface of the river, just behind a long procession of factories with idle smokestacks, is the escarpment of a city that does not look even remotely magical.

When Shug returns, Henry points to a squall of black flakes swirling over the meticulously terraced royal jute fields that lead to this side of the river's edge. "Is that ash?"

Shug shakes his head and says, unconvincingly, "No. That is snow. Himalayan snow."

"Really? In September? So where are we off to, Shug?"

Shug walks and Henry follows. When he catches up, Henry can see that the small, dour man has now miraculously shifted into an even lower gear of seriousness, and for the first time his smug exterior seems to have been shaken. "Shug?"

Shug stops, takes a breath. "We are going to see the prince," he finally says. "I have been told that the prince has specifically requested your presence."

His Royal Smallness

After Henry is frisked for a second time, an aide instructs him to "please be seated until the prince has completed his fitness regimen." He sits and looks out upon the enormous ancient hall, which has been transformed into a glistening modern fitness center. At the far end of the hall, silhouetted against a row of floor-to-ceiling windows, Henry can detect some kind of movement, the bends and twists of distant bodies. Presumably the prince, but it is so far away Henry cannot be sure.

Dozens of large plasma monitors are mounted every ten feet or so, including a row directly in Henry's line of vision. He expected some combination of the BBC, CNN, Al Jazeera, a Tokyo business report, and *Good Day Galado,* but instead it is all movies, some American—*The Dark Knight, Iron Man, The Hangover, The Curious Case of Benjamin Button*—but mostly, he presumes, Indian. Musicals and thrillers, fantasies and love stories, playing to the overdone bass of the house music pulsing through the room.

Unaccompanied by musical scores and dialogue, Henry thinks, the films seem diminished, rendered silly, broad pantomimes of events nothing at all like life, unless, he thinks, life is this simple, this stereotypically predictable.

A few minutes later another aide in a *gho* approaches. Henry rises and offers to shake the man's hand, but the gesture is ignored. "You are not under any circumstance to touch the prince. This is expressly forbidden. Under no circumstances are you to ask him anything, or speak unless spoken to, or address him as anything other than Your Majesty."

"Sure, that's—" Henry begins, but the man raises a hand, silencing him.

"In addition, any discussion of the Galadonian political situation, international trade, human rights, the environment, the health of the king, or the prince's recent trip to Graceland is also expressly forbidden."

"Gotcha," Henry answers. "Ixnay on the Elvisay."

The man stares at Henry for a moment, then looks to Shug as if he is considering calling the whole thing off. But it is too late. Someone across the hall has waved for them to approach. The man lifts his chin at Henry and says, "He is ready for you."

Henry looks at Shug. "Aren't you coming?"

Shug shakes his head. "The prince prides himself on his command of English. My presence would be an insult."

When Henry is halfway across the room, the new chaperone stops him. From the flat bench-press station near the wall of windows at the end of the room comes a high-pitched, extended grunt as the weights—what look to be three forty-five-pound plates on each side of the bar—rise and fall in short, pistonlike bursts. A final exaggerated squeal is the signal for the royal spotters to grab the ends of the bar and safely place it in the forks of the rack. When the bar is secured, the spotters stand back and the lifter sits upright, then jumps up onto the bench, where, squealing again, he begins to execute a series of moves that are a combination of bastardized bodybuilder poses, World Wrestling Federation bravado, and a six-year-old's interpretation of kung fu. The music playing on the sound system, Henry realizes, is "Get Your Head in the Game" from Disney's *High School Musical*. It is during this routine that Henry notices that even though the lifter, presumably the prince, is standing on the bench, he is the same height as his seemingly average-sized spotters.

"Holy crap," he says. "His Highness is a Smallness."

The chaperone looks at Henry. "Any discussion of height is also—"

Henry cuts him off. "Understood. Is bodybuilding something of a national obsession here?"

"No. This is the only such facility in the kingdom. The prince discovered the benefits of weight training and nutrition during a visit to the San Francisco Bay area several years ago."

For his final pose the prince rolls his black Lycra shorts down to his knees, then bends and thrusts his hard, thickly veined bubble butt toward the rest of the room, Henry included, shaking it to the final chords of the Disney tune. After the prince pulls his shorts back on, one of his assistants gives him a high five and another helps him into a shiny lavender Adidas sweat jacket before whispering into his ear and nodding toward Henry.

When the prince sights Henry, he hops off the bench and bounds toward him.

"Remember," the chaperone says under his breath, "no touching."

But the prince is quickening his pace and spreading his short, incongruously muscled arms as wide as they will go. "Mister Henry Tuhoe! What's up Yo-Town!" he says, and embraces Henry, who looks over the prince's shoulder at the chaperone.

Is it more dangerous to return the royal embrace or to ignore it? What's up with the princely enthusiasm? And on what planet is this place called Yo-Town? He gets no help from the chaperone, just a sinister sort of smile. Finally Henry raises his arms less than a foot away from his outer thighs and gently wraps them around the prince's back.

"Welcome to my kingdom. It is an honor."

"The honor is mine, Your Highness. Thank you for having me."

"Go, Huskies."

"Pardon?"

"Go, Huskies. You are a fellow Northeastern man, yes?"

Henry blinks. Aren't princes supposed to go to Harvard or Yale? "You know Northeastern?"

"Go, Huskies! Class of '01, Yo-Town!"

"Really? I was '00."

"I know. This is partially why I granted you an audience. You were a geology major, no?"

"Actually, I majored in English, with a geology minor."

The prince stops smiling, and for a moment it looks as if he might cry, or have Henry or whoever gave him the slightly inaccurate biographical information put to death. As if on cue the Disney music stops, but Henry can still hear music. It is coming faintly from the iPod headphones dangling around the prince's neck.

"The Hold Steady?"

The prince tilts his head, again not sure if this is a slight or some insider's lingo that he doesn't know about. Either one would be bad for everyone involved. But Henry points at the postage-stamp-sized music player. "The Hold Steady. 'Sequestered in Memphis.' I like their sound."

The prince looks at his headphones and then at Henry. He smiles. "The Hold Steady. Absolutely, bro!" He slaps Henry on the small of his back. "Come," he says. "Let me show you around. It is such a pleasure to have an American here to appreciate what I am trying to do with our archaic little society in Galado. Ancient ways. Ancient places. Spirituality. Too much, you know, can have such a corrosive effect on the culture."

Henry decides it's best not to comment on this. The prince waves off the members of his staff and leads Henry into a room off the thousand-year-old iron-pumping room. It's a smaller, more formal space, with one wall of windows looking out on an expanse of royal gardens.

Against the near wall is a one-thousand-gallon fish tank, at the bottom of which floats one eighteen-inch-long, wrinkled, and grotesque fish. Henry has to bend closer to make sure that the fish, a gray, black-spotted, seemingly eyeless being with a long pocked and whiskered nose, is alive.

"Ah-hah," the prince offers, bending alongside Henry to observe the barely moving creature. "This is Gally, a rare specimen indeed. Gally is the last known living evidence of the bottle-nosed Galadonian riverfish. Gally has become something of a pet project of mine, and a symbol of my government's commitment to preserving the indigenous species of Galado. It is blind."

"Excuse me?"

"It uses sonar to catch other fish. But now, after twenty million years, it is threatened. Every day teams of scientists from the Ministry of Wildlife scour our streams and rivers, in hopes of finding one blessed partner for lovely Gally to perpetuate the species."

"Is Gally male or female?"

In response to the question, the prince stands up and cocks his head.

"I'm just saying it would be a shame if it was a male and after all that work the only fish they found was another male."

The prince doesn't answer. "Come," he says, waving Henry away from the last living bottle-nosed Galadonian riverfish, "There is much to see." He strolls to a long, knee-high table in the middle of the room, upon which are two scale models of two versions of the same urban landscape. In the center of the table is a laminated sign that reads *The Shangri-La Zone*. Before the model on the right is a smaller sign that reads *Present,* and before the model on the left, which is considerably larger and features a number of large office towers, banks, hotels, brand-name luxury boutiques, and a huge cineplex, is a sign that reads *Very Near Future.*

"What do you think?"

Henry bends and then decides to kneel to consider the models more closely. After giving the past a casual glance, he decides it's better etiquette to linger on the future. "That's quite a cineplex."

"Twenty-eight theaters, with a grand auditorium for world premieres and, of course, the film festival. Just like Cannes."

In front of the mock cinemas are tiny limousines and tiny paparazzi, and at the entrance high above the street is a two-inch likeness of the prince standing atop a grand, red-carpeted semicircle of stairs. Henry says, "I like the movies too."

The prince comes alongside him and, looking at the model, asks, "Have you seen the film *Walk the Line?*"

"I have. I love Johnny Cash."

"Of all the types of film, I enjoy nothing more than a well-done biopic. Biopics make me cry, because if created with love, they make me consider the only cliché that still has the power to make me laugh and care and thrill and fear, and that is the finite arc of a life that, inevitably, ends."

Henry turns away from the models and looks at the prince. He didn't expect this kind of insight from the man who only minutes ago had addressed him as Yo-Town. "You know," he quietly answers, "I've often had that same thought. Whether it's about Cash or Ray Charles or Marie Antoinette, even though the stories are often completely predictable and the endings universally known, if they're told well enough, they leave me in the most profound, contemplative I guess, funk."

The prince puts his arm over Henry's shoulder. "The inevitability of mortality, yes?"

Henry rises and the prince's arm falls away.

A servant knocks at the door. He is holding a silver tray with two drinks. The prince nods. As the man approaches, the prince says to Henry, "Protein smoothies."

Henry accepts his glass and sniffs the drink.

"Do you lift?"

"I belonged to a gym in Manhattan but didn't—"

"Fantastic. We can train together!"

Henry takes a gulp of the cold orange smoothie. As he swallows, he wonders if it is possible to detect orangutan testosterone in pureed mango.

The prince points back at the models. "So what do you think, Henry Tuhoe?"

Henry licks his lips and nods. "I think it is grand and ambitious."

"For charter corporate partners, like your company, for instance, the Shangri-La or Free Zone will offer tax-exempt status and other perks."

Henry can think of no reason why a bottled water company would want a storefront presence in the Shangri-La Zone, but says, "I would think that a lot of companies would be interested in such a deal. I admit, I'm not an expert on Galado—in fact, until recently I'd read very little about it—but from what I understand it has, if anything, resisted corporate involvement, outside involvement, industrial development, and even tourism. Is this an issue?"

The prince takes the last sip of his protein shake and hands the glass to the servant. He shrugs his shoulders and torques his neck left, then right. Then his lips twist to the side in such an exaggerated fashion—pained? disgusted?—that Henry is certain he has gone too far. Only after the prince takes three deep breaths does Henry feel that things might be all right between him and the prince after all. "I appreciate the candor," the prince says. "Most of my advisers are so terrified of me, and rightfully so, they go to extremes to placate, to avoid conflict."

"I was just curious. Not seeking conflict."

"Obviously, Henry Tuhoe, things are changing in my little country. We can continue as we have for centuries, shut off from the world, economically challenged but spiritually pure, while our Chinese and Indian neighbors to the north and south, the two biggest rising powers in the world, thrive. Or we can find a way to engage with the world while remaining spiritually one with the universe. We can welcome the Internet, the global brands that bring jobs and prosperity. We can begin to tap into its rich natural resources and embrace industry. Did you know that right now if a citizen of Galado wants to cut down a tree—a single tree—he must first get permission from the king, or, under the current circumstances, me. And if I want to cut down a tree, I must gain permission from two thirds of Parliament. Preposterous. Do you know that until five years ago there was no television in this country? Granted, only state-run programming is permitted now, thanks to me, and it was quite a struggle, but it's a start."

"Do the people want it?" Henry asks. "TV? Internet? The freedom to wield their own chain saws?"

The prince waves him off. "They don't know what they want, but it is coming. I have been laying the groundwork for years, making alliances in Parliament. Getting my father to champion my legislation as his. It is forbidden to talk about it, but already we have steel mills burning night and day in the valleys to the north. Coal mining to the north and south. Timber harvesting in the hills. And it has made a difference. Because of my changes, our GNP per person, which Parliament refuses to acknowledge in lieu of the preposterous and unmeasurable spiritual indicator gross national karma, has risen five percent in the last year, but it is still the second lowest on earth.

"They want more monasteries," the prince continues, and then points at another building on the model, a towering modern edifice of spiraling glass and steel. "I want more of this."

"Which is?"

"The Royal Galadonian Academy of Ideas. Designed by the people who worked with people who did the Bird's Nest Stadium in Beijing. Some years off, but the Academy of Ideas itself already exists within the walls of this palace, at the very site in the country that is your place of work. One day I will give you a virtual tour."

"That would be nice," Henry says, still looking at the models, surprised that, under the circumstances, he is so interested in the future of a place that three weeks ago he didn't know existed. "What about tourism? I know it's strictly limited, but I would think as a revenue source . . ."

"Tourism will come and it will absolutely become a source of profit. But for now, until I get the next steps of our plan in place, limiting tourism and the unwanted attention of undesirables is one of the old rules that I actually agree with."

Henry raises his chin in the direction of the scale models. "So this is the next step?"

"Exactly. We first needed industry before opening the doors to commerce and development. Right now we are in discussions with dozens of leaders from the top brands and multinationals in the world. For the most part I have decided to bypass governments and political diplomacy in favor of corporate diplomacy. When you think of it, the modern CEO of a multinational conglomerate is more powerful than any ambassador, more of a head of state than any president or other despot."

"Is there a model in the free world that you're patterning yourself after?"

The prince shakes his head dismissively. "We want to be the next Bangalore. The next Beijing. The next Bollywood. Silicon Valley. Technology *and* industry *and* the arts. The Academy of Ideas. A state-of-the-art sports stadium."

"More democracy than monarchy, then."

The prince aggressively shakes his head. "Oh, no. The people don't want democracy. The monarchy will still rule. Brandocracy, if anything. Plus, of course, we need to strengthen our army. Our nuclear arsenal."

"Do you have one?"

"Technically, no."

"So you aspire be a nonviolent Buddhist brandocracy with nuclear capability."

The prince considers this and smiles. "Perhaps."

Henry begins to laugh, but, realizing that the prince wasn't going for a laugh, he transitions to a clearing of the throat. "Well, I don't know what to say, other than, you know, good luck with all this, Your Highness."

"Not so fast, Henry Tuhoe. You haven't heard my proposal."

"I think you're overestimating my importance in the grand scheme of things here."

"Oh, I'm not overestimating a thing. I know who you are, and just from speaking with you for this short time, I can see that you are my kind of person. I make it my business to meet with almost every new dignitary, corporate or political, who enters our kingdom, and ninety-nine percent of them I dismiss as unenlightened, incapable of seeing the way things can be. But you and I . . . you got to admit, we totally hit it off."

"Sure, but—"

The prince puts his forefinger to his lips. "What is your principal responsibility here on behalf of Happy Mountain Springs bottled water?"

"To set up a back-office customer service call-center operation."

"Exactly. And this will no doubt include the training of Galadonians."

"Yes."

"Galadonians who speak English."

"Yes."

"And when these English-speaking Galadonians are being trained, what colloquialisms and accents will you be looking for, what country's ways will you encourage?"

Henry stares at the prince. He knows the answer but isn't sure where it's going. "Okay, I guess that would be American. The more convincingly American they can sound, the better."

The prince smacks his hands together so forcefully it startles Henry. "Bingo, Yo-Town!"

"I don't follow."

"Despite your economy, your widening cultural void, your anti-intellectualism, your reality-TV approach to electing leaders, your fast-food addictions and thickening midsections—despite all of this, what the world wants most is to act like America. And at this moment in time I think that there is no greater job, no calling that better captures the era, than what you are doing here. Teaching the art of being American."

"Okay."

The prince returns to the models, looks at them while speaking with Henry. "What you are doing for your water company is teaching this on a lesser scale. Important, yes, but what I would like is to be able to hold your model up as an example to other companies that are considering doing business here, to show them that our people are capable of acting like and doing business with the best."

Henry nods. "That's fine, but I haven't even started yet. I need to make my own little thing work before using it as some kind of—"

The prince waves him off. "I have no doubt you will succeed."

"But, again . . . I'm not . . . I . . . ."

"I'm sure your company would not mind at all, Henry Tuhoe, if you helped out casually, every now and then, as a friend of the state, as a corporate liaison. As a favor to me, because in this economy I could use all the help I can get."

Henry decides that it's best to go along with it for now. Later he will call Giffler and speak with whomever he needs to speak with to see how to handle this. But right now, jet-lagged, disoriented, frightened, and freaked out, he decides he's in no position to take a stand on anything. Rather than formally committing, he answers the prince with a question. "So to make all of this come to pass," he says, sidling up to the edge of the models, "what is the single most important thing that needs to happen?"

The prince steps back and fixes his gaze on Henry. He stares at him for an uncomfortably long time. He wants Henry to know that not just his question but every aspect of him and everything that he represents is being considered, being judged, and that the answer the prince is about to give is not something to be taken lightly.

"What needs to happen first and foremost, and sooner rather than later, Henry Tuhoe, is for the heart of my father to stop beating."

One Man's Spa

Spiritual enlightenment and state-of-the-art luxury, it turns out, are not mutually exclusive.

After sleeping for most of the hour-and-a-half drive from the capital, a gradually ascending, late-day trek over deep-rutted, unpaved roads bordered by rice paddies and jute fields, Henry awakens when the Range Rover jerks to a stop.

Shug looks at him in the rearview mirror and clears his throat. Several times at the beginning of the journey Shug tried to get Henry to discuss his conversation with the prince, but all that Henry would volunteer, to Shug's growing consternation, was that one day he might work out with the prince at the palace. When it became clear that Shug wasn't going to get any political insight or royal gossip, he decided to give Henry the silent treatment.

Henry sits up and rubs his eyes. To his left, the edge of the road gives way to a sheer granite precipice. Looking down through the lavender twilight, he sees a gray mass of smog trapped in the valley, and through the smog he can barely make out the rooftops of a village and the black snake of a river.

Shug points to the nearest bend in the snake, to a modern building north of the village. "Your place of business is down there. In the valley." Then he looks up and to his right at a lavish edifice partially built into the smog-free mountainside. Sunset rays illuminate a spectrum of brilliant colors and ornate Galadonian spiritual carvings.

"And here . . . once again, here are your lodgings: Ayurved Djong and Spa." Two men in white *ghos* scramble down the front steps of the spa to greet them.

Madden may have been right. "What happened to having an apartment in the valley, near the office park?"

Shug glances at him in the rearview mirror again. "You were supposed to. But the prince upgraded you. Last week the head of Sri Lankan Trade stayed here in the presidential suite, until the head buyer of Old Navy arrived and bumped him to a lesser room. Anyway," Shug continues by way of farewell, "these men will show you to your accommodations. In two days, Monday, I will be waiting here at eleven a.m. to take you to your new headquarters in the valley."

At once Henry's door and the back luggage hatch swing open. A smiling young man steps back and opens his arms. "Welcome to Ayurved Djong and Spa. I am Ratu, your personal concierge."

Eating a room-service cheeseburger in his boxers alone in his suite, listening on his headphones to Dylan's "Sad-Eyed Lady of the Low-lands" from *Blonde on Blonde*, which, if he's not mistaken, was written in a hotel room, in the Chelsea.

He'd asked for the cheeseburger and fries to mess with Ratu, who seemed especially proud of the organic vegetarian menu, but the man, despite seeming pure of heart and mind, did not blink. "Absolutely, Mr. Tuhoe. Would you prefer waffle or shoestring fries with that?"

Ever since that morning in the focus group room with Giffler, Henry hasn't had a chance to stop and collect his thoughts. And now, still unable to sleep and too tired to engage in anything beyond music, he is finally doing just that. And the results of collecting and giving these thoughts even the most casual scrutiny are disturbing. Losing a marriage, a job, a house, and a country, all in . . . what, two, three weeks? Jesus. This song, he decides, concentrate on the song.

Written for Dylan's wife Sara, right?

On "Sara," on *Desire,* he sang what?

Stayin' up for days in the Chelsea Hotel,
Writin' "Sad-Eyed Lady of the Lowlands" for you . . .

But it's no use. He is sweating all over, and clearly it's not that hot out; this is the mountains, he thinks, not the goddamn tropics. And it's too soon to have contracted, like, typhoid, right?

He places his hand over his heart, which is racing considerably faster than the six-eight time of the song, and now he can't concentrate on the lyrics or even the specific things he's trying not to concentrate on, but instead of not concentrating on individual issues, or let's call them themes, the themes of his totally fucked-up life, he is overwhelmed by their inseparable blind totality.

Telling himself, At least you didn't go through with the vasectomy, at least you still have this or that, doesn't help, only reminds him of . . . an even greater totality that now includes fundamental penis/procreation/cuckold/witchcraft issues as well. He rises and walks away from his half-eaten burger, the untouched pile of shoestring fries, and walks to his window, which looks out over the now black valley, the unseen village, the river.

A heart attack, he thinks. So this is what a heart attack feels like. Here, of all places.

On the intro tour, whatshisname—Ragu? Ratu?—showed him mud baths, yoga, meditation pods, sundry wraps and scrubs, wine tasting bars, infinity pools, massage suites, flora and fauna, using the language of religion to preach the gospel of self-indulgence, telling him he can achieve a higher sense of purpose without having to give up the creature comforts, that he can go on a one-of-a-kind metaphysical quest without sacrificing a thing. Right here. And now, he thinks, here you are in one of the world's most exclusive enclaves of relaxation, eating a cheeseburger and shoestring fries, and you're having a massive heart attack. Like Martin Sheen in *Apocalypse Now*.

He tumbles facedown upon the pure white bedding and tries to breathe, but the air is slow in coming. As he begins to roll onto his back he is startled by a small patch of red on the sheets. An aneurism! Great! He pulls out his earphones and touches his ears for signs of blood while leaning in for a closer look at the stain. Ketchup. That's what you get for ordering red meat in an Ayurvedic spa in a Buddhist nation. Bad condiment karma. On his back now, breathing deeply, still gasping, he takes stock of his arms, the right in particular. No pain to speak of, shooting, throbbing, pulsing from the heart. And other than not being able to breathe, he feels no pain in his chest, the general neighborhood of the heart.

He thinks, Maybe I'm not having a heart attack in an Ayurvedic spa in a Buddhist nation after all.

Maybe it's only an anxiety attack.

When he asked what the word *djong* meant in relation to the resort's name, Ratu answered, "Monastery fortress." When he asked how many centuries old this monastery was, Ratu answered, "This is not technically a monastery. Or a fortress. It was built two years ago, a fusion of the old and the new culture, as part of the prince's grand plan."

The likelihood that this is an anxiety attack, not a heart attack, isn't as comforting as he'd like. An anxiety *episode* would be preferable, he decides, much better than an attack, but it's nice to be relatively sure you're not about to die.

On the nightstand, wrapped in a strip of green banana leaf next to a vase of white lilies, is a spa menu. Still on his back, he reaches for it and opens it. Listed in calligraphy within its eight vellum pages are dozens of categories and subcategories of treatments. Facials. Wraps. Mineral baths. In-room spiritual consultation.

The entire centerfold is dedicated to a variety of massage options.

A man answers the house phone. "How may I help you, Mister Tuhoe?"

"Ratu?"

"Yes."

"I would like a massage."

"We have many massage options. Have you considered the menu?"

"I have not. Look, Ratu. Between us, I'm not doing so well right now, stresswise. Do you know what I mean?"

"Yes, Mister Tuhoe. I believe I know exactly what you mean."

"It's been a crazy couple of days, with no relief in sight. My wife . . . I feel like I'm about to explode."

"Say no more. I can have someone in your suite within fifteen minutes."

Fourteen minutes later there is a knock at his door. A pretty Galadonian woman with her black hair cross-thatched in a loose bun smiles and bows at him. "My name is Lacy." She is wearing a white doctor's smock and holding a black leather work bag.

Henry returns the bow and motions her inside. Lacy tells him to remove his clothes and lie facedown on the bed.

As he takes off his T-shirt, he begins to explain his trip and his new job, but she shushes him and twirls her finger to indicate that he should spin around, get on the bed, and shut up.

Warm lavender-scented oil drips onto his back, forming an S-shaped bead. When Lacy's hands touch him his body spasms; he is not so much startled as, after months of real rejection and fraudulent sexual recuperation, unaccustomed to the touch of another human. He takes a deep breath, finally with ease, and closes his eyes as the masseuse works her way from his neck and trapeziums down to the balled mass of muscle in the center of his back. It's all feeling quite good and he's thinking that this was a great idea, when the towel over his ass is slowly peeled down and a well-oiled index finger begins to probe the outer perimeter of his rectum.

"Excuse me, Lacy?"

"Yes?"

"I think I'll skip the prostate massage this evening, thank you."

After a moment Lacy shrugs and moves her hand north along his spine. "Maybe later, then."

He shakes his head, which is facedown in a rolled-up ring of white towels.

Several minutes later, Lacy's hand finds its way back under the towel. Warm fingers scoop underneath his buttocks and begin to softly squeeze his recently reprieved testicles.

"Hey—whoa, no. No, thank you."

"I think that trimmed privates is very sexy, Mister Henry. Does this not feel good?"

It does. Besides the chronic pre-surgery-that-never-happened masturbating jag and the two times, post-non-op, that he faked ejaculating while with Rachel, it has been a while. Months. And technically and legally, he is separated. But no. Not here. Not tonight. Whoring in the second world with jet lag, fifteen minutes after having either a heart attack or an anxiety attack, or a combination of both, sporting a pair of fuzz-covered testicles upon which a virility curse has just been placed, isn't how he wants to begin his postmarital love life. He'd rather get on with the anxiety attack.

He pushes his chest off the bed and turns. Lacy is naked. Her hair is down, unbound, almost touching the tops of her small breasts. The white smock is in a lump on the mahogany floor. "Sorry, Lacy. But I can't."

"Can't, or won't?"

He doesn't know what to say.

"Maybe you want a boy instead?"

Henry shakes his head.

"You want me to continue, but without returning to . . . ?" She looks at his midsection.

He looks at his midsection. "No." He doesn't trust himself. "But thank you. Really."

While she bends to pick up the smock, he swings his legs around and sits on the edge of the bed with a small towel covering his crotch. He tries again to explain the month he's had, the chest pains, but Lacy doesn't seem to be interested. When she is done buttoning the front of the smock, she walks to a mirror on the wall and pulls back her hair, ties it into a kind of soft knot.

She walks to the door and puts her hand on the knob without turning to say good-bye. Henry calls her name. She stops. "Yes?"

"You wouldn't happen to have any knowledge of the occult, would you?"

Cue the Motivational Video

Early Monday morning the phone in his room rings. "What's shaking, studly?"

Giffler. Henry rubs his eyes. He's been sleeping on and off for almost two days. "The eco-lodge is a whorehouse."

"Book me a VIP suite ASAP," Giffler replies, back in New York City, via sat-phone.

"It's like Canyon Ranch, but with prostitutes on the spa menu, right next to seaweed wraps and morning Pilates."

"That's my kind of inconvenient truth. And absolutely consistent with my prediction that with time, green will become so increasingly complex and fractured it will be impossible to separate the good from the bad."

Henry opens his mouth but decides not to speak. Outside his window on the lawn of a lush garden he sees a group of American and European guests in *ghos* being led through a series of yoga moves. He's fairly sure that the instructor is Lacy.

"Have you met the prince?"

"I have. We . . . well, we seem to have hit it off."

"Splendid. I hear he's bonkers in a cute, occasionally homicidal way. What's up with the call center?"

"I just got here, Giff. I'm supposed to go meet the local management team and tour the new building in about an hour."

"Here's a little tip: your best bet right off the bat is to go all empire on them."

"Pardon?"

"Empire. Gun-to-the-head, no-nonsense leadership. Make an example of someone within the first five minutes of the meeting. The third world expects this from us, or they will rob you blind."

Henry considers telling Giffler Madden's theory that Galado is about to transition from third to second world, but again chooses not to reply.

"I imagine as part of the orientation you're gonna screen the motivational creation myth video. You have seen the video, haven't you?"

"The Happy Mountain Springs video?" He hasn't. "Sure."

"It's brilliantly manipulative. Show them that. Hopefully they won't be too offended by the lesbian marriage thing. If they are, downplay it. No, deny it. Just say that's the way hard-core environmentalists look in the Vermont section of the United States."

"Okay."

"If that fails, just keep emphasizing how much money they can make compared to abject poverty, then give them the sample customer service scripts so they can start justifying themselves."

"Gotcha," Henry answers, then adds, "By the way, were you or anyone back in New York or Vermont aware of the fact that more than three quarters of the country of Galado is drought-stricken or has no access to potable water?"

"So you think there's a bottled water opportunity there?"

"No. I think it's sort of a sensitive issue that we might want to be careful with. Maybe we should consider a token investment in their infrastructure. Wells. Filtration membranes. Treatment plants. LifeStraws. You know, consistent with the whole Happy Mountain Springs ethos. We could even get someone from marketing to film it and use it as a PR tool."

"So, these Galadonian whores," Giffler responds. "Are they hot or skanky?"

"I have to go."

"Wait a sec. I gotta run, but someone wants to say hi."

He hears the jostling of the phone, then a woman's voice saying hello.

"Meredith?"

"Giffler tells me you're smothered in prostitutes."

"I forgot, you work for the man without a conscience now."

"He needs someone to keep track of all the people he's firing."

"How's Warren?"

"He's gone. To India. He did get his job back."

"Do I dare? Do I dare disturb the universe?"

"Nicely observed, Tuhoe. How are your testicles?"

"Filled with shame and healthy swimmers. And your quadruple Es?"

"Apparently they are recession-proof. When the markets crash, men seem to have an uncontrollable desire to seek the solace of very large, digitally convenient breasts."

"I don't know what I'm doing here, Meredith."

"Would you rather be *here*? What's here—abandoned cubicles and defaulted loans? Endless memos about armpits?"

"Divorce lawyers."

"Exactly. Have an adventure, Henry. You're in a mysterious land. A mountain kingdom. Disturb the universe. Get your freaking 'nads back."

He is greeted in brilliant sunshine outside the call-center-to-be by a group of twelve employees, several local dignitaries, and a small chorus of sweet-singing, orange-robed schoolchildren accompanied by a dranyen, an instrument similar to a folk guitar. He can't make out the words to their song, but as he watches them tightly grouped with the white-peaked Himalayas as a backdrop, he is fairly sure that they have embedded his name into the chorus—*Tuhoe Tuhoe-Tuhoe*—and he finds it all strange and moving.

When the song is over, a bass drumming commences and two shirtless, barefoot men in bright skirts of red and yellow and lavender silk with porcelain fish masks on their heads begin enacting a dance that mimics rainfall and swimming and drinking. As they dance his eye is drawn to a gathering of peasants on the other side of the stone fence. Their robes are worn and tattered, and the expressions on their faces are the opposite of the brilliant smiles of those formally assembled before him, for him.

He applauds when the dance ends, then accepts from two young girls a bouquet of wildflowers and a porcelain fish mask all his own.

"It is a bottle-nosed Galadonian riverfish," explains Maya, a Galadonian woman in a black Western-style skirt and jacket who is to be his second in command, pointing at the mask. "Soon to be extinct. The river teemed with them before the factories, but now there is only one known left in the world."

"I know," he answers. "I saw it yesterday in a tank in the prince's game room."

Maya narrows her eyes and looks Henry up and down, as if he is about to be extinct. He meets her wide, dark eyes for a moment, but can't hold her stare for long.

After bowing to the performers and the assembled group in a gesture of thanks, he turns to hand the gifts to Shug, but Shug takes a step back and gives him a look of incredulity. *Are you kidding me?*

The new building in which the call center is to operate is more substantial and better constructed than Henry had expected. It's a long, rectangular structure with white-painted concrete walls and an asphalt-shingled roof. Inside there are four rows of cafeteria-style tables that stretch the sixty-foot length of the open space and dozens of metal folding chairs stacked against the windowless walls. He stands in the center of the room taking it in, flanked by Maya and the Galadonian minister of future commerce. He waves at the gathered employees and in unison they bow in his direction.

"The telecommunications service is not yet in place," the minister of future commerce, a tall (for Galado), thin man with a shaved head, tells him. "It's simply a matter of running lines through the mountains, wiring the building, purchasing the devices, and negotiating a contract with a provider."

Henry nods. "What's the official relationship with outside telcos in Galado?"

"Presently," the minister answers, "they are forbidden. Mostly because of the Internet. But the prince is in negotiations with several large multinationals, and a piece of legislation is being drafted that we are confident will soon rectify the situation."

"I see," Henry says, and when he looks up, Maya is glaring at him. He shrugs: *What?* She turns and stomps away, shaking her head.

"Will that be all for today?" the minister asks.

Henry looks around. "Yes," he says. "I think it will."

The next morning Henry's first speech to the employees seated before him inside the call center is straightforward and measured, devoid of Giffler's suggested threats and any hint of a malevolent empire. After thanking Maya, he tells them that on behalf of the founders of Happy Mountain Springs, he is excited about the opportunity to live in such a beautiful place and that he looks forward to working with them. He tells them that in a few days the American conversational etiquette expert from Kashmir will arrive and they will begin training. "In the meantime," he says, "after we view this short film about the Happy Mountain Springs way, we'll hand out a folder with additional background as well as some sample call scenarios you can familiarize yourselves with. Okay?"

No one answers until Maya steps forward and excitedly says something in Galadonian to the employees, who answer in unison, "Okay!"

The film commences with a beautifully composed scene of a drop of water forming on the ice-glazed, leafless tip of a maple branch. The camera pulls back to reveal a snow-covered Vermont forest thawing on a golden early spring day. One drop becomes a thousand becomes a trickle down the face of glacial granite into a gently moving brook. A drumbeat mimics the building momentum of the dripping and trickling. Brooks converge as a string section joins the percussion, forming a tumbling and foaming river coursing through a narrowing gorge. Already bored, Henry turns to glimpse the others and is surprised to see that they are transfixed by the lavishly filmed hydro ballet, or, better yet, hydro porn.

The music all but vanishes as a cupped hand reaches into the blue-black current. The camera pulls back as it follows the hand rising from the water, revealing two athletic thirtysomething women in dungarees and flannel shirts kneeling at river's edge. One woman raises her cupped hand to the lips of the other, who drinks from it. Henry again turns to the others to see if there are objections to the homosexual overtones, but either they don't care or they don't get it.

For the next three minutes the two women, Audrey and Pat, walk through the Vermont countryside as they share the abridged, media-friendly story of how they came to found Happy Mountain Springs. A deep, abiding love of nature. A commitment to purity of mind and taste. And an unabashed shared desire to change the world for the better. With this they each lift a sixteen-ounce plastic bottle of Happy Mountain Springs water and the picture match dissolves to the image of two bottles in the plant. Then a dozen. Then thousands of bottles, flowing toward the viewers like an infinite, synthetic, nonbiodegradable river.

Which prompts a collective gasp from the small gathering.

Henry takes a closer look at the tidal flow of branded bottles on the screen to see what has prompted the gasps and now the whispers and head-shaking. Two women in the back of the room rise and walk out of the building. Several others begin to hiss and don't stop until the scene switches back to Audrey and Pat and two Irish setters in front of the crackling stone fireplace in their New England farmhouse.

Henry looks at Maya. "Did I miss something?"

"Plastic."

"What, some kind of pagan plastic deity? A sex toy?"

Maya smiles and looks down before forming an answer. "The plastic bottles. Seeing so many in one place shocked them."

"Because of their water situation? Did they feel that seeing so much clean water was offensive, a taunt?"

"There is that," Maya answers. "But it's really what the water is inside of that offends them. Plastic bags and bottles are forbidden in the kingdom."

He looks back at the group. As the credits begin to roll, the whispering returns. "Didn't they know that Happy Mountain Springs is a *bottled* water company?"

"That's a good question. Even if they did, I think the seemingly endless quantity was a bit of a shock."

"Well, it's not as if we're bringing all those bottles *into* the kingdom. So," Henry continues, looking at the remaining members of the group, "do you think they're okay with this—that they're not so offended they won't want to work for us?"

Maya nods, then slowly tilts her head from side to side. "I think they're okay with it. Poverty has a way of making people okay with all kinds of things."

Outside, the sunshine and mountain view have vanished, smothered in roof-high clumps of tangerine smog. Henry does a three-sixty, trying to get his bearings.

"The wind shifted from the south," Maya explains. "When it's this color, it's coming from the coal furnaces. When it's from the concrete and steel mills, at sunset the particulate becomes a shade of violet that, despite the source, is almost beautiful."

"According to outside reports, Galado didn't have any heavy industry."

Maya glances at her feet. Almost smiles. She's in on the maudlin joke about the ubiquitous industrial complexes they're not permitted to discuss, but she won't allow him that. "Yes," she says, "that is what I have heard too."

At the rough piled-stone wall on the edge of the property, two small girls and a boy no older than three stare at them. The girls are shoeless. The boy's left arm ends in a stump just above the elbow. Henry gives them a quick wave, then looks away.

"You don't want to be here, do you?"

"In a tiny village in the middle of nowhere teaching workers from a drought-plagued region how to talk about crystal-clear water that comes in a container that, incidentally, is forbidden here? What makes you think that?"

Maya narrows her eyes and looks past him, into the smog. "I think that the way you are feeling right now, wherever you happen to be is the middle of nowhere."

Double Blind

Maya leads the way, walking along the edge of the muddy street and through the stone archway of a restaurant that has no sign. After four days of no progress, of blank stares from the operators in training, of gruff responses and eye rolls from Maya, and after four nights of self-doubt and loathing back in his room in the eco-lodge, he told her that they had to talk. To clear the air, to make a plan or to bail.

Henry had suggested dining back at the lodge, but she said no; she was not a fan of the eco-lodge.

"This is my favorite place in all of Galado," Maya explains as they pass through a narrow alley lined with empty cedar food crates and into an outdoor courtyard. She is in a lavender dress, and her hair, usually pulled back at work, falls in a graceful sweep of black across her forehead to her shoulders. "And this is not only because it is owned by my cousin and has been in his family for more than six hundred years." At the end of the courtyard they pass under another, smaller arch and emerge on a small stone patio cantilevered over the side of a sheer ledge.

Henry asks, "Why does everything beautiful in this country seem to be clinging to the side of a cliff?"

"That's how it is here. On the precipice of sublime beauty and total catastrophe. Spiritually, physically . . ."

Henry stares over the cliff edge, waiting for Maya to finish. In the valley, black coal smoke seeps from riverside stacks into the gray dusk sky. From above he can hear the voices of monks reciting a sutra.

" . . . and of course," Maya adds, "politically." She joins him at the stone railing and considers the view. "Did you get everything that you needed done back at the lodge?" She pronounces *lodge* as if it is the name of a nemesis, a pimp—as if it is cursed.

He nods. After leaving the call center this afternoon, he had Shug drive him back to the lodge, where he changed clothes and checked his messages. Corporate spam from Giffler. A long-winded note from the American manners expert from India, whose arrival is still a few days off. And then there was the e-mail from Rachel telling him that their house is worth $150,000 less today than it was the day they bought it, and that the Realtor says they should be happy if they get that, because the market is completely dead. Then she said he might want to know that before he left she took a lock of his hair while he was sleeping and she has now given it to a witch to create another, more damaging spell, which they will invoke under the light of the next full moon. It ended with a passage written in a language he's never seen; however, after two of the words she provided the English translation, *death* and *penis,* in parentheses.

He turns to Maya. "So you're obviously not a fan of the lodge. Any reason?"

"Truth without consequences?"

He nods.

"Well, first I should clarify. Because I am from this," she says, waving her hand over the valley, the mountainside, "going to such a place would be inappropriate, and, honestly, for the same reason, because I know so many people who work there, it would make me uncomfortable. The pampering. The excess."

"But for me," he responds, "it's okay? The excess and pampering?"

"For you it's a different social and philosophical dynamic. I shouldn't judge and didn't intend to. It's up to the individual to decide what is ultimately best, and for some the lodge is the pinnacle."

She turns and looks at Henry's face, his eyes. Something about her smile makes him wonder if her pals already told her about his

botched massage experience. If she thinks he's a whoremonger. Or
gay. "You know, originally I was scheduled to stay somewhere
else—more modest, I imagine. But without telling me, the prince
had me moved."

"Oh, yes," she says. "The prince is quite fond of your lodge. He
says it is a symbol of the new Galado, and he uses it to impress anyone who he thinks can make his vision come to pass. Shall we sit?"

To their cliffside table for two, a young man in a *gho* who is Maya's
nephew brings them two cups of *ara*, a local rice-and-barley wine.
He places a butter lamp on the top of the railing, then lights a stick
of cypress incense in a stone dish two tables away.

"When I met the prince," Henry says, "he showed me some of
his plans for the new Galado. Pretty ambitious."

Maya sips her wine and nods, but doesn't answer.

"I have no stake in any of this one way or the other," he says.
"You can speak freely with me about whatever you want. Politics.
Bottled water. Buddhism. Pampered Americans. The other night, I
thought I was having a heart attack in my room. So I decided to try
a massage. They sent me a prostitute."

She tries to suppress a wince, but her eyes betray her. They close
for two seconds of disgust before reopening, unfazed. She points to
the peaks on the other side of the valley. "Do you see the tallest, to
the right?"

It is almost dark, but the snow-glazed mountain caps glow as if
they retain sunlight. Henry nods. "Yeah."

"It is more than twenty-two thousand feet high, and is one of
the highest unclimbed mountains in the world. It's forbidden for
climbers to try to scale it because our culture says it would disturb
the spirits."

"Do you believe that it would?"

Maya shakes her head. "I don't know. But I'm happy that it's
forbidden. That preserving and considering the spirits and the
nature is an important aspect of our culture. Our laws, which the
prince has already been altering to meet his needs, mandate that seventy percent of our land must remain forested and protected. It's a

beautiful law with sincere intentions, but I'm not so naive as to think that we can remain like this forever. We're poor. We are technologically isolated and grossly uneducated. We have no economic power or military leverage. To survive as a culture we have to change, but will excessive or hastily enacted change ruin the culture? Will it compromise happiness?"

Henry takes a bite of his appetizer, a cheese dish heavily spiced with hot green chiles. His face reddens and his eyes begin to water.

"Drink the wine," Maya says.

He drinks, wipes his mouth and eyes with a napkin. "So you think the prince is moving too fast?"

"Opening up the country to trade and light industry, to the Internet and more outside visitors, if done gradually and moderated carefully, I think is a good thing. Breaking down every wall and law without regard to our land or culture, creating a Las Vegas–style sensibility with Western trinkets with total disregard for the consequences, is the sociological equivalent of giving alcohol and guns and smallpox-tainted blankets to your American Indians."

"I don't mean to sound rude, but how did you learn to speak English so well? How'd you get such a balanced view of the world?"

This time she doesn't hide the wince. "Whether you mean to or not, and I believe you do, what you say sounds and is rude. I was allowed to go abroad for my education because at one time I was part of the in crowd at the palace, and because I was the oldest daughter of well-connected and enlightened parents. I went to Princeton. Majored in economics, with a minor in philosophy. I liked your country very much, but despite the present situation, I love it here in Galado."

"How does the prince get away with it?"

Before answering, Maya waits until the waiter finishes placing before them two more dishes—chile-spiced pig's feet and buckwheat dumplings with bok choy and poppy seeds. "You mean, how does the essence of a physical place, built upon pillars of spirituality and peace, become a breeding ground for greed and power? Money and brilliant timing is how he gets away with it. For a while, at first, there was so much coming in, from China, Europe, and the U.S., that he was able simply to buy people's compliance. Including, in a way, mine. A year ago I was teaching English one day a week in the palace school. Now I make more than my parents, brothers, and sisters combined. And of course the short-term result of his changes is that the economy, or, more importantly, our standard of living, did get better. Until recently, anyway. There were more jobs for people like me, more money for schools. But now he is panicking because he feels the economic momentum slowing, and he is willing to try anything. And again, at what cost?"

Henry swallows. In a perverse way, the chile heat appeals to him. "What's your threshold?"

"Excuse me?"

"At what point would you refuse to do something because it compromises your ideals?"

Maya doesn't immediately answer. With the end of the chopsticks that doesn't touch her mouth, she transfers red rice from a bamboo bowl onto her plate. "Look at the flaming stacks in the valley, from factories burning coal to feed the Chinese machine. Look at the prayer flags alongside the factories, on the tops of our mountains, asking the gods for peace, compassion, and wisdom. Think about your spa, your lodge, where Westerners come and switch philosophies the way a diva makes wardrobe changes. Wealthy people served by the previously impoverished. Win-win or obscenely wrong? And what about our company and our jobs, selling something that can be gotten for free from a sink, a stream, or a cloud in the sky for billions of dollars? It all comes down to what it is you're compromising. It's complicated."

"It is," Henry agrees. "But there are a lot more despicable things one can do than create jobs selling bottled water."

"We'll see. What you need to understand is that right now Galado is a petri dish in a grand experiment being conducted by a madman. A double-blind experiment, where neither the individuals nor the researchers know who belongs to the control group and the experimental group. Every act has implications and consequences. In any place, especially in a country this small, at such a critical time, our presence, even at this table, has a significant and possibly irreversible social impact."

Maya's nephew reappears as she finishes speaking and asks if they would like more wine. Henry begins to say yes, then catches himself. He looks at Maya. "Why do I feel like whatever answer I give will cause irreparable damage to all mankind?"

After the third glass of rice-barley wine, the topic switches from bottled water and Galadonian politics to their personal lives. "Why did you come here?" Maya asks.

"Circumstances pointed me here. It was a choice, but a choice based on a passive rationale."

"You were forced?"

"Not really."

"You chose?"

He shakes his head as she stares at him.

"You don't know why you're here, do you?"

"I've had an interesting time of it lately."

Maya sips her wine while she decides whether she wants to know more.

"For starters, my wife threw me out the day I lost my position at work, because, in part, I falsified my vasectomy."

"Okay."

When he sees that she hasn't winced, he decides to continue. He tells her about the first time he met Rachel and their move to the country, their adventures in conception, the debacle of Meat Night, and even about the pagan spell that was cast on him this evening, moments before he left for dinner. He has to recite the chronicle of his falsified vasectomy a second time before she understands what he is talking about.

"You *have* had an interesting time of it lately."

"As you said," he reminds her, "it's complicated. Every act has implications and consequences."

"You know," she answers, "you are the first American I have met who is so . . . forthcoming about his . . ."

"Shortcomings."

"Yes." Maya laughs, and for the first time Henry thinks of her as a fully realized person instead of as a businesswoman or a threat or an ideologue. He's not proud of this. But when you meet so many people every day in meetings and hallways, on conference calls and through e-mail and text and tweets, there is little time for the personal, the human.

"So then," she continues, "you came here to escape?"

Henry tries without success to locate the peaks in the darkened sky. He thinks of Meredith and the Eliot poem. Escape. Finally he says, "Escape implies that some planning, some actual thought, went into it. It takes a certain amount of passion or nerve to escape from something. The truth is, I came here because it was the next thing that life told me to do."

For several minutes neither speaks, but it is a comfortable silence. Now that the monks have finished their sutras, Henry considers their absence, the way the absence of a thing can make it feel more powerful than an abundance of it.

"You know," she says, "I really did not like you."

He shrugs. "These days I'm not exactly in love with myself either. So how come you're no longer rolling with the royal posse?"

After a lag, Maya quietly says, "I had a child. She died when she was sixteen months old. I grew up near the palace. My father was an intellectual and a teacher who had the blessings of the king. That is where I learned English and received an education that few in Galado are fortunate enough to have access to—America, Princeton, travel—and why I am not working in a field today. Five years ago, soon after I became pregnant, the prince began to undermine his father, and to institute decrees against intellectuals of a certain type, artists and cultural hardliners. By that time the king was already losing his senses. We were among many who were ostracized, and in a way we were lucky, because my father had known the king since they were little boys. Others were sent to prison or killed. But my father, who in grammar school had taught the prince to read poetry, to understand the philosophers of the West, was permitted to move out here with our relatives in the country and work in the taro fields."

He listens, more transfixed by her story than he's ever been by his own. She drinks the rest of her wine, her fourth glass to his two, before resuming. "When my father fell into disfavor, my husband, who had a clerical job in the palace, told me that he could not abide my presence if he were to have a career. We were a distraction. He didn't know that I was expecting a child. I was so young I barely knew myself. She died from diphtheria. From, you'll be interested to know, tainted water. Had we lived near the palace, she could have been treated and perhaps saved, but the roads were impassable because of the monsoon rains, and at her age she passed quickly."

"What happened to your father?"

"He died in a taro field. Heart attack, I imagine. A person raised as an intellectual can't be expected to survive as a peasant field-worker at the age of seventy-two. It's no matter, because the prince built a dam that dried up the rivers, and the fields died soon after that."

"I don't know what to say, Maya."

She signals for the bill. "You know, the way you spoke about your wife, I don't think that is how you truly feel about her. Maybe you are no longer in love, and maybe you were not meant to be married, but you should respect her. The desire for a child, the loss of a child . . . you can't begin to fathom."

Continuous Partial Attention

Two nights later, after ten on a Sunday, Madden is in Henry's room, sitting on Henry's bed, drinking Irish whiskey out of the bottle, when Henry returns from a late dinner alone in the spa restaurant, followed by a garden stroll.

Madden's presence doesn't startle him. Already he's reached the point where nothing in Galado surprises him.

"I thought I told room service not to bring me the drunken Aussie until after eleven."

Madden smiles, toasts Henry with the half-consumed bottle of Jameson. "Well, according to the concierge, you're a flaming homosexual, so I thought I'd stop by and give you a proper buggering."

Standing at his desk, Henry checks the messages on his laptop. He's been away for only two and a half hours, but there are more than a dozen, including several apiece from Giffler and Rachel, plus one with a video attachment from Norman. But he has neither the curiosity nor the desire to open any of them.

"You realize," Madden says, "that anything that goes through their network is being deconstructed and analyzed by no less than a dozen security hacks back at the palace. The prince may indeed like you, but the truth is, he's put you here, just as he's put dozens before you here, because it makes you that much easier to keep an eye on."

"What will they make of your late-night presence?"

Madden stands and stretches. His fingertips and the bottle top reach the ceiling. Henry had forgotten how large the man was.

"They'll scratch their heads a bit over it, but ultimately they'll think it's a good thing. Back at the palace, anyway. They don't entirely trust me, but I'm a rainmaker, and these days the prince gives rainmakers special privileges."

For the hell of it, Henry calls up his iTunes library on the laptop and pushes Party Shuffle. "No Fun," a dance song by Vitalic, begins to pulse. He's not particularly fond of the song, but he downloaded it anyway, because he read that the front man claimed to be a part-time gigolo as well as a Ukrainian trubka player from a family of sea otter fur traders. For a moment he thinks of sharing this backstory with Madden, but Madden speaks first.

"So are you ready for a bit of an adventure?"

Henry waves at his room, toward the foreign darkness outside his window. "I hung with a prince. I had dinner on a cliff. I'm staying at a holistic whorehouse. Don't you think I'm already sort of engaged in one?"

Madden laughs derisively. "This? Come on, mate. Grab a jacket. Let's take a ride. I've got some business to tend to in the hinterlands."

Henry looks at his watch, which is still running on New York time. "Now? It's got to be pretty late here, right?"

"Why not? Unless you've got some young massage boy scheduled for a midnight quickie."

In the passenger's seat of Madden's Range Rover, careering around a winding, guardrail-free mountain road, Henry declines yet another offer to hit off the bottle of Jameson.

"Here, then," Madden says, rising off the seat to reach in his pocket. "Grab the wheel for a sec, will ya?"

The truck is going straight toward the edge of a cliff and certain death while the road ahead veers sharply to the right. Henry lunges across the seat and gives the wheel a yank. "What the hell?"

Madden retakes the wheel. He mumbles, "Nicely done," because he now has a small metal pipe clenched in his mouth. "I knew you were a man of action."

"Is that a crack pipe?"

"Not crack. Hashish, mate." Using his thigh to control the

wheel, Madden flicks a butane lighter and puffs the pipe's contents to life. After he's taken a second hit, he offers it to Henry. "Galado doesn't have much to offer in the way of nightlife, but it may well have the very best hashish on this planet."

Henry says no, but when Madden waves it closer, he takes the pipe. As he's inhaling his first hit, Madden says, "Of course, if you're caught with it on your person here, it's punishable by death."

When he stops coughing, Henry looks at Madden to see if this is true.

Madden shrugs.

"What kind of business are you doing up here?"

"Timber."

Henry tilts his head. "I thought there were strict rules regarding timber. Special permission from the king to fell a tree. Et cetera."

"This is true. But many of these rules are about to be tossed out the palace window. When this happens, some people are going to get very rich. Might as well be me and my constituents."

Henry accepts the pipe again. He thinks about his recent conversation with Maya about every action impacting something. "What about the people? They spent centuries trying to preserve their culture, then it's all gonna change overnight?"

"It's my opinion that people spend way too much time trying to preserve their so-called ways. If they're worth a damn, they'll preserve themselves." Madden takes his foot off the gas and stares at Henry. "For instance, you Americans get your underpants all up in a bunch when someone tries to pirate your culture, but it's really not about preserving your culture. It's about protecting your right to shove it down someone else's throat for a healthy profit. You just shook your head."

"I did."

"Oh, please." He raises the whiskey bottle to his lips and takes a gulp. "Get off your high horse, Mister Bottled Water in the Land of Poisoned Rivers and Dried-up Wells. The fact is that every successful modern country polluted its way to prosperity, only to worry about the environmental consequences later. Now that the U.S., Japan, and the UK are obscenely wealthy, they suddenly want to get all green with their rules, which basically will ensure that no one else will."

"I just wonder if globalizing a place—"

Madden interrupts. "Oh, horseshit. We are the opposite of a global village. We live in a global kingdom. With the select few in the castle, and those who serve them comfortably living in the kingdom, and everyone else flailing in the muck and pestilence outside the walls, hating them, suffering them, warring with and dreaming of destroying them."

"What I meant," Henry responds, "is that introducing commerce and technology to a place shouldn't mean it has to abandon its traditions. It's just a disconnect that such a spiritual people would be forced to change so—"

Madden interrupts again. "My spiritual belief is a grand unified theory of pragmatism. I believe that God lives in our synapses, in the last chemical link before action is taken. They whine about losing a species like a blind riverfish, but it's a fair trade for the untold billions to be made in development. Soon many other two-and-a-half-world countries will be forced to make similar decisions. We'll choose who prospers and who lives in poverty. Which species will thrive and which will not make the cut. Darwinian economics."

"By 'we,' I'm assuming you mean people like you and a steroid-taking prince whom you have called, if I'm not mistaken, a sociopath."

"That is correct. One man's liberty is another's control. You think the answer is to democratize them. To Americanize them."

"I didn't say that."

"But no one gives a shit about that," Madden says, smashing his right hand on the dashboard. "They sure as hell don't. I don't. And the people at your company, they don't. We just want them to want our shit. Our Walmarts."

"Our Big Macs."

"Our bottled water, but without the water."

"Our domains."

At an abandoned roadside shack Madden slows the truck and turns onto a one-lane dirt track that slices across a small valley in the ridge between two peaks. Henry, stoned and disoriented, thinks of the forbidden peak that Maya pointed out earlier in the week and can't help but feel that right now he and Madden are disturbing all kinds of spirits.

Madden fills another bowl and begins talking, unprompted, about his marriage. He's been married fourteen years and separated for the last three. "The day our marriage was officially over was the day that we started telling each other the bald truth. About our bodies, our friends, and our lovemaking skills. The irony is that this was a relationship that transcended love in its intimacy and purity. Because only people in love would never say those things. They would only think them. The final straw came when I found out that she had lost most of our savings playing online poker. I thought from her behavior that she was having an affair. After she told me the truth, I would have preferred it to be a fucking affair."

"So you asked for a separation then?"

"No, she did. She said I suffered from continuous partial attention syndrome. This is because I'm always doing five things at once—talking on the mobile, reading a magazine, working on the laptop . . ."

"Driving on a mountain road while swigging whiskey, telling a story, and lighting a hash pipe . . ."

"And, according to her, doing none of it particularly well. Especially when it came to giving her even a sliver of my continuous partial attention."

After a while Madden turns to Henry and asks, "And you?"

For the second time in two days Henry tells his story, which he has by now edited and honed into a crisp piece of performance art, with exaggerated pauses, ironic inflections, and revelatory notes precisely integrated for maximum impact. This time, most likely because he is tired and disoriented from the growing buzz of the Galadonian hashish, it actually sounds to him as if he is telling some other loser's story.

Madden downshifts as they turn onto another unmarked road. When Henry is through, Madden says, "You know, researchers in Denmark have found that men who have had vasectomies have an increased risk of dementia and language loss."

Henry looks at Madden, who is smiling, and says, "I have no words to respond to this claim."

"You need to know all the wrong people to get anything done here."

Madden has stopped the truck about twenty yards from a stone farmhouse. It is after midnight, more than two hours since they set out from Henry's room at the spa. Wood smoke is spiraling out of a stone chimney and electric light shines golden in the windows. It's too dark to see what lies between the truck and the house. From the backseat Madden grabs his green field jacket, and from the front pocket of the jacket he removes a pistol, a .40-caliber Glock semiautomatic.

"Pardon me for noticing, but most of the business meetings I attended in New York were primarily firearm-free events."

"It's just precautionary, mate." Madden sticks the gun in the back waistband of his jeans, opens the door, and walks to the rear of the truck. Henry gets out and follows. From the back hatch Madden removes a large canvas duffel bag.

"What's that, a weapon of mass destruction?"

Madden smiles. "Just follow my lead and everything will be fine."

Together they walk to the front door of the farmhouse, which on closer inspection appears to be some kind of community hall. The combination of altitude, cold mountain air, and paranoia makes it difficult for Henry to draw a proper breath. He braces himself for gunshots, but instead the door opens, revealing more than a dozen smiling men and women. They are not wearing *ghos* or Western clothing but locally made thick woolen pants, sweaters, and fur hats. One of the men, a burly peasant with a long black beard, gives Madden a hug, and when Madden introduces Henry, he gives Henry a hug as well. Henry has never smelled a yak but now thinks he has a good idea of what it might be like.

They are led to a large wood-plank table in front of a fire blazing in a ceiling-high stone chimney. Upon the mantel sits a bronze Buddha, and mounted on the stone and mud walls are tapestries. On the plastered wall across the room above an altar is, according to their host, a Shambhala fresco depicting a parallel universe, a mythical idyllic kingdom hidden beyond the peaks of the Himalayas. "People insist this place exists," the host explains. "But what's more important is that you *believe* that it exists." He looks at Henry. "Correct, brah?"

Henry nods. "Yeah, man."

One of the younger men pours them each a cup of butter tea. Madden takes a sip and then makes a show of hoisting the duffel bag onto the table. He unzips it and begins pulling out several dozen pairs of sneakers—all kinds of brightly colored, older-model Nike running shoes. The people immediately set upon the sneakers. They take off thick fur boots and rush to try on pairs of Shox. Meanwhile, Madden continues to pull trinkets out of his bag: stacks of CDs, six dozen Slim Jims, and a generic brand of digital camera for everyone. Watching the Galadonian peasants scramble to claim their share of the booty, Henry can't help but think of Maya's statement about the smallest act being capable of causing irreversible change. He thinks of the Pilgrims, the Dutch, and even Lewis and Clark swapping their own sparkly knickknacks with Native Americans from Plymouth Rock to Fort Clatsop, and inevitably he thinks of what those transactions led to.

After the gifts are sorted and stowed, a semblance of order is restored. Only one of the Galadonians, the bearded man who greeted Madden and Henry at the door, can speak English. He sits at one end of the long table, speaking on behalf of and translating for the others. Madden takes the seat at the opposite end, with Henry occupying the chair next to him.

From what Henry can gather, the purpose of the meeting is fairly straightforward. The forty-year-old National Forest Act, which nationalized a great deal of private woodland, is about to be rewritten by the prince, and the families of many of the people in this room will soon be able to reclaim of some their timberlands through restitution. Madden is here to try to claim more than a small portion of that land—or at least the timber rights—for himself. By the time he is distributing his leave-behind—a contour map of the area and a sample contract—Henry's concentration has drifted away from the table and toward the Shambhala fresco. One more bowl of Madden's hash, he thinks, and he just might believe such a place exists too.

The meeting ends not with gunplay, as Henry had anticipated, but with more hugs and butter tea and a version of the hot-chile-pepper-and-cheese dish Henry had at dinner with Maya.

Afterward, standing outside the Range Rover, Madden takes the pistol from the back of his pants, slips it into the pocket of his field jacket, and tosses it into the backseat. "So what d'you think?"

Henry concedes to Madden that yes, he's happy that he came along. It was a worthwhile adventure.

Soon after that he is asleep, his face pressed against the cold glass of the passenger's-side window as Madden smokes and drinks and drives his way back to their lodgings.

Buddha Clause

As he rocked in and out of sleep, Henry was aware of Madden talking to himself, but now he hears Madden yelling. "Fuck, no! These bloody—" Henry is wide awake before Madden shoves him. "Move! In the back, grab my gun from inside the coat!"

Henry leans over the seat without asking for further information. As he feels for the coat, the truck lurches to the right and then spins 180 degrees. Henry spins with it, toppling into the backseat. He sits up just as Madden floors the gas, then is immediately slammed into the back of the front seat as the brakes are applied with equal force. Finally he finds the jacket with his left hand, and he is checking the pockets with his right when the doors swing open and gun barrels shove in out of the darkness. Madden is hollering and the men outside the truck are yelling in Galadonian.

Henry lets Madden's coat fall to his lap and raises his hands. He watches Madden being dragged outside and closes his eyes as a pair of hands grab him by the arm and pull him into the mountain darkness. A hood or a hat that smells of smoke and sweat and his interpretation of yak is pulled over his face and he is shoved to a kneeling position on the ground. The TV news phrase *execution style* sounds in his head, but for some reason he isn't wetting his pants. Soiling his pants. Blubbering in any way. Why? he wonders, as someone pats him for weapons. Because you're fearless? Or hopeless?

Or maybe this is exactly what you've been waiting for all along.

"Sorry about this, mate." Madden. Close by.

"What do they want?"

"It's my fault. They say I don't know my place. I grabbed for too much and profiteers like us are set on ruining their culture."

"Us? What are they going to do with us?"

"I reckon they're going to kill us. That's what one is saying, anyway."

"Kill us? Isn't the culture they're determined to preserve based on nonviolent Buddhism?"

"Well, I reckon these fellas here are what I'd call *lapsed* Buddhists. Though when they come back, I'll be sure to share your point with them."

Neither speaks for a while. The bandits are talking rapidly near the truck, opening and closing doors. Henry is acutely aware of the wind pushing against the mountain's edge, chilling the thin air. He thinks of the land of Shambhala, but already he has forgotten the particulars of the fresco he saw earlier.

Why, he wonders, is so much of a culture based on places that can't or are not allowed to be reached? Mythical kingdoms. Forbidden peaks. What kind of spirits want you to believe in them yet not disturb them?

A gun barrel presses against his temple. The engine turns over on the Range Rover. A foreign voice next to Madden, presumably the person who has a gun to *his* head, begins shouting. Henry doesn't understand anything but the intent of the words. Angry. Threatening.

"Did you tell him about the Buddha clause?"

"I did," Madden answers.

"And?"

"They said they'll try to be better in their next lives."

"You really think they're gonna kill us?"

"Actually . . ."

Henry doesn't wait for the rest of his reply. Surprising even himself, he shoves the gun away, rises, and begins to take the hood off his head. "Screw this," he says.

He wakes up shivering on the edge of a cliff. Immediately he knows where he is. On the edge of a cliff on a remote mountain road in a mysterious Himalayan kingdom, abandoned by bandits and his lunatic traveling companion.

Believing it, that's a whole other matter.

On the back of his skull is a throbbing, swollen contusion. Beats a bullet hole, he thinks, gently stroking the tender knot with his fingers. When he sits up, it feels as if a sluice gate opens, dispatching every drop of blood in his skull to his belly, prompting him to quickly lie back down before he vomits, or passes out and rolls off the cliff into a remote Galadonian crevasse.

His second attempt at rising is more successful. The cliff, he can now see, rests atop another cliff, so if he had rolled off, he wouldn't suddenly have died. More likely he would have broken his legs or spine and died gradually.

Calling out for Madden is a possibility, but he's not completely sure that the bandits have left, plus calling out for Madden means having to be prepared to deal with the consequences of Madden's potential response.

He stands and walks toward the center of the road. The sky is black and pulsing with stars, but a faint glow over presumably eastern peaks hints at the coming of dawn.

They may have kidnapped Madden. Or they may have killed him. But Henry doesn't think they killed Madden, because if they had, in all likelihood they'd have killed him too.

Regardless of what's happened to Madden, the truck is gone. As he takes another step downhill, toward his room at the spa, however far away that might be, Henry's foot comes down on a soft object. Kneeling, he sees that it is Madden's down-filled coat. Inadvertently dragged out of the backseat along with Henry. Inside the right hip pocket he finds the Glock. He scans the darkness once more and, detecting no sign of Madden, weighs the gun in his right hand before sliding it under his jacket and into the back waist of his pants.

A moment later a moan breaks the silence. Uphill on the mountain side of the road, a body slowly rises. As it begins to approach, Henry calls, "Madden?"

"Correct." Madden is rubbing his head and limping.

"You all right?"

"No, I'm not all bloody right."

"Did they hurt you?"

"They took my vehicle. My belongings. My recreational drugs. But no, they didn't hurt me. They only hurt people foolish enough to play the hero. Admirable stuff, mate, but damned foolish."

"What about your head?"

Madden laughs. "I smoked a gram of hashish, drank a fifth of Jameson, and slept on the side of a frigid mountain road. If my head wasn't splitting, then I'd be worried."

"Do you have any idea how far away we are?"

Madden scratches his head. "I reckon about an hour, but—"

Henry interrupts, "An hour's not so bad."

"An hour by truck, Tuhoe." Madden cocks his neck from side to side, then commences the downhill walk home.

Henry catches up and calls, "Hey."

As Madden turns, Henry tosses his jacket to him.

"Found it in the middle of the road."

Madden weighs the jacket and squeezes both pockets.

Suburban Shambhala

"Why, exactly, did you decide to resist them?"

They are shuffling down the ragged mountain road. Sunrise came with a spectacular flourish, igniting the airborne factory particulate brilliant hues of orange and then red before dimming to a languid gray smog that obscures the peaks and valleys.

"I don't know. In a sense it was an involuntary reaction, but while I was kneeling there, I was thinking about a lot of things."

"Like, apparently, suicide."

"Not really. Just about what a conventional, wasted existence I've had. It's certainly not the first time this has occurred or been pointed out to me, but the gun to the head, you know, kind of gave it a bit of an exclamation point."

"No more Galadonian hashish for you, Tuhoe."

"Have you ever met Maya, the local woman who's been working with me and Happy Mountain?"

Madden strokes his goatee. "Some kind of botched connection to the palace? Not bad on the eyes?"

"Yeah, that's her. We had dinner the other night."

"I know all about it. A pair of Nikes goes a long way with your concierge. And don't tell me you had a raucous night of sex with her, because you definitely came back to your room solo."

"No, not that."

"Then what?"

"We had a good talk. She sort of hates me. But she's, you know, cool."

"Well, good for you, mate. So this new, post-hijacking you, you're wondering how to live a meaningful life. To follow your heart, your dreams. Will it lead to disaster or bliss? And if that's the case, if you're doing what you feel you must, then technically even disaster should be fulfilling, right? A victory of the spirit."

"Something like that."

"Good Christ."

"What? Then why are you here, doing this?"

"I came here to get rich and/or to disappear. Whichever comes first. The desire to disconnect completely has always appealed to me, but you know, it gets tougher to disappear every day."

Henry disagrees with Madden's hypothesis—that the urge to disappear is somehow more admirable or at least more understandable than feeling compelled to live a better life—but he says nothing. He's tired. His head throbs. He's in fucking Galado. From a place far behind them he thinks he can hear the faint whine of an engine. He cocks an ear to see if it is coming toward or going away from them.

"Do you know how many fucking people like you I've come across in my travels, Tuhoe? A million. All thinking they have to travel to the ends of the fucking earth to find so-called meaningful experience, only to get a case of the trots or the clap and major karmic disappointment once they discover the reality. What I want to know is, why can't you find meaningful experiences back in your conventional world in—"

"The suburbs of New York. A Manhattan cubicle. But I never said that—"

Madden waves him off. "Why the fuck can't you simply act like a man, or a decent human being, and find meaning and fulfillment in your neighborhood, your cul-de-sac, your bloody job, instead of having to go all W. Somerset Maugham or Indiana Jones?"

Henry walks with his head down. The vehicle is still far away but definitely coming toward them. "That doesn't accurately describe what I did or why I'm here," he says somewhat forcefully. Then, almost whispering, he adds, "I was transferred."

As the truck rounds the curve above them, Madden steps into the road and begins to wave his arms. When the truck, a work-battered Toyota flatbed, squeals to a halt, the large Australian limps over to the driver and begins to speak with volume and emphasis in Galadonian. He points back up the mountain and then to a place somewhere below the smog in the valley. When he is finished, the driver is shaking his head and laughing.

Once they're up on the back of the flatbed, which, coincidentally, is filled with recently felled cedar timber, Henry reaches under the back of his jacket and takes the pistol out of his pants. Holding it by the barrel, he offers it to Madden.

Madden considers Henry for a moment before grasping the gun handle and slipping his forefinger onto the trigger. Before putting the pistol inside his coat pocket, he says, "I was wondering how long you were gonna hold on to the bloody thing, mate."

"And I was wondering, if you go to the trouble of carrying it, why didn't you use it?"

"Because it was in the backseat. Because I got complacent. Which, as it turns out, is a good thing. Last thing I need is to explain a bunch of bodies on the roadside to the authorities in this hellhole."

A small crowd is gathered in the pandanus- and bougainvillea-lined driveway outside the Ayurved Djong and Spa. Shug, Ratu, Maya, even Lacy the masseuse, are standing with arms folded as the timber truck lurches to a stop. With stops and engine trouble it had taken the truck more than four hours to make the drive. As the idling diesel engine rattles and coughs black smoke into the early afternoon air, Henry and Madden rise and stretch, then notice the others.

"Looks like you've been missed, mate," Madden growls, before tapping Henry good-bye on the shoulder and hopping off the other side of the truck.

"You *are* late, Mister Tuhoe," Shug admonishes after Henry has climbed off the truck's left sideboard.

"Well, as you can see, I ran into a few complications."

Shug shakes his head and begins to answer, but Henry steps forward, placing his face within inches of the older man's face. "Your job is to take me where I want to go and to translate what I ask you to translate. If I'm not mistaken, your job is *not* to shake your head with disgust, or to judge, or to scold. If I've gotten any part of this wrong, please tell me. Otherwise I'm politely asking you to stay out of the way and keep your mouth shut."

Shug takes a step back. Henry turns to Ratu, the concierge.

"And your job is to satisfy my requests, not share my itinerary with any stranger handing out Western gifts. Agreed?"

Ratu steps back and looks at Shug. "Agreed."

"I appreciate the prince's hospitality, but as soon as possible I'll be checking out and moving into the lodgings I was originally booked into."

Shug turns to Maya and raises his eyebrows. "USAVille?"

Maya shrugs. "We'll look into availabilities as soon as possible." After Henry turns and begins walking up the stairs toward his room, Maya calls after him, "I was wondering, will you be joining us at the call center this afternoon?"

He laughs, but can't bring himself to turn around.

For Tonight's Performance, Playing the Role of the Disgruntled Caller Is the Man Playing the Role of Henry Tuhoe

He spends the night and the entire next day holed up in the room he demanded to leave. Sleeping, mostly, even though he thinks he has a concussion, but also doing some work and talking to the States. Rachel calls and texts him dozens of times in a period of hours. He doesn't pick up. Doesn't respond. But he does read and listen to them all. Some are pure rage: *How dare you? I hope you catch swine flu. You know, Vegas wasn't the first time I've cheated on you.* Others are pure sadness. *I'm afraid. How could you leave me all alone? If I were married to me, I wouldn't have gotten snipped either.* And others are pure craziness. Which makes him sadder. He calls Rachel's younger sister and then her mother to ask them to check on her. But her sister tells him to fuck off and her mother says, *Where were you two yuppies when I needed you?*

The only person who agrees to check in on Rachel, to call and if necessary take a train up to the house, is Meredith.

Late in the afternoon of the second day, while he is staring out his window at clouds gathering at the top of a distant peak, a note is slipped under his door:

I'm sorry to impose upon you like this. But your presence would be most helpful back at the call center. Our protocol liaison has arrived two days early from Kashmir and is

awaiting your instructions. If you will not be in the office
tomorrow, please advise.

—Maya

"Hello, Happy Mountain Springs, where purity is our passion, how
may I help you?"

"Again!"

"Hello, Happy Mountain Springs, where purity is our passion,
how may I help you?"

When the group finishes, the man standing before them, a
dark, thin twenty-five-year-old in Levi's, red Chuck Taylor Converse
sneakers, a Los Angeles Dodgers cap, and a black Sean John sweatshirt, claps his hands together and says, "Wah-TER! WahTER! Sell
those *rrrr*'s! Again!"

Henry stops at the door, reluctant to enter. He's been gone three
days, but it feels as if he's never been here. "How long have they
been doing this?"

"Hours," a woman tells him and Maya. "Since ten a.m. at least."

"Have they read through any of the caller scenarios?"

"Oh, no," the woman answers. "He says they're not nearly ready
for that. He tells us a lot of stories about how he did it in India. How
his team sounds more American than Americans."

In the front of the room, the man yells, "Again!"

"Anything new on getting an actual working phone system?"

Maya shakes her head. "I called the minister of communication
again this morning, but his voice mail wasn't picking up."

Henry rubs the back of his skull. "I don't know if I can deal with
this right now."

Maya turns and considers him. "Deal with what? Your job?
Life? I need to know exactly what you can and cannot deal with,
because we have work to do here, and in addition to your employer,
these people are depending on you."

He stares at her. When she is angry, he thinks, she is terrifying,
and when she isn't, she's beautiful. Right now she is both. "Okay, "
he answers. "You're right. Let's get to work."

"Come," she says, signaling Henry to follow her to a kitchenette in the back of the center. "In our effort to make you feel more at home, we have purchased a coffee machine. Starbucks."

He's a tea guy but takes a black coffee anyway. He rubs the back of his head again. Pain bursts with pulsing regularity from his brain stem to the sockets of both eyes.

"What happened to your head?"

"I think the answer to that question, and any additional questions about that night, have to be tabled until I have a few tall glasses of *ara*."

"This is what you get for doing business with a man like that."

"Madden? I wasn't doing business with him. He asked me if I wanted to go for a ride. I shouldn't have but did. Is he that bad?"

Maya sets her jaw and looks at the man in the front of the room. He is telling the others a story about a cousin who drove a taxi in Los Angeles for three months.

"What do you think of our American expert?"

It's hard to understand exactly what he's saying, but Henry is fairly sure he hears the name Keanu Reeves invoked, to silence. *The Matrix* gets a similarly blank response.

"I think," Henry says, "that Happy Mountain Springs is in deep shit."

"He comes highly recommended."

"He's from Kashmir. I thought all of the outsource call centers were supposed to be in Bangalore and Mumbai."

Maya shrugs. "Do you really want to move out of the spa?"

He almost forgot. "Sure. I mean, yes."

"Okay, good. I can make this happen this afternoon."

During a break, Mahesh Singh, the cultural liaison, introduces himself to Henry. Henry asks Mahesh if there is anything that he needs. Mahesh removes his Dodgers hat and pushes back his long black bangs. "Actually, it would be very helpful if corporal discipline were permitted."

"Physical punishment?"

"Only for the most extreme cases. One simple act can work wonders among an entire group."

At a loss for words, Henry turns to Maya and then back to Mahesh, who suddenly breaks out into a smile and holds up his hands. "Just joshing, brother, okay?"

Henry half nods and says, "Okay," but he's not sure he believes the part about the joshing. "Anything else?"

"Well, seriously, yes. Since you are an authentic American, I wonder if this once you could help me in a simple role-playing scenario for the sake of the trainees."

Henry wonders if it is possible to role-play when one is already fully immersed in a much more demanding long-term version of the game.

Mahesh picks up a nonexistent phone receiver. "Hello, Happy Mountain Springs, where purity is our passion, how may I help you?" He is sitting on a metal folding chair on one side of a small desk.

On the other side sits Henry. "Yes, I'm—"

Mahesh interrupts. "Please," he says. "The receiver."

Henry picks up a nonexistent receiver. "Would you like me to dial and make a ringing sound?"

"This will not be necessary." Mahesh picks his invisible receiver back up. "Hello, Happy Mountain Springs, where purity is our passion, Ryan speaking, how may I help you?"

"Ryan?"

"Yes. We must not reveal our Hindu—I mean, our Galadonian given names. It undermines the aura of neighborliness. Ryan speaking, how may I help you?"

"Hello, I'm calling from Aurora, Illinois. I recently had a dozen five-gallon jugs delivered for home use, and to tell you the truth, the water in this first jug tastes sort of, well, funky."

The smile on Mahesh's face vanishes. He pulls the invisible phone away from his face and stares at Henry. "What exactly do you mean by funky?"

They decide to switch roles. For some reason Mahesh insists that this includes switching seats. When Henry rises, a wave of nausea and dizziness washes down, from head to belly to legs. He braces himself against the desk and manages to move to the other seat.

"Ring ring . . ."

Henry answers. "Hello, Happy Mountain Springs, where purity is our, er, passion. Henry speaking. How may I help you?"

"Your water tastes like yak piss, dude."

"Excuse me?"

"What, do you have dog cum in your ears? Your water, it tastes disgusting. Like it was strained through a month-old feminine napkin. My whole family is fucking sick with the typhoid."

Henry looks at Mahesh to see if he is serious. Not only does Mahesh seem serious, he seems genuinely angry and a bit dangerous.

Henry finds Maya in the group and forces himself to focus on her face when the room flashes red and his knees buckle.

USAVille

It's morning in America, or a reasonable facsimile thereof.

Outside, a rolled-up newspaper lands with a thud in the middle of Henry's driveway. Or the driveway of wherever he happens to be. He gets out of bed and looks out his second-floor window in time to see the newspaper boy turning around his bike (is that a Schwinn?) and slowly pedaling away. There's a mailbox at the end of the driveway, and on the other side of the street a clumsy necklace of two-story raised ranch homes is strung out in both directions. None of the neighboring houses have lawns or plantings of any kind. None of the other houses have vehicles in the driveway or flags on their porches or toys in the front yard.

Except for the fast-vanishing newspaper boy, the scene is devoid of life.

It's seemingly morning, but he has no recollection of the night. Or how he got here.

He lies back down, stares at the slowly spinning ceiling fan above him, and attempts to place himself by taking an inventory of recent events. The inventory, if true and not the imagined drivel of a damaged mind, frightens him. It also does not answer the question looped on his internal PA system: Where the hell am I?

A second look out the window reveals either a recently abandoned or a nearly completed mall at the end of the cul-de-sac, replete with half a set of golden arches and a box store with a giant red K on its incomplete exterior. This scene of ghostly mall, silent streets, and empty driveways could be anywhere back in the America of credit crises, bank failures, and economic doom. But with the Himalayas looming in the background behind the inadequate arches, he realizes that he is in some kind of alternate, experimental, unfinished America.

Retrieving the paper, which he has no desire to read, seems the natural thing to do. He pulls on his jeans and sneakers, which he has no recollection of removing, and makes his way downstairs. The house is sparsely furnished and randomly decorated. There is a kitchen table and chairs but no window curtains or wall coverings. A glance toward the living room reveals a leather couch, an easy chair, and a fifty-seven-inch flat-screen monitor hanging on the wall above the unused fireplace, but there are no books or DVDs on the shelves, knickknacks or magazines on the end tables, or any sign that other humans may have once inhabited this space.

At the end of the driveway, he bends and picks up the paper. He is impressed to see that it is the *New York Times,* then less so when he sees vaguely familiar headlines and a nine-month-old publication date. Lifting his arms overhead, he stretches from the waist, left and right, down and up, before straightening back upright and tilting his head toward the presumably rising sun and closing his eyes.

"Howdy, neighbor."

He opens his eyes. To his right in the next driveway stands a tall black woman in a black pants suit, with a black leather knapsack draped over her shoulder.

"Morning."

She takes a step toward him. "You know, I was here when you arrived last night. On a gurney."

"How unlike me. That's usually how I depart from a place."

His reply draws her a step closer. "Maya asked me to stick around and keep an eye on you this morning."

Henry slowly nods. "Thanks. I have no recollection of . . ."

"They knocked you out, gave you a couple of somethings to settle you down. Maya spent the night, making sure you were all right, but she had to go home this morning to take care of some personal matters."

He doesn't know how to respond to this, other than to nod.

The woman crosses the small patch of thin lawn between the lots and extends her hand. She's tall, more than six feet. "Madison," she says. "Madison Ellison."

"Nice name."

"I created it. The names of my favorite avenue and my favorite writer. Anyway, welcome to the tentatively titled USAVille. I'm the only other person dumb enough to live in this botched sociological experiment, but at least I have an excuse: I have to. Or at least I'm being handsomely paid to." After he releases her hand, she places it on his shoulder and steers him toward her house. "Come, I made breakfast."

Henry follows, as if doing so is as normal as following Marcus and Gerard and Victor across a tiki-lit patio on Meat Night.

Unlike the house he just stumbled out of, Madison Ellison's house is thoroughly and beautifully decorated with a warm and colorful mix of African and Galadonian art and furnishings.

"It ought to be," she explains, sliding a spatula-sized portion of omelet onto a plate. "I've been here for six months, and the prince was very generous with my lifestyle budget. The idea, I imagine, was for my place to be a sort of model home that others like you could visit and better imagine the possibilities."

He sits slump-shouldered at the head of her kitchen table as annoying boy-band music plays in the background. If he had to guess, he'd say Jonas Brothers. Unless Hanson has made a comeback. "I saw what appeared to be a shopping center at the end of the street. And one golden arch."

She retrieves two pieces of browned wheat bread from the toaster. Keeping one for herself, she places the other on his plate. "The second arch is supposedly en route," she explains. "Their ambitious intention, in case you haven't noticed, is to create a Western, distinctly American community here, with authentic American amenities to put at ease homesick corporate types like yourself who do not want to go the native Galadonian route."

"This is delicious. By 'they' I take it you mean the prince."

She nods.

"So is this the Shangri-La Zone?"

"Nope. That, at least in theory, is big-time commercial. This is residential with some commercial accoutrements."

"How come there's no . . . well, life here?"

"Money. And momentum. Or at least a more formal type of commitment from some of the better-known multinationals."

"What's the holdup?"

"For starters, in addition to the worldwide economic collapse, they're waiting for more aggressive measures to be taken by the Galadonian government to stimulate foreign investment and development. Plus they have legitimate questions about cultural restrictions, infrastructure deficiencies, political instability, and, frankly, the emotional stability of the man in charge of the whole shebang."

"Apparently Happy Mountain Springs didn't get that memo. With those obstacles, why would anyone consider it?"

Madison Ellison sits down next to Henry. "A market the size of a nation, even a micro-nation like this, is a terrible thing to waste."

"So what are you, like the royal Realtor or something?"

"Nope," she answers. "PR. Last year the Galadonian government contracted my parent company to maintain its stellar magical-little-kingdom image in the world while cleaning up any potential messes that may occur during the upcoming, let's call it transitional phase."

"What company?"

Before she responds, her phone rings. She holds up a hand as she rises to take the call. "Yeah. Yes. Well, if that's the case, then why not do a video press release about something positive, about how, I don't know, these new state-of-the-freaking-art factories are actually *empowering*, not enslaving, women, giving females from rural areas opportunities they never could have experienced prior to the prince's social renaissance. Two *s*'s in *renaissance*." She clicks off the device and stares out the window, gathering her thoughts before returning her attention to Henry.

"Is that what this is?" Henry says, gesturing at the house and beyond. "Ground zero of a social renaissance?"

"Absolutely. It remains to be seen whether that which is being reborn is good or bad. But it's a renaissance nonetheless."

"That is, if you're sticking with the literal versus the humanistic variation of the definition. What company are you with again?"

"I didn't say. But it's not one you'll have heard of. We had to do a totally separate spin-off after the prince contacted my old blue-chip firm, which you surely have heard of. Had to because of the risk, because of the potential PR fallout for our corporate umbrella brand if our name were to be attached should this all go horribly awry. If you want a hint, it's the same Madison Avenue firm that China hired to put out fires before the Beijing Olympics."

"Tainted milk," Henry says, counting on his fingers. "Lead in toys. Choking pollution."

She takes a bite of toast and, with her mouth full, answers. "Exactly. And don't forget Darfur and all those pesky human rights issues. We didn't make them go away, but we certainly spun them the best possible way."

"Tibet be damned."

"I mean, what do you remember about Beijing? Michael Phelps's eight gold medals or a couple of human rights crazies protesting outside that French supermarket?"

"Darfur be damned."

Madison Ellison waves him off. "Please. What are you gonna do, blame the brands, the quarter-pounder with cheese and the twelve-ounce can of Coca-Cola, for the mess the world is in?"

Henry holds up his hands. "Hey, I'm supposed to be teaching people in a toxic watershed to talk about crystal-clear bottled water. I'm in no position to blame anyone for anything."

Madison Ellison stares at a text message flashing on the screen of her device. It's important enough to divert some of her attention from him, but not enough to stop her from replying. "In a sense, you know what we are, the people such as me who assign made-up stories to real world events? In an indirect but very accurate way, we're the historians of our time. Not necessarily the work we do, but the things that our work is a *response* to. Because if someone in my position creates an alternate or modified version of an event, it's highly probable that there is a much more interesting and troubling reality behind the spin. Poison in the paint. Blood on the blueprints. Electoral deceptions.

Unravel that spin, backtrack through the diversionary press releases, the shiny happy viral e-mails, the pithy sound bites and paid advertorials, and you'll get a jaw-dropping three-sixty view of how the twenty-first century truly works."

"Other than the fact that I could not disagree more, I understand."

"You'll see."

"Curators of alternate realities."

"I'll take it."

"Okay, then," Henry asks. "What's the story behind the story of this place? What is it a response to?"

"This place? This has more made-up stories per square inch than any place on earth. Right now it's quiet, but we've been formulating preemptive responses to a number of scenarios, for when it all, knock on wood, goes kerplooey."

"You're kidding, right?"

Madison Ellison shakes her head. "We make a lot more money on triage than on preventive medicine."

"Is this really the Jonas Brothers?"

She nods. "Makes me think of home."

Henry wipes up the last bit of omelet with his toast and looks up at Madison Ellison. "Sounds like you could use a little break from your Galadonian adventure."

She laughs. "They make me think of home in a negative way. Reminds me of what I left. The truth is, there's no place I'd rather be than right here."

On the short walk back to his place after breakfast, Henry stops and watches a mud-splattered Toyota Land Cruiser roll down the street and turn in to his driveway. A young, angry-looking Galadonian man is driving. Maya gets out of the passenger's side. She opens the back door and takes a brown paper bag out of the rear seat and says something to the driver before closing the door.

Henry knows that he has no right to feel this way, but the presence of the man with Maya fills him with jealousy.

"How are you feeling?"

"Much better. I'm assuming that strange Indian man at the call center wasn't a dream?"

Maya smiles. "Mahesh? He's about as real as real gets."

"What happened?"

"You passed out. Probably from the blow to the head. Exhaustion. Lack of sleep and food. Culture shock. Narcolepsy. Whatever it was, you were out. Here, I brought you some essentials."

He accepts the bag and bows from the waist. "Want to come inside for a cup of . . . whatever might be in this bag?"

"No. I'm going back to work. There's no need for you to come in today. We're still practicing the basics. There's two more pills in the upstairs bathroom if you need them. You should rest."

He thinks about protesting but knows the last thing he needs right now is more pseudo-American role-playing with Mahesh and the gang at the call center. "Thanks," he says. "It's been a bit of a frenzy since I got here, much of which I brought on myself. And thanks for keeping an eye on me last night. Madison filled me in."

Maya says, "Not a problem," and pivots to head back to the Land Cruiser.

He can't help it: "Who's your friend?" As soon as the words come out, he wishes he hadn't said them.

She turns, no longer smiling. "He's just that," she says. "He's my friend."

iVoid

Losing his marriage, his job, his home, his mojo, and, twice in the last week, his consciousness is one thing. But now Henry has apparently somehow lost his music—5449 songs in all, the entire contents of his meticulously curated iTunes library. It's not in his library, not on his hard drive, and he can't find his iPod, which holds only a fraction of it anyway. The thought of living here, or anywhere, without his security blanket of life-stage-appropriate songs paralyzes him with dread.

He never would have told Maya that he was content to languish alone around a strange and barren house in a foreign land if he had known it would be without music.

Rebooting the machine and searching the hard drive doesn't help. Nor does slowly banging his forehead against the kitchen tabletop. Calling AppleCare from Galado, for the time being, isn't something he's up for.

It's not just the music. It's the combinations of songs. Their precise order. The quirky titles he gives to each grouping. Painstakingly created for certain situations. Distinct responses to specific events. Similar, he thinks, to Madison Ellison's definition of PR, except with music he is the solitary victim of his own spin.

Though it would cost thousands of dollars, it might somehow be possible to recall and repurchase a great many of the missing songs. But the mixes, the playlists, which reflect nothing less than the syncopated rhythms of his soul, he could never come close to replicating.

Looking around the vacant home, dwelling on the silence, he thinks, Now I know how a junkie feels. Only a junkie, in theory, gets a little better every day that he goes without.

Without music, he realizes, what I really feel is alone.

Staring at the laptop screen, trying to will the songs back from the digital void, he sees an instant message clicking into his in-box. It's Rachel. She did it, he thinks. She's stolen my manhood and my soul and now she's stolen my songs, with witchcraft.

—Howz Galado?
—Where's my music, Rachel?
—Pardon?
—You know what I'm talking about. Give me back my music library.
—OMG. It's gone?
—Don't play innocent, witch. Undo thy spell.
—There is no spell, Henry. How many times have I told you to back up your files? And lay off the witch stuff. I'm just having some fun.
—At my expense?
—To an extent, yes. Absolutely. Plus what's so wrong with believing in something? What do you believe in, Henry?
—
—That's what I thought.
—Shambhala.
—What?
—An unreachable utopia. I believe deeply in that, and nothing else. Unless of course someone's casting spells on me.
—What's a spell, Henry, except someone else's version of a prayer? A proactive wish.
—Last I checked, prayers were supposed to be for redemption, forgiveness, love, and the helping of others. Not the condemning and punishing of souls. Not for revenge, thievery, and the emasculation of soon-to-be ex-husbands.
—Oh, that. I was drunk. Sorry, but it made me feel good. I needed a spiritual outlet.

—

—Couldn't we have simply joined a Unitarian church?

—It won't happen again. I'm coming to terms with us. Past and
   future tense.

—How's the house?

—Worth another 25% less than last time we spoke. You heard
   about our bank, right?

—No.

—It no longer exists. Bought out by a brokerage firm that may or
   may not be in existence by the end of the week. Our nest egg,
   fittingly, is gone. So, I ask once more: how is Galado?

—Maybe Galado, I am learning, is what I deserved. Hypocrites.
   Criminals. Lunatics. And now—no music.

—Maybe that's a good thing.

—

—Henry?

—Look, Rachel. I'm. . .It's obvious that you deserved better. Not at
   first, maybe, because I wasn't so bad for a while. . .but if you
   want to make a case for later. . .

—

—We loved each other, right? Now, not so much. So we move on.

—Well, this is sort of why I'm writing.

—You met someone?

—Living with. Sort of.

—Okay. Mr. Las Vegas?

—Yeah.

—How romantic. Did you work that into your pickup line—Hey, my
   husband's having his balls snipped as we speak, at my
   insistence, in fact. . .wanna have sex?

—It wasn't like that.

—

—Anyway, I just wanted you to know. And to tell you to, you know, to
   take care of yourself, Henry, and that I hope things turn out
   well for you over there.

—

—?

—I'm glad you're happy, Rachel.

He stares at the last passages onscreen for a while, wondering if something else will pop up or if that will be the end of it between them, with all future communication initiated by her attorney. His in-box is filled with messages, all work-related. There was a time when he had a circle of friends who would call and later e-mail each other, but after he moved to the country he let more and more time go between sending and replying to messages. As the weeks turned into months, the incoming e-mails slowed to a trickle, and by the time last year that he decided to do something about it, most of his alleged friends' addresses had changed and his wry suggestions for long-overdue get-togethers were kicked back to him unopened. To be sure, there were more ways than ever to track his old acquaintances down—Google begat Classmates begat Facebook, LinkedIn, Twitter, and all the subsequent social networks—but he made no further attempts. He found a sad sort of solace in the fact that he had at least tried to reconnect, once, and something else entirely in the epiphany that he hadn't really wanted to in the first place.

The effort mattered more than the result.

He's still staring at the screen when it blinks off, then on, then off again. The fridge motor has also shut down, and looking up, he sees that the light over the kitchen sink is out too. At the spa there were backup generators for Galado's frequent power outages, but in USAVille this is not the case.

There Are No Bonus Rooms in the Ruins of an Imagined Future

Two hours of solitary is enough.

He laces up his hiking shoes, grabs a sixteen-ounce bottle of Happy Mountain Springs water from the package Maya brought him, and heads out into the abandoned neighborhood.

A sheet-metal sky of factory particulate is suspended just above the base of the surrounding mountains, obscuring the post-noon sun and shearing off the rooftops of the empty homes of the valley. At first he purposely holds to the center of the broad paved street as he walks, content to contemplate from a distance the dozens of peripheral structures in various stages of incompletion. But the further he walks away from his driveway, the more he begins to wander onto the pale, hard-packed dirt of the unclaimed front yards and within arm's reach of the timber webs of unsheathed exterior walls and roughly framed saber-toothed gables.

In his life he has been guided through developments in progress where there was a palpable sense of what's soon to come, the kinetic buzz and tease of anticipation. The pull of the imminent. But walking on the cross-hatched two-by-twelve floor joists of one of a hundred three-bedroom townhouses indefinitely frozen in Phase Two, he isn't feeling the thrill of what's yet to come, or what *might* one day come, so much as the cold surety of that which will never be.

In his life he has also explored many ruins, including an 1850s Colorado silver-mining town, a burned-out Victorian hotel on the lake of his youth, and an abandoned Boy Scout camp deep in the

Adirondacks. And those places, while spooky, held a different fascination. Their splintered and crumbled walls were dusted with the residue of human experience. There were memory shards in the rubble, and in the surrounding air the morbidly thrilling sensation of lives lost and unrequited dreams floated like a phantasmagoric presence.

But this place. Yeah, it's a sort of ghost town, only one in which no one has ever lived or died. Which is something he finds in many ways eerier and more disturbing than a Civil War battlefield or a graveyard at midnight.

This place.

The ruins of an imagined future.

He hops off the first-floor platform onto the chalk-hard earth and takes a swig of Happy Mountain Springs' finest while surveying the frozen residential landscape of USAVille.

If music were an option, he decides that the song for this moment should be "Where Is My Mind?" by the Pixies (the Purple Tape, seventeen-song original demo-check).

> *And you'll ask yourself*
> *Where is my mind?*

He tries to remember the rest of the lyrics, but without his iPod he can't. Can't recall anything beyond the only part of the song that had interested him in the first place: its self-indulgent, fatalistic hook. Any alt-rock lyric that celebrated alienation or disillusionment in the most remotely clever way, he realizes, resides on one of his playlists, wherever they are.

At the end of the cul-de-sac, just before the entry to the would-be mini-mall, sits a house much closer to completion than the others. Its exterior is sheathed in plywood, wrapped in Tyvek, and more than half covered with white composite clapboard. All of the doors and most of the windows have been installed and trimmed, and inside the framing studs are covered with untaped Sheetrock.

This, Henry thinks, is very close to the condition his house was in when he and Rachel first toured it. Even then, following their

Realtor from one subdivision to another, or to the rare yet out-of-their-price-range lone colonial on a hilltop, he didn't feel anything close to a great sense of anticipation, or that a wonderful new phase of their lives was about to begin. He remembers feeling that looking for the house, buying the house, and finally moving there was simply something to do, a thing that perhaps they ought to do, if only because at that point, though they never articulated it to each other, they were at a loss for what else they might try.

What he also remembers about his first pass through the nearly finished rooms—besides stepping over the black cords of the carpenter's momentarily discarded power tools and hearing himself actually asking the Realtor, because Giffler had told him to, if there was a bonus room, even though he had no idea what a bonus room was or why, in a house this size, he'd need it—is a distinct sense of dread. But he knew that it was a lesser dread than he'd have felt if they had done nothing at all.

It occurs to him now, dragging the top of a thumb through a layer of construction dust on the Corian countertop, that buying that home with Rachel was a form of marital nihilism, of relationship suicide, and that subconsciously they both knew it. Otherwise why else, without children, let alone a plan for having a family, would they move to twenty-first-century suburbia like moths to . . . no, moths don't know that beyond heat and dazzling light the flame will suddenly destroy them, while Rachel and Henry, they certainly had warnings.

If anyone was a moth to suburbia's flame, he thinks, it was his grandparents. In the late forties the concept was flush with momentum and promise. The latest incarnation of the American freaking dream. The thing to do after coming home from the blasted forests of Ardennes, the bloody waters of Leyte Gulf. After surviving naval assaults, artillery bombardments, and bayonets in the hedgerows while it seemed as if half your generation didn't, the prospect of living far from the noise of the city in a generic subdivision of affordable prefab homes probably didn't seem so bad.

When it came time for his parents to decide where they were going to live their lives, there was much more data to draw from. For starters, having grown up in suburbia, they were aware of and had experienced most of its benefits and shortcomings. They were the damaged children of Cheever and Rabbit and *Revolutionary Road,* just as they were the fortunate and comforted children of homecoming dances and firemen's parades and *Father Knows Best.* More than once while growing up his parents had no doubt seen the air taken out of the suburban dream (adultery, alienation, cultural depravity), as often as they had seen it resuscitated (community, belonging, adultery). And most likely they knew exactly what they were getting into before they decided to sign the lease on their own contemporary ranch with detached garage and enough room in the backyard for an aboveground pool.

They had at least considered the data and made a decision.

But what data had he and Rachel considered? For sure they'd been exposed to an even broader cultural sampling than their parents had. Plus they'd had more than a taste of life away from suburban life, in college in Boston and later as young Manhattanites. By the time they had made their decision on that inbound train from Westchester after the harvest festival at the home of people whom, incidentally, they would never see again, they had generations of data to work with.

And Henry can honestly say right now that they ignored every last bit of it.

Which plays right into his relationship suicide theory. They had chased the absolute worst aspects of the suburban cliché to give themselves an excuse to unearth the reality of Henry and Rachel more rapidly: They were flawed. And their relationship—not suburbia—was flawed.

Suburbia, like USAVille, is simply a vessel waiting to be filled by angst or contentment, a lifetime of hopelessness or generations of happiness. Unfortunately, he and Rachel had seen suburbia as nothing more than an opportunity to ramp up their already escalating pangs of hopelessness and desperation and expedite the inevitable.

Of course he hadn't been able to see it then, and Rachel undoubtedly has her own theories on the subject, but he does see it all quite clearly now, as he sits six time zones away from his past, pacing the length of the front porch of a home that may never be inhabited.

Back in New York he always made a point of avoiding the malls in and around his hometown, especially the large, enclosed malls, which seemed to have their own ecosystem, fed at the top of the food chain by human spirit and money.

He used to tell Rachel that every aspect of the mall experience depressed him, but she wasn't sympathetic to his claims. She used to answer, "No shit. You think I like doing the zombie walk past the Candle Castle, the World of Womanly Lotions, and six different versions of the Gap? The days of mall as novelty experience—going to admire the atrium fountains and the latest-model Saabs parked in front of the Sunglass Hut—are long past. We go because we need shit, Henry, and for you to pretend that you are above it and won't go because it's not stimulating enough, or because it reflects too much truth about the world you refuse to engage, is an insult to my intelligence."

Yet this mall, dark and decaying, never complete and never new, he has no intention of avoiding. If anything, the ghostly emptiness sprawled before him is an attraction. As he enters the doorless center of the concrete-block edifice, bats alight from the aluminum header for a would-be interior storefront. Strolling down the darkening entry venue, he imagines Rachel's atrium fountain at the end of his sightline, flanked perhaps by a Jamba Juice stand and a discount perfume cart. To his immediate right, maybe a Stride Rite shoe store, a crappy jewelry shop, a Bath and Body Works. To his left, he's thinking a Chili's or an Applebee's. Something with aspirations a quarter-step above fast food, with a serviceable bar.

Much better to imagine it than experience it.

A second floor of retail ruins overlooks the first-floor atrium, but there are no escalators. He locates a concrete stairway on the back wall and makes his way up. Stacked on the edge of the far walls are bundles of aluminum wall studs and iron rebar, waist-high wooden wheels wrapped full with copper wire, and a half-dozen pallets of bagged mortar. He wonders why, with so much poverty all around, the materials here and in the surrounding homes haven't been looted, stripped clean, reused, and resold. He decides that maybe the locals look at this place as a repository of bad spirits, like the forbidden peaks that Maya showed him, an evil place not to be disturbed. As he continues, he can't help but be thrilled and relieved by the fact that none of this has come to pass, and in all likelihood never will.

Far above, a blue plastic construction tarp flaps, wind-frayed and brittle, along the edges of the large atrium skylight hole it was meant to temporarily cover. Standing in what could only be the food court—he's thinking Sbarros, Burger King Express, some American-owned Chinese chain with the word *panda* in the name—he stares at the ragged hole in the sky, sun blinking through the synthetic fray like a semaphore, and he marvels at the absurdity of it all, a Western-style mini-mall in a remote rural region of a Buddhist nation.

After several minutes he looks away from the opening and reconsiders the condition of the mall that never was. He wonders how much Himalayan wind and snow, sun and rain it will take to bring it all down again.

From below, a noise. Henry slowly tilts his head and sees movement in the atrium. It is a barefoot boy, maybe eight or nine, in a burnt-orange *gho*. His head is clean-shaven and he walks with a limp. Several times the boy passes from the front entrance of the mall to a place out of Henry's line of sight, where Henry's hypothetical Applebee's might have gone. Probably stealing shit after all, he thinks. Or vandalizing, doing a little Himalayan graffiti tagging on the bare walls, and who can blame him, really.

Several times the boy returns and disappears. Henry is certain that the boy is unaware of his presence, but on his last pass before disappearing, he stops and looks up, directly at Henry.

They stare at each other for a moment, until Henry blinks and waves. Instead of waving back, the boy presses his hands together at his chest and bows gently and slightly from the waist.

The boy is gone by the time Henry makes his way back downstairs. He calls after him anyway, his American voice echoing off the garish walls of made-in-China cement. Outside, the sunset wind has begun its crawl down the backs of the peaks and into the valley. As he looks for a sign of the boy, who vanished like a phantom, he hears fabric flapping in the rising breeze. Overhead he sees the boy's hand-iwork: the breathtaking, brilliantly colored squares of a prayer flag, strung across the broad expanse of the vacant building's entrance. Five rows, each more than twenty flags long. He steps away from the building to get a better look and stops after a dozen steps, when he is out from under the shadow of the walls and can see the mall and the swirling flags framed by the sun-dashed tops of the surrounding peaks.

The blue, white, red, green, and yellow cloth squares represent, as Maya explained to him at dinner at her nephew's place, the five elements: sky/space, wind/air, fire, water, and earth. Maya told him that as wind passes over the flags, the surrounding air is purified and energized with peace, compassion, and wisdom. Finally, if he remembers it right—and he's fairly sure he remembers everything Maya has told him during their brief time together—at the center of the flags is the image of a wind horse, which combines the speed of wind and the strength of the horse to carry the blessings of love to all sentient beings in the universe.

"Including capitalists and liars?" he had asked her.

"As long as they're sentient capitalists and liars," she had replied.

Walking back to his temporary house in the development that never was, he can't stop thinking about the boy and the sunset flags outside the mall and how beauty and absurdity battle over every pulse of his existence.

Uninvited Guests

The first death threat arrives via the opposite of a prayer flag, a handkerchief-sized homicide flag with his arrow-riddled likeness Sharpied onto red-white-and-blue fabric. He finds it nailed into his front door when he comes home after his visit to the abandoned mall. And now, inside, he is finding even more threats via different mediums—text messages, phone calls, and words slathered on his bedroom wall with what he is hoping is the blood of a chicken or some animal other than human.

All saying pretty much the same thing: *Go away or we will kill you.*

In the upstairs bathroom he washes his hands and face, strips down to his boxers, brushes his teeth, and climbs into bed. But falling asleep proves difficult with *Die Imperialist Yankee* scrawled in mystery blood on the opposite wall, next to a framed Thomas Kinkade *Snow White Discovers the Cottage* print. He stands and considers doing something about the visual assault, but the best solution he can come up with is to turn the print around, with Snow White facing the wall.

He's getting back into bed when his cell phone rings again. He's reluctant to answer. Receiving prerecorded death threats is one thing, but he's not ready to handle them in real time. Sitting on the edge of the bed, staring at the tiny screen, he sees that it's not a would-be Galadonian political assassin. It's not even Rachel. It's Maya.

"Maya?"

"Yes. Just checking to see if everything is all right."

He rises and begins to pace the new ivory broadloom. "Other than the threats on my life, the knots in my stomach, and the uncontrollable trembling, yeah, I'm just splendid."

"Death threats?"

He parts the curtain and peeks out at the darkened street, at Madison Ellison's empty driveway. Was our meeting this morning a hallucination, he thinks, or does such a woman actually exist? "Yes," he says to Maya. "Death threats."

He tells her about his walk through the neighborhood and the empty mall and what was waiting for him when he returned.

Maya sighs. "These are the actions of the Cultural Preservation Movement. I doubt that they will carry through with any of it."

"I was hoping for a little more assurance than 'doubt.'"

"Going on midnight adventures with an individual such as your friend Madden, drawing that kind of attention to yourself, is not the best way to ingratiate yourself to them."

"I imagine working for an American multinational and living in a subdivision called USAVille isn't the most diplomatically subtle move either."

She laughs. "Do you want to return to the spa?"

"No. Hopefully, I can get to sleep. I've been trying, but I don't know why it's taking—"

"Maybe because it's only seven o'clock, Henry. And last night you slept for more than fourteen hours."

"Oh."

"Have you told your chaperone about this? Shug? Perhaps he can come and make sure that—"

"No, thank you. I'd rather deal with political assassination than character assassination."

"Shug is a better man than you think. Have you eaten?"

"Not since brunch with the PR person to the despots. Would you be interested in joining me?"

Maya pauses. Henry thinks he hears an adult male voice speaking to someone on her end. The guy he saw in the car with her?

"That won't be possible tonight. Why don't you eat some of the rice and vegetables I prepared for you?"

"Can you guarantee it hasn't been poisoned?"

She laughs again. "I'm calling to make a plan for tomorrow. We should meet at the call center first thing in the morning."

"For what? Trust falls? Our annual holiday party? A meeting of the board of directors?"

"Not far off, actually. I guess you haven't been checking your e-mail."

"I kind of lost interest after I saw my corporate profile pic PhotoShopped onto the body of a man hanging from the national tree. What's up?"

"Audrey and Pat are coming."

Henry walks over to the Kinkade print and turns it back around. The river in *Snow White Discovers the Cottage,* he decides, bears an eerie resemblance to the emotional high point of Audrey and Pat's Happy Mountain Springs creation myth video. "To Galado?"

"Yes. According to . . . is it Giffler?"

"Uh-huh."

"Well, according to Mister Giffler, the sale of a supposedly eco-friendly company like Happy Mountain Springs to a huge corporation, despite being welcomed by the financial markets, has apparently proven to be wildly unpopular with the loyal, environmentally responsible Happy Mountain Springs base. In fact, he said that his suggestion that they visit was based on one of your earlier ideas."

Henry approaches the wall and traces his finger along the dried blood of the letter *D* in *Die.* He likes it that she used the phrase *supposedly eco-friendly.* "Wow. What a shocker. I mean, who would have thought that selling out to a soulless conglomerate would have such a negative impact on a core group of spiritually enlightened, environmentally responsible consumers?"

"Irony, yes?"

"Yes. And they feel that making a trip here and publicizing it will be a way to make some kind of karmic corporate reparations?"

"This, in essence, is correct."

"When?"

"According to Giffler—"

"Who is an absolute looney toon."

"Well," Maya continues, "he says they are scrambling to pull this together ASAP. He wants us to come up with a tentative agenda by end of day tomorrow."

"Eight a.m.: meet and greet with psychotic delusional prince."

"If you like," she says, "I could pick you up."

"Nine forty-five: press conference with nonexistent members of the electronic Galadonian media."

Maya, deciding to play along, adds, "Eleven a.m.: photo op alongside dried-up riverbed. Noon: explain female homosexuality to a population that does not have a word for it, let alone acknowledge the concept."

"Now we're talking!" He laughs, and it feels as if it is for the first time in weeks. "Are you sure you don't want to brainstorm tonight? We could go back to your nephew's place."

Another pause. Another voice in the background, this time a child's.

"Just kidding. You have a good night, Maya."

"I'll pick you up at eight-thirty. Sleep tight, Henry Tuhoe."

The Lake That Fell Through a Hole in the World

Maya arrives alone in her truck and taps the horn. He sees her through the kitchen window. He finishes his cup of Galadonian red tea, his third this morning, and puts it in the sink. He wonders if it's caffeinated, then decides it doesn't matter. He's been up for hours. In fact, he's fairly sure that he never went to sleep last night.

As they back out of the driveway, Henry notices Madison Ellison bending at the curb to pick up her daily nine-month-old paper. She glances up and waves at them with a level of enthusiasm that unnerves Henry, who responds with a cool nod of the head and a half-smile.

He wonders if Madison Ellison gets death threats too.

Maya turns right onto the dirt road outside USAVille and heads east across the valley and toward the river. The opposite direction, he discerns, from the call center.

Her hair is pulled back under a white woolen skullcap and she's wearing a black sweater and dark blue jeans, making her look— besides adorable, he thinks—much younger and slightly smaller than she looks in business clothes.

He's wearing dress-down Friday khakis, a red pinstriped Brooks Brothers shirt, and brown Top-Siders, which under the circumstances makes him look and feel about sixty-seven years old.

"So you are alive," she declares, adjusting the rearview mirror.

"Yes. Quite. Though part of me is disappointed, because I've always wanted to be able to say that I survived not one but two assassination attempts."

Maya smiles. The morning air is clear and bright with sunshine, and the road in front of them is devoid of vehicles and pedestrians and surrounded on both sides by browning autumn jute fields. "You're quite funny."

"Thank you."

"Especially when it comes to dealing with the truth. The harsher the truth, it seems, the better the joke."

"Which would make me the perfect date come the apocalypse."

"But you use it as a shield, to deflect."

"Actually, it makes a hell of a weapon too."

She looks away from him and concentrates on the narrow, rutted road.

"Would you rather that I dealt with harsh truths with anger? Or bitterness? Or . . . what, despair?"

"No. But sometimes, to be taken seriously—"

He interrupts. "The more seriously someone wants to be taken, the more dangerous he is."

"If I may, I'm saying this because I think that you have much to offer and you use your humor and your cynicism to protect what is essentially smothered idealism."

For this he has no pithy comeback. He presses his face against the window glass and stares at mountains too large and sharply defined to be real.

After several minutes, still facing the window, he asks, "Where's your friend today?"

Maya takes a breath, as if trying out several responses, before answering: "He's working."

They drive without speaking in the general direction of the river for a dozen miles. He's sure now that they are traveling farther and farther from the call center, but he doesn't care enough to ask. Maya doesn't seem like someone to go off on a journey without a purpose.

With each mile the land becomes more barren. Colors fade, life evaporates under the rising sun. Blue pine forests give way to spent jute and sunflower fields, which give way to an empty land pocked and webbed with deepening crevasses. After more than an hour of rough driving, Maya pulls the truck off the road and comes to a stop at the edge of an empty lakebed whose shattered and fissured bottom looks as if it were used up and thrown down from the heavens.

He turns to her. "Odd venue for a meeting."

She doesn't smile. "This is where my family used to live. This is where we were sent when the political situation changed. At first it wasn't so bad. Beautiful, even. Before the factories and the dam, it was seventy miles around. Fishing villages lined the shores. Everything else was rich farmland. On this road there was a constant line of carts filled with produce making their way to the river."

"What happened?"

She shrugs. "Some people actually believed it all dried up because they insulted the gods by taking more fish than they needed. It happened so fast I guess I don't blame them, because really, how could humans ruin so much so fast?"

"Where'd they go?"

"Most left to work on the dam and at the factories that had already ruined their lives. Of course, many simply died." Without warning she opens the door, gets out, and begins walking onto the lakebed.

When he catches up to her, she turns to face him. "He's not my man. Okay? He is my brother."

He nods. Okay.

When she resumes walking, he is alongside her. "It's going to get much worse here before it gets better. There is a rising opposition that is in direct proportion to the prince's irrational ambition. My brother, if he could, would like to see the prince and anyone associated with him dead. And if the prince knew what my brother was up to, he would have him arrested and eventually killed. Just as he has with anyone who has dared to oppose him."

"What about you?"

She stops, pulls the band of the white cap higher on her forehead. "I don't want to kill anyone. I'd just like some, you know, human progress. Some kind of ethical balance. But in a country that supposedly embraces balance, all that I see are extremes. Absolute spirituality or absolute greed, with not much wiggle room in between, all at the expense of contentment. We're so concerned about losing our identity if we open up too fast to the world, which is fair enough, but what exactly is the identity we're saving? Cloistered? Corrupt? Spiritually rich? Economically impoverished? What the prince is doing will absolutely have a devastating impact on our future. But if it somehow comes to pass that the opposition, that my brother and the cultural preservationists, defeat the prince and his modernity movement, I'm not so sure that life here will be any better. Just righteously corrupt versus morally corrupt. And they'd kill in the name of spirituality as quickly as the prince kills for greed."

"Are you sure there's not a clearly defined good or bad side? Because, you know, it would be so much easier if I could simply choose a side." Henry smiles after he says it, but Maya doesn't smile.

She smacks him.

He doesn't touch his reddening cheek. He keeps his arms at his sides and stares at her wet, agitated eyes. The heat rises where her fingers landed, and a mountain breeze conjures a cloud of powdered, ruined earth.

"Listen," he finally says, adding another melodramatic pause before continuing. "I know you think I don't take life seriously, but everything I've ever taken seriously, I've lost."

As Maya considers his words, he readies for an embrace, an apology, the solace of a friend and the understanding of someone more. He prepares for her to tell him that she knows he's been through so much, that she knows that this has been an especially trying time for him and that he has handled it with uncommon dignity and fortitude. Perhaps even a kiss.

But instead Maya smacks him again. With the opposite hand. On the opposite cheek. Then she says, "Wrong answer, Henry. Here's the deal. Nobody cares about your emotional crisis. About the difference between a vocation and a calling and—what did you say the other day? A finding! My goodness. I lost a child. My family lost everything. Our life expectancy is fifty-three point three years and our culture is being raped by a gang of logos and you're afraid to take something seriously because it might not work out? Please. All things considered, Henry, I find your sentiments pathetic and incredibly offensive."

Being smacked twice in the face by a woman who then tells you that what you had thought was a sincere, heartfelt, and difficult confession was in fact pathetic and incredibly offensive would normally mean that she's just not into you. But Henry feels differently. After the face-smacking and moral condemnation, he feels a strange sort of release, accompanied by the feeling one experiences when given an unexpected, perfect gift.

In this instance, the gift is truth.

Giddy is how he feels.

As they resume their drive toward the river, following the shore of the phantom lake, he decides that if music were presently a part of his life, the playlist selection for this moment would be "Bling (Confessions of a King)" by the Killers. He begins singing the song in his head, but when Maya begins to talk, he instantly forgets the words, forgets the song ever existed.

Equally liberated by the physical release, Maya begins to narrate as she drives, assigning stories and insights to subtle changes in the landscape. The man walking bent over far out on the lakebed is a crazed diviner, a former monk who thinks that the lake fell through a hole in the world and that if he can simply find the exact spot, all will be well with his villagers. The empty cluster of cinder-block huts around a solitary well is a "cancer village," where textile factory runoff polluted the groundwater and the irrigation channels that fed the farms, killing and deforming the villagers and finally driving the survivors away.

When Maya's stories begin to appear one-sided, to sound like a biased diatribe against the crimes of the government in power, she switches positions and begins lambasting the old ways, the traditional practices of their supposedly tolerant, peaceable culture.

For instance, the fact that slavery was not abolished in this part of the country until 1979. Or that in the 1990s, tens of thousands of Nepali-speaking Hindus, many of whom had entered the country through a narrow pass to the north and had lived here for decades, were forcibly expelled, and hundreds were killed during pro-democracy demonstrations.

Closer to the river, the land begins to show signs of life. A man on an empty horse-pulled cart shares the road with them. An old woman in a straw hat plows a field of dark soil with yoked bullocks. A flock of black-necked cranes banks low above the valley floor and soars overhead, casting a shadow that passes through the road like an arrowhead.

As if sensing that Henry is taking pleasure in, or at least is less depressed by, the more favorable conditions, Maya counters with more words and stories. "At this small stone farmhouse on the left"—she points as she slows the truck—"the one with the frayed prayer flags near the kindling pile, a lifelong girlfriend of mine was bludgeoned to death with field stones by her in-laws, for the capital offense of bringing an insufficient dowry to her marriage."

Henry stares at the farmhouse. Wood smoke discolors the sky from a tin elbow pipe punched through the roof.

"Her in-laws," Maya adds, "still live there."

"No wonder this place has such strict limits on tourism."

"They claim it's in order to protect our culture and our natural resources, but really it's to keep outsiders from discovering the truth. And not just now. For decades. Every generation has an entirely new type of truth it wants to keep the outside world from discovering."

Madison Ellison, he thinks, before adding, "Both absurd and brutal."

And Maya answers, "Exactly."

Several minutes before noon they reach the river. Maya stops the truck at a small, seemingly uninhabited village. But as soon as they open the truck doors, brindle mutts waddle from behind tin-roofed shacks to greet them. Mountains hover on the other side of the tar-black water, larger than anything he's ever seen. Beneath them the living world is diminished, reduced to a humbling dollhouse size.

Noting his astonishment, Maya lifts her chin toward the peaks. "The only way to live in a place like this," she offers, "is to trust them, respect them, and then hopefully forget about them. Otherwise you would become completely intimidated. Overcome by feelings of insignificance compared to something so enormous, and paralyzed with fear that one day they will smash down and crush you."

"Does that actually help?"

She smiles. "Oh, no. We are merely specks compared to them, and eventually they may come down and crush us either way."

"I see."

"But at least until then we will have been able to live in relative peace."

They walk to a rectangular slab of granite that forms a natural bench and sit facing the river. When the dogs see that they have no food scraps to hand out, they skulk away. Three wooden dories in various stages of disrepair are flipped over on the gravel low-tide bank, and a row of iron chains looped through iron hooks embedded in anchor stones indicate that perhaps a dozen working boats are out on the water. At an eddy at the water's edge, foaming clumps of waste float like cotton, piling high and swirling with the ebb against a rotting piling.

Maya points at the toxic cluster. "Cyanide, arsenic, and factory lye. On the rare occasion that the water in the river appears clear, it's a sure sign that there are going to be inspections from some global watchdog. Amnesty. UNICEF. Or, more importantly, a visit from a corporate dignitary. For them, they shut down the factories far in advance. Same thing with the highways. Days before this next conference, they'll pull all the cars off the roads to the capital and douse the stacks and everyone will leave impressed with the quirks of our magical, spiritual mountain kingdom."

As Maya is speaking, children appear. Many of them know her. One by one they approach, smile and bow at Maya, then give Henry a tentative, skeptical nod. One, a boy of ten wearing American blue jeans and a rugby-style shirt, kisses her cheek. His face is blotched burgundy with chemical burn and the visible skin on his forearms bulges with more gray tumors than Henry can count.

"This is my nephew Sanjay," Maya explains. "My brother's son." After Henry shakes the boy's hand, Maya stands and for several minutes speaks rapidly in Galadonian to the group. The children listen intently, and when she is done they all laugh before scrambling back to the small shacks along the dirt path. "I told them we're hungry," she says.

"Don't they go to school?"

Maya laughs. "In the new Galado they boast that health care and education are free! But the reality is, they are almost completely unattainable, particularly in rural areas, where there is rampant illness and illiteracy."

While lunch is being prepared, Henry gets up to watch the children. They are playing a makeshift game of cricket on the hardscrabble lot near the river. At one point Maya's nephew calls something to her. "He wants to know if you want to play," she tells Henry.

He shakes his head. "Tell him I don't know how." He takes the level swing of a baseball player. "Tell him my game is baseball."

After relaying this to her nephew, she says, "He wants you to teach him."

Henry smiles and starts to walk toward the boy. Sanjay holds out the handmade bat, made not of willow but of plywood. Looking at the bat's warped striking face and rough edges, Henry pauses. He looks at the other children, then back at Maya. "I have a better idea." As he speaks he points at the bat, at Sanjay, and then at himself. "Why doesn't Sanjay . . ." Here he takes an intentionally pathetic downward cricket swing with a phantom bat, which already has the children laughing. "Why doesn't Sanjay teach me?"

After he makes a fool of himself to the delight of the children for fifteen minutes, Maya says that lunch is ready. When he sits down beside her, she passes him her cup of butter tea. He senses that she is pleased with him, but she won't say it. Instead she says, "While we eat, how would you like to hear my thoughts on a possible agenda?"

He shrugs, nods, still looking at the mountains, thinking how strange it is that talking shop in a place like this can feel like the most normal thing in the world, still not quite grasping how a seemingly random transfer from a parity job in Underarm Research could possibly have brought him here. "An agenda for Pat and Audrey's visit?"

"Uh-huh," Maya says. Then she extends her right arm and waves her hand over the foaming river, up the base of the humbling mountains, then back toward the leaning shacks, the hungry dogs, and the toxic children, as if issuing a blessing, a decree. "And for this too."

Divining Purpose

Henry listens.

He eats. Good stuff. Chile-spiced rice, some kind of fried taro patty. He thanks the kids and shakes their hands and even pets the goddamn brindle dogs, and then brings food to his mouth with the same hands, without Purell, without fear of catching rabies or fleas or whatever horrible condition Sanjay has. This, he realizes, has nothing whatsoever to do with personal growth, or selfless bravery, or resurgent nihilism. It has nothing to do with anything and much to do with Maya.

He keeps his mouth shut.

He stares at the mountains, still listening to Maya, but also trying to imagine their insane and explosive rise from the earth. In his mind it happens in minutes, or seconds, like a Hollywood CGI special effect, sharp peaks piercing the crust of an unsuspecting planet replete with snowcaps, mythological legends, and harrowing tales of alpine tragedies.

He listens, falling in love and falling to pieces at the same time. He knows it. Knows that in all likelihood the falling-in-love part will not be reciprocated. Shouldn't be, really, because who can blame her?

And also knowing, no, *feeling* more than he's ever felt anything that the falling-to-pieces scenario, that is an absolute. A sure thing. A matter not simply of if, but of when.

And how completely.

In small part this rush of feeling and purpose and fatalism is happening and will happen because of Maya's proposed agenda. Because of the way she is laying it out. Simply. Rationally. Selflessly.

But mostly it's happening because of who she is.

And that is someone who is infinitely better than he will ever be.

He listens and forces himself to keep his mouth shut to the extent that every time he senses the urge to blurt out words that have the potential to make him appear less than serious, or frivolous, or shallow, or crazy, he devotes some of his substantial continuous partial attention skills to things like the Hollywood-style rise of the Himalaya mountains or the hundreds of priceless playlists that he's lost, perhaps through the same hole in the bottom of the lake sought by the diviner.

He listens because he loves her now, he's sure of that. Not that he's going to tell her or anything, because that would totally blow it, but yeah, these past five, six, seven minutes have clinched it.

He loves her.

Which is all the more reason to keep his mouth shut, because the last thing he needs is to get himself double-face-smacked again.

Or is it?

Because to get a Buddhist so frustrated that she smacks you in the face a *third* time in one beautiful, brutal, absurd, and lie-changing day must mean that, at least to a degree, she digs you.

Right?

What Henry finds so impressive about Maya's plan isn't that she wants to initiate a coup or violently overthrow the government or break so much as a parking law. She doesn't want to close the borders to development, undermine centuries of cultural traditions, or even write a sharply worded letter back to the home office.

What she wants to do is give a few hundred people access to clean water.

Here, in succinctly reasoned, Princetonian, MBA-style bullet points is how:

- Make the call center operational enough to flatter and impress Pat and Audrey and corporate; this includes working with—no, *supervising* Mahesh to help train the operators to at least look like they know what they're doing in time for Pat and Audrey's visit.
- Convince them that beyond the good PR buzz potential of the call center, they have an opportunity to generate much more globally newsworthy publicity with an ambitious yet viable and scalable plan to bring fresh water to people in villages such as this. This would be done with the affordable, life-saving LifeStraw (which Henry first learned about from Madden), a product whose mission is consistent with the broader Happy Mountain Springs ethos. This could be enhanced by entering a partnership with a not-for-profit organization such as UNICEF (Tap Project) or Charity: Water.
- Exploit the Happy Mountain Springs project as a shining example of how corporate goals, cultural ideals, and environmental sustainability can work hand in hand in the new Galado, and convince the palace to create a Ministry of Corporate and Cultural Sustainability.

When she is finished, Maya puts a hand on Henry's thigh and looks him in the eye. "You know the only reason I thought of this, the only reason they may even consider this, is because of you, Henry."

Does Henry agree with the goals of Maya's agenda? Absolutely. Does he think they have a chance in hell of achieving any of them? Absolutely not. Will he share his opinions with her? Of course not. He loves her.

He places his hand over hers and says, "It can't hurt to try."

They depart from the village and head for the call center shortly after lunch. This time Henry is behind the wheel. After directing him onto the only paved road in the region, Maya curls up in the passenger's seat, pulls her black wool sweater up snug about her neck, and sleeps. He passes yak-drawn carts on the side of the road. Young men on smoke-spewing two-stroke scooters. Billboards for South Korean computers and cell phones, on stilts deep within rice paddies. Prayer flags alongside billboards covered with desecrated images of the prince, Galadonian graffiti spray-painted in yellow over the young despot's smiling, airbrushed face.

Far ahead smog hovers above the capital city like atomic fallout.

He doesn't think much of the first red-robed person he passes sitting cross-legged at the side of the road until he passes a second, a mile later. A half-mile later there is a third, like the others male, cross-legged, neither smiling nor frowning but staring straight ahead as he zips past at seventy-five miles an hour. After passing three more men, he finally sees a woman in the same position as the others. Henry waves, but she doesn't respond and probably didn't see him to begin with. As he gets closer to the capital, the red squatters, now close to an even mix of male and female, appear with more regularity and in increasingly larger groups. Ten. Twenty. Now groups of a hundred, shoulder to shoulder in something akin to prayer along the roadside.

When red-robed squatters line both sides of the road, he considers waking Maya but decides not to unless the squatters do something dangerous or threatening. As if sensing the change outside the truck window, she awakens, but she shows no sign of being surprised or concerned by the demonstration.

"AAD," she says by way of explanation. "The Alliance Against Dictatorship. They are protesting the prince's policies. I forgot that today was the day."

"Are they legal?"

"Barely. So far the protests have been nonviolent. They wear red and line the roadside to the capital. Last week they gathered outside the airport, and there were clashes with the military. But from what I hear the military is split, like the rest of the nation, over which side to take."

"What does the prince make of this?"

"Oh, I imagine he is insane with rage. Citizens wearing red in the capital have been beaten and thrown in jail if they fight back.

Several months ago the opposition color was yellow, but when HM wore yellow for a speech, the opposition realized that was a royal color on Mondays and Wednesdays, so for a while there was much confusion about what to wear if you wanted to express your disgust with the government and simply not get killed."

Henry slows the car after noticing flashing lights up ahead. It's a military checkpoint. A half-dozen armed soldiers stand in front of two dark green personnel carriers blocking the road. Henry looks down at his untucked shirt, a white Brooks Brothers with a thin red stripe.

"Calm down," Maya tells him as the truck eases to a stop. "We're fine."

A soldier approaches Henry's side and raps on the window. Before Henry can speak, Maya leans across the seat and begins to converse in Galadonian with the soldier. Henry sits back, crosses his bare forearms across his potentially incriminating red-striped shirt, and stares ahead. On the side of the road three soldiers are thrashing the legs of a young man in a red robe with riot sticks. Maya sits back in her seat and rummages through her valise for a document. She hands it to the soldier, who looks at it but doesn't seem to read it. He smiles, steps back, and waves them on.

"I told you we'd be fine."

He touches the lump on his head that he got from his night out with Madden. "Never doubted you."

As they ease through the tight space between the two military vehicles, Maya nods at the soldiers. There are no red-robed protesters on the other side. "Too close to the city for the prince's comfort," Maya explains. "He had the military shut it down out here, but according to the guard back there, it's getting increasingly difficult. Too many demonstrators at too many locations. And according to some others I'd rather not mention, it may all change if the prince loses the faith of the military."

"How would that happen?"

"If the monks get involved and HM asks the military to crack down on them. It's one thing to ask a soldier to cane an intellectual, but a monk? Many soldiers depend on them for spiritual atonement. Giving food and assistance to them helps bring you to a better place."

"Look, I don't want to seem any more callous and offensive than I've already been, but why would any company want to do business here? Didn't someone, some corporate type, do a little preliminary research into the situation before diving in with an investment?"

Maya inhales deeply and rolls her eyes. "From what I've seen, I doubt it. But in their defense, they're not alone. The prince has been doing this dance with multinationals for a while, and the protests, they are nothing new. They've been getting bigger and bigger, but because up until now he's been able to control the flow of information, to an outsider it probably seems like more of the same."

Less than a mile from the checkpoint, two miles from the city limit, Maya instructs Henry to turn off the highway and head back toward USAVille.

"Shouldn't we head to the call center?"

She shakes her head. "It's late. Better to rest up one more night, give our plan a good think, and dive in with them tomorrow."

After a few moments on the new, unpaved, and significantly rougher road, Henry says, "What do you think? Do you think what we just saw is more of the same?"

"I do," she answers. "But who knows how long that will last."

In his driveway he puts the truck into park but doesn't shut it off. Before he can ask, Maya says, "I really have to get going, Henry. I have a lot to do tonight."

Endorsed (or at Least, to the Best of Our Knowledge, Not Yet Officially Condemned) by the Gods

Shug is in the driveway at eight the next morning. After several miles of silence en route to work, he asks Henry if he is feeling better.

"I am, Shug. And you?"

The older man smiles. "I am well. And, if I may, your employees are excited about your return."

Inside the call center Mahesh has the team gathered around a television. As Henry gets closer, he sees that they're not re-viewing Pat and Audrey's corporate creation video or a customer service lesson but watching a bootleg DVD of the American situation comedy *30 Rock*. On the table alongside the TV are two half-empty boxes of Dunkin' Munchkins. After an onscreen punch line is delivered and no one in the group laughs at the appropriate time, Mahesh shakes his head, pushes Pause, and with a blue marker on a white board begins to diagram the joke for them.

It takes Henry two pronounced clearings of the throat before Mahesh finally acknowledges him. He motions with his forefinger for Mahesh to come to him. Mahesh responds by holding up his forefinger. *Just a sec.* Henry shakes his head and mouths the word *Now*. Reluctantly, the young man walks away from the TV screen and stops beside Henry.

"What's going on, Mahesh?"

"Training. Immersion in the culture."

"Watching a pirated sitcom?"

Mahesh taps his temple with the same just-a-sec forefinger. "Not just any sitcom. Two-time Golden Globe winner. Out-of-the-box thinking, bro."

"Where'd you get the doughnuts?"

"Had them overnighted. Verisimilitude."

"Tell you what," Henry says. "If they want to eat doughnuts and watch sitcoms, they can do it on their own time. Extra credit. With you. But right now we have to teach them basic phone protocol. Get them to buy into the fundamental mission of the company that's paying them. Paying us. You down with that, bro?"

Mahesh lowers his head, nods. "I am."

Ten minutes later, Mahesh, who today is wearing a blue-and-gold Los Angeles Lakers hat and a seemingly ironic T-shirt that says *Worldwide Economic Downturn: Team Leader,* deviates from practicing the call scenarios and launches into a long story about how he was almost cast as an extra in Mumbai during the filming of *Slumdog Millionaire.*

"You know what the director, Mister Danny Boyle, said to me?" he asks the group, and they shake their heads in unison. "He said I would be perfect but I looked too American. Can you imagine that?"

Henry can't. When the story is complete, even though he hadn't planned it, he steps in front of the group and says, "Thank you, Mahesh. Have a seat, please, while I go over a few things. If I speak too fast, raise your hand, and Mahesh and Maya can help translate. But you know, soon callers are going to be talking fast too. In English. Without subtitles. And I hate to say it, but Happy Mountain Springs can't afford to have people working these phones who cannot hold a basic conversation in English. If you need extra help, practice at home with a friend or coworker. If you can't keep up, then I can't use you until you are able to. You may find this harsh, but I find it harsh that people who I was assured were, if not fluent, at least conversant in English expect a paycheck from me even though they are not."

Mahesh raises his hand and begins to speak before he's acknowledged. "But—"

"Not now, Mahesh."

Mahesh stands. "But—"

"Not. Now. Mahesh!" He smacks his right hand on a work-
table, knocking a stack of documents to the floor. For the first time
in a professional environment he has raised his voice. And it has an
effect. Mahesh sits. The others sit up straight. The response surprises him to the point where he momentarily loses his train of
thought.

In the back of the room, Maya subtly nods her head. *Go on.*

"Now, to put it bluntly, we are fairly well screwed. We are a *call*
center"—he picks up an untethered placebo telephone—"without
working telephones!" For punctuation, he drops the phone and
laughs, enthusiastically enough that the others decide not to join
him. Next he picks up two empty sixteen-ounce bottles of Happy
Mountain Springs water and holds them out toward the group. In
the front row, two women lean back, like people in the front row of
a bloody boxing match. "If that's not bizarre enough," he continues,
"we're pimping on behalf of a water company in the middle of a
region that has no access to water and where plastic bottles are out-
lawed!" He throws the empty bottles over his shoulder and then,
more delicately, says, "This must be . . . horrible for many of you.
But I didn't create this situation. All that I can do, and all that we
can do, is to try to make it work, right? If we do, our lives may get
incrementally better. And if we don't, in this economy, they will
shut us down in a heartbeat. Any questions so far?"

An older woman in the back row raises her hand. Henry points
at her. "Yes, in the back?"

She rises, straightens her blouse, and asks, "What does *pimping*
mean?"

After the others stop laughing, Henry picks up one of the laser-
printed decks of stock calling scenarios they'd been practicing and
tears it in half. "In the morning," he says, "we will have new, better,
simpler ones." And because no one else has a question, he decides to
proceed by having each person stand up, say a little bit about him- or

herself, and then answer a few simple questions as honestly as possible. Without fear of retribution.

A sampling:

Tell me three positive things about Happy Mountain Springs bottled water: It is bottled fresh from a clear mountain stream; it does not contain arsenic or other carcinogens; it increases sexual stamina.

What kinds of things do others who do not work with us tell you about Happy Mountain Springs water? It will deplete your sexual stamina; it is a false front for a chemical weapons operation created by the prince; it will make you barren; it will make you insane; it actually does not contain water; it is laced with heroin; it will corrupt my dreams; it will dilute my karma; it caused tumors in laboratory mice; it will turn me into a woman who makes sex with other women.

Do you think it's true that the gods do not approve of water sold in bottles? Yes (unanimously).

Do you really believe that Happy Mountain Springs is owned and operated by evil spirits? Yes; not really; not necessarily owned and operated by but most likely guided by them.

If you were president of Happy Mountain Springs, what new policies would you institute and what old ones would you change? I would eliminate the bottles; remove the narcotics; give us working telephones; give the water away for free.

Finally, why do you think that Happy Mountain Springs has chosen to open a call center in Galado? You were sent by the gods to test our resolve during the drought; to pretend you are good global citizens; to exploit our cheap labor and corporate naiveté; the spirits decreed it; no other country would have you.

———

One by one he refutes, clarifies, or confirms their claims and statements. What impresses them most, judging by their body language, is the number of their assumptions that he more or less agrees with. For instance: Yes, I can absolutely understand how water sold in bottles might upset the gods; Yes, to an extent the company is here to take advantage of Galdado's affordable labor and favorable tax codes; and, While I don't exactly agree that the company is run by evil spirits, I can confirm that there is no shortage of evil deities skulking around the boardrooms back at the home office.

Before he gives control of the room back to Mahesh, a woman in the front row holds up her hand. "Yes?"

"We appreciate that you have been so forthcoming with us, Mister Tuhoe. That you have acknowledged truths and discredited rumors. And that you have shown an interest in our lives outside of this building. But what we would like to know is . . . what we've all been wondering is, why have *you* come *here*? And a little bit about your personal life too, please."

"Yes," he says, stepping back into the center of the room. Behind him, Alec Baldwin's face is frozen in a smarmy sitcom smile. It takes him aback, and for a moment he considers turning off the TV, but since he doesn't know how, he continues. "Of course. Well, I started working for Happy Mountain Springs' parent company when I got out of coll—"

Then he stops. He stares at a blank spot on the far wall, puts a closed fist to his mouth, and thinks, What are you going to do, tell them about Oral Care and Non-headache-related Pain Relief? The brief stints in Laxatives and Silicon-based Sprays and Coatings? Fucking Armpits? Will they understand or care? Should they?

There's nothing more pathetic than reducing one's life down to bullet points on a résumé. Especially one that ends with a midlevel stint in Armpits.

He looks to Maya for a sign. But this time, instead of nodding, she looks down at her feet.

He thinks, Should I say I'm here because for the last ten years I have let the tedium of a dispassionate life lead me wherever it wanted? As a young man I took a job I never coveted for a company whose mission and values I never bothered to learn or question or improve upon, and I bounced from job to job in that same company until I was far from a young man, making just enough more each year to keep me comfortable enough to stick around, content enough not to question any of it—that is, until the process began to reverse itself, at which point I became less and less comfortable with my job, my marriage, which was a by-product of the job, and of course myself.

What about Rachel? he thinks. Should I share that as well? Witchcraft. Falsified vasectomies. The vastly depreciated home and spirit. Did I want to come here? Oh my God, no. I came here because the life I had there was over and in typical jackass fashion I jumped right in with whatever life presented to me next.

"I came here," he finally says, "because I made something of a mess of my life back in the United States, and I needed a change. A chance to do something worthwhile with my life. The good news is that Galado is the most interesting place I've ever been. Crazy interesting, but what's so wrong with that? And since I've been here, and these last few days in particular, I have begun . . . I've begun to sort of, you know, for the first time, to feel a real sense of purpose about what I'm doing. What we're going to do. So, uh, that's why—with the help of you, and Maya, and Mahesh—I'm going to do whatever I can to make this thing we've got going here work, not just for Happy Mountain Springs but for you and your families. Okay? Okay. Any more questions?"

No one stirs. In the back of the room, Maya is smiling. Finally Mahesh stands and begins to slowly clap his hands as he walks toward Henry. Following Mahesh's cue, the others begin to clap as well. When he reaches Henry, Mahesh wraps his arms around him, squeezes, and whispers into his ear. "Beautiful shit, bro," he says in Henry's ear. "A little scatological but very heartfelt. Very *Jerry Maguire*-esque."

———————

As an inspired Mahesh resumes his lesson, Henry approaches Maya in the back of the room. "Nice," she says.

"Did I go overboard with the personal revelations?"

"Perhaps," she says. "But from what you've told me, it could have been a lot worse."

Same Cliff, Different Menu

The next night, after a long, productive, and somewhat encouraging day at work, during which they often separated from the others to discuss their larger plan, Maya invites him to have dinner at her cousin's place. Because it is dark when they arrive and cold air is blowing off the peaks, early autumn prophesizing an early Himalayan winter, they have a drink on the terrace but take dinner at an inside table.

"Who do I have to speak to get the phones working?"

Maya sips a glass of *ara*. Without asking, her cousin had brought out two glasses and a carafe of the rice-barley wine. Before speaking she takes a second sip, finishing the glass. "You should know, this is a problem with me," she says, nodding at the glass while Henry gives her a refill. "Not out of control, but there are times when I can't . . ."

He shakes his head. No need to explain.

"Anyway," she continues, "the phones. That would be the minister of future commerce."

"Whom I already met and who blew me off."

"Correct."

Henry says, "What about our friend the minister of communication?"

"Sure. But to speak with him you must go through official channels."

He takes a long drink of wine.

"Your best bet is to speak directly to your new BFF."

"HRS?"

Not quite following, Maya tilts her head to the side.

"His Royal Smallness."

She almost chokes on her wine. "I like that," she says, smiling. "Though if I said it in his presence, he could technically put me in prison for the rest of my life."

"All right, then," Henry says. "I'll try to arrange a meeting."

"No need." Maya reaches into her valise and pulls out an envelope that bears the royal seal of Galado, a fire dragon on a mountain peak. "Your friend Shug dropped this off at the call center late this afternoon, while you were telling Mahesh that the Statue of Liberty is not in Las Vegas. Anyway." She opens the flap and hands him a cream-colored invitation. "Looks like you've been asked to exercise and then dine with His Royal . . . the prince at the palace tomorrow."

Maya is on her fourth glass of wine when their entrées arrive. While they eat they continue to refine their plan: Henry will crank out some new scenarios tonight and start to share some of their better thoughts with Giffler, and Maya will develop a corporate sustainability program for HMS in Galado, as well as a template for other companies planning on doing business here to follow. Perhaps, it's agreed, Henry can seed the idea of sustainability coexisting with growth, if things are going well, with the prince.

He asks, "What exactly were you thinking we should propose as far as a goodwill project?"

Maya takes another drink, brushes her hair away from her face, and plays with the candle in the center of the small table. "Water, of course."

"Okay. But there are a lot of different—"

She interrupts. "Wells, ideally. But for now, you know, the filters."

"Filters?"

"The straw. The inexpensive straws that purify water. It was your idea. You told me about it the first day we spoke, and I think it's brilliant."

"You mean the LifeStraw. Actually," Henry says, "it was Madden's idea. I'd never heard of it before he kind of tossed it out there the first time we met, when he thought about the absurdity of a bottled water company opening a—"

She cuts him off again. "Madden!" she says, waving her hand. "Madden is a pig and a plunderer."

"That may be the case," Henry says. "But he's the only person I know in this country who could help pull something like that together. Unless you know of someone else, under the circumstances he is kind of perfect."

She answers by raising her glass.

Henry drives her truck back to USAVille.

Outside the restaurant after dinner he went straight for the driver's seat, and Maya didn't protest, didn't seem to notice. Now that they're away from the small cluster of buildings and out on the mountain road, he offers to drive her home first, wherever that is. "I can pick you up in the morning," he says.

But she shakes her head. "Just go to your place," she says. "We'll figure it out from there."

She gives him general directions—"right at the second pass, left at the first dirt road after that, then look for the obnoxious faux-Western architecture"—before settling back into her seat, and, he thinks, sleeping.

There aren't a lot of navigational choices to make in Galado once you're pointed in the right direction, so he isn't worried about getting lost. Getting hijacked or forced off a cliff or hitting a yak that has wandered into the middle of the road—these are all realistic concerns. But getting back to USAVille in the dark, not so much.

"You didn't mention your wife today."

Her voice surprises him. After ten minutes of silence had passed, he had assumed that she was asleep.

"What, no more curses on your virility?"

He takes a breath, then decides to tell her about his last e-mail exchange with Rachel.

"So," Maya says when he is done, "that's that, then. All is forgiven. Best of friends again."

"Apparently."

"Did you at least consider the fact that she may have had some other motive for telling you this?"

He shakes his head. "Not really. I didn't have time to think about it. She told me and I guess I believed her because, to tell you the truth, I was relieved, mostly."

She claps her hands and says derisively, "Hah!"

He takes his eyes off the road and looks at her, not to observe her more closely but to register that he has taken note of the change in her demeanor. Apparently six glasses of *ara* trumps the legendary Galadonian humility and kindness. "The night we first came here, you told me not to be so hard on her."

"That was before I began to care about you."

Inside the house, rather than suggesting a nightcap, he puts on a kettle of water for tea. While Maya slumps on the living room couch, he makes a cursory scan of the first floor, looking for additional signs of foul play, death threats. All that he finds is a large wicker gift basket on the kitchen counter from his new and only neighbor, Madison Ellison. A closer inspection of the basket—cookies, chocolates, exotic fruits—reveals that his gift is a regift. Madison Ellison has neglected to remove the original card from the basket, which was sent to her from her "friends in Corporate at Target."

He's still contemplating the contents of the gift basket when Maya comes up behind him and places a hand on his shoulder. He turns around, not sure what to expect. A kiss? Another slap to the face? Knee to the groin? Who knows?

For a moment they stare eye to eye, lost. Then she leans in and puts her arms around his waist and hugs him. A comfort hug, he decides, but he can't be sure if that's all, if it may elevate into something more. It's her hug; she's driving it, and he's going to let her take it wherever she wants. He rides it out by staring at the regifted basket, the card he wasn't meant to see, the teapot simmering under the blue flame of the stove.

When she finally releases him, Maya takes a step back and stares at him differently than she did pre-hug. But he's still not sure what she's thinking, and since she still hasn't spoken, he decides to keep his mouth shut as she turns and heads back to the couch. He watches her drop onto the never-before-been-lounged-upon cushions, then checks on the water. Not quite at a boil when he shuts it down. Because he's not sure what to do next, what to say or what will happen when he finally returns to Maya in the living room, he takes his time removing a matching pair of USAVille™ mugs from the cabinet, rinsing them under the faucet, and opening up two individually wrapped pouches of Earl Grey.

When he returns with the steeping tea, she is asleep. Of course she is. Not curled up and cozy, as she appeared to be earlier, in the truck. Her head is tossed back, black hair spread in a mass over the back of the couch, and her mouth is open. Her arms twist at her sides like randomly dropped pieces of string. Her legs are outstretched and splayed, shoeless feet hanging at awkward angles over the wall-to-wall carpeting.

He puts her mug down on the end table and checks his watch. Midnight in Galado, but he's far from tired. Maya is snoring, but the act doesn't seem to bother him. Good sign, or bad? Does it say that he doesn't really care what she does or that he's willing to forgive anything that she does? When the snoring modulates and settles into its own rhythm, he decides that it is finally safe to lift her legs and feet onto the couch and to turn her lengthwise.

From his bed upstairs he grabs a pillow and the comforter. When the pillow is propped under her head and the comforter carefully draped from feet to neck, he takes two cushions from the matching love seat and places them on the floor alongside her, lest she fall.

Outside, it begins to rain, the first he's seen or heard since arriving in Galado. Rooftop thrumming away the midnight silence. New waters course downhill in excavated rivulets, pooling in empty driveways. He sits alone at the kitchen table, listening, drinking from both mugs of tea, staring at Maya in the darkness of the adjoining room and wondering if this is the onset of the rainy season or some weather anomaly or simply more bad juju from a pissed-off god or witch or river dolphin.

In the morning he'll ask her. In the morning they'll have reached another level in their relationship. A new level of trust, the result of each having revealed an unfortunate aspect of their worst selves, somehow without alienating the other. This, of course, in addition to the attraction.

What he had needed was a fling. That's what some had told him after things got bad and then untenable with Rachel, and what he had almost allowed himself to believe. What he had needed was a passionate, decadent interlude with some young hottie from work, a neighborhood MILF, an upscale bar pickup, all mutually guilt- and expectation- and consequence-free. To get over Rachel. To get over failure. To just have some fucking fun.

But that has never been the way with Henry, and not because he's a prude. With Henry and any relationship with a female, there will always be expectations and consequences, always something to feel guilty about, no matter how unconditional the hookup, no matter how brief the relationship. To Henry, a fling constitutes at the very least a failure of character, and ultimately a failure of ego. How could I enjoy my time with you knowing that we both want it to be finite, to have a moment and get it over with, that no matter what, you neither want nor plan to spend more than a fixed amount of time with me? How could I respect you yet have no intention of ever taking our relationship to a level beyond booty call? Even when they'd just begun to date, Rachel used to tell him that he should stop thinking so much and just do. Just live. But he never could. And still can't.

Already with Maya he's neck-deep in the muck of expectations and consequences, already contemplating the extent of the wounds that are sure to come, even though he and Maya have yet to kiss. The difference here is that despite his anxiety and low expectations, he is willing to go through with it anyway.

One magnificent thunderhead rumbles over the peaks before crashing through the valley like an avalanche, rattling windows and sweeping the night away on a sonic wave. He opens his laptop and turns it on. As the application icons slowly reveal themselves onscreen—the colorful stamp-sized globes and cameras, calendars, gears, and guitars that coordinate so much of his life—he thinks he has never felt more disconnected, more doomed to fail, more convinced that he does not belong in a place than he feels now. Yet when he peeks over the top of the flickering screen and sees Maya, legs kicking in drunken REM at an antagonist of her unconscious, he decides that it doesn't matter.

In New York, Meredith immediately responds to his e-mail, the subject heading of which reads "Is Kevlar a Billable Expense?"

She writes, after updating him on the latest round of layoffs, defaulted loans, and corporate misdemeanors, that she will research what he is proposing and get back to him ASAP with everything she can find about their company's green and sustainable practices, including a full dossier on Happy Mountain Springs and Pat and Audrey.

And this time, rather than ending with her usual sarcastic sign-off, she writes, "Sounds interesting and potentially worthwhile, Tuhoe. In fact, this wins my Least Offensive E-mail of the Day Award."

At 1:45 a.m. he decides to do something about the telephone lines. Maya's right. He can ask the prince to help, but he decides that it is more prudent to save his royal favors for the greater good of the project, or simply to save his ass. Instead, after digging up the man's royal business card, he e-mails the minister of future commerce and tears into him, threatening him with his own deepening relationship with the prince and the prince's high hopes and unflagging interest in the project. It would be a shame, Henry concludes, to have a simple misunderstanding between well-intentioned colleagues undermine the prince and his grand plan and cause him so much duress at this critical juncture in the nation's history.

If this doesn't work, he tells himself, pushing Send, then I absolutely will speak to the little bastard in person.

———————

Even at two a.m., Madden, not surprisingly, is up and awake. He answers his sat-phone before the second ring. "At this hour, whatever you're up to better involve sex, drugs, or immortality."

"Nope. Water." Henry gets directly to the point and asks for Madden's help connecting him and perhaps brokering a deal with the people who distribute the LifeStraw.

"I can set something up tomorrow," Madden replies. "Tonight, if you're really fired up about saving the world."

"Can't. I have a playdate with the prince tomorrow."

"Then day after. I'll pick you up."

"Thanks. I owe you."

"Duly noted."

As soon as he hangs up, he immerses himself in the work he and Maya had been outlining all day. Part social manifesto, part business plan. Part Maya, part Henry. He goes online and pulls quotes and headlines, statistics, images, and video clips. He researches desalinization plants, reverse filtration membranes, aquifer depletion, and deep-earth river disputes. He investigates UNICEF and the Tap Project and Charity: Water. He becomes fluent in the Walmart effect (in which big-box stores appear in remote third world regions and eliminate the culturally invaluable mom-and-pops), and the impact of upstream waste on downstream village wells in rural India, and the five most deadly waterborne diseases caused by pathogenic microorganisms known to man.

He employs the personality archetypes of Joseph Campbell to demonstrate desirable brand attributes.

He quotes from Robert Frost's poem "Going for Water":

The well was dry beside the door,
And so we went with pail and can . . .

He uses Ben & Jerry's sustainability programs as a case study.

———————

Through the template magic of Keynote a deck begins to emerge—
"Happy Mountain Springs: The Purity Flows Through Us All"—
that makes more strategic and ethical and monetary sense than he
ever could have hoped for.

Halfway through the working night, on a whim, he clicks on the
icon for his music library. And it's there. Every song and playlist,
miraculously restored. He stands, backs away from the computer,
and walks to the window. The rain has stopped, and wet dirt lots of
the empty neighborhood have taken on a moonlit gloss.
    It's a sign.
    Of course it's not, you wack job.
    It's weather.
    It's a miracle.
    No, it's a wonky computer.

Back at the kitchen table, he scrolls back and forth through it all,
stopping to consider favorites as if looking at photos of loved ones.
Having so many songs at your fingertips is amazing, but there are
times, like now, when he wishes there were a more tangible aspect
to the digital music.
    Something to touch, or read, or clean your weed on.
    To avoid waking Maya, he puts on his headphones before push-
ing Shuffle.
    Here's what comes up: "Smile Like You Mean It" by the Killers.

At 5:30 a.m. he finishes his final sentence, clicks Save, and e-mails a
copy of the file to Meredith. Then, as a wild-card entry, he sends a
copy to Norman, his Percocet-addicted former personal trainer
and aspiring viral filmmaker. "Read this," he writes. "Then make a
film about it. Something that would make a group of sociopathic,

egomaniacal corporate muckety-mucks want to implement it. Whatever you want, as long as it's three minutes or less."

Upstairs in the guest room/home office, he turns on the complimentary laser printer and spits out two sets after it has warmed up. He fans through the pages, stopping twice to read a particularly satisfying paragraph or look at the hard copy of a downloaded image.

It's good. With feedback and input from Meredith and Maya, and encouraging news on the LifeStraw from Madden, it might be good enough for the likes of Giffler and Dworik, Pat and Audrey.

Back downstairs, he places one deck on the table next to Maya's car keys. He stares at her for a moment. Outside, the sun is starting to backlight the mountains, and the rising cream glow enters the room like a ghost through the wall of a dream.

When he wakes up two hours later, Maya is gone.

The deck is gone too.

Next to the laptop is an empty water glass that wasn't there when he went to bed. He touches the space bar and the Recently Added section of his music library appears onscreen. At the head of the section is a track called "Water Music." The artist is listed as Maya. It's a pop song, in the *rigsar* genre, a fusion of Indian, Nepalese, Bhutanese, and Galadonian music old and new, featuring a fifteen-string electronic version of the dranyen.

Even though he can't understand a word of it and the melody is a little more techno-driven than what he normally prefers, in a strange way he kind of likes it.

Mister Henry

Shug is in the driveway at nine a.m. He's chatting with Madison Ellison, who has picked up her wet plastic-wrapped newspaper and is fussing with the dried-up buds on a rhododendron near her mailbox.

Henry hadn't planned on it, but it occurs to him that Madison Ellison might be worth talking to.

"I hear you're meeting with the prince today," she says after an exchange of matter-of-fact hellos in this most improbable of locales.

"I am. In fact, if you have a minute, before Shug and I leave, I'd love to run something by you."

They walk into her house, leaving Shug fidgeting against the truck in the driveway. At her kitchen counter, he walks her through the deck in broad strokes.

When Henry is done, Madison Ellison, who knows her way around a multimedia presentation, says, "Interesting. The sustainability card. What exactly do you want from me?"

Henry shrugs. "An opinion. Some advice. Your take on what the prince will make of it."

"Well, you're not a client, but since the prince is and this ultimately could ladder up to his ultimate yet—off the record—almost certainly unattainable goal, I'll tell you what I think. I think it's ambitious, and though it's a bit rough around the edges, it is well intentioned, well stated, and, most important, well reasoned."

"Say I get approvals on my side and we're able to cut a deal with the LifeStraw people. Do you think it has a chance?"

She steps back and considers Henry, then the open presentation deck on the countertop. "For anything to have a chance with the prince, the first thing you have to do is make it seem as if it is *his* idea. His royal lightning strike of inspiration. Even if you know and he knows deep down that this isn't true, for appearance's sake, you have to serve it up to him just so."

"Okay."

"And what you also have working in your favor is the fact that right now he's desperate. He'll consider any proposition thrown his way if it will somehow trigger some momentum and resurrect interest in this place. To lessen, if not stop, the bleeding. Every day it seems as if another multinational is either scaling back or reneging on its promise to be part of his master plan. Look at this development. Six months ago it was all systems go. Trucks filled with workers and materials were coming in and out of here every ten minutes. Then things started falling apart in the States, then in the banks in Europe, and then here in USAVille. In the Shangri-La Zone. And now they're—no offense to you and me—ghost towns."

Shug beeps the horn in the driveway. Henry looks over his shoulder and can't help but be impressed by the man's audacity.

Madison Ellison continues. "For what it's worth, if he doesn't pay my company within the next two weeks, I'm going to be pulling out the tent stakes too. I imagine your company must be on the fence with this place as well."

Henry says, "I guess," though in truth he has no idea. "They've had so much internal turmoil the last few months—layoffs, mergers, defaults, takeovers—I'm not sure they've been paying a lot of attention to the tiny operation in the works here. So you think he might like this?"

She pauses again before answering. "I do. If it's properly pitched. If he's on the upswing of the manic-depressive, steroid rage pendulum. If he doesn't further suspend human rights in the name of capitalism and democracy. If he has a good meeting with the Wal-mart delegation. If there isn't a nonviolent coup. Or a successful assassination attempt. If he doesn't find out that your friend Madden is cutting deals behind his back and, on the other side of the ideological spectrum, that your girlfriend hates him with every bone in her body. All very distinct possibilities, from what I've heard."

The horn beeps again. Asshole. "If things really are this bleak," he responds, "or if there's a distinct possibility that any or all of this might come to pass, why are you still here?"

For the first time during the conversation, Madison Ellison smiles. "That's easy. If any or all of it comes to pass, it will create an entirely new and different set of circumstances, which will present us with an entirely new and different set of opportunities. And clients. You see, Henry, the reason this place works for me is, beyond growing my business, I'm not emotionally invested in it. I don't fucking care. And I'm hoping, for your sake, that you don't either."

"We will be late," Shug tells him, tapping his watch. "You were expected at the call center at nine-thirty."

Henry surprises Shug by getting into the front passenger's seat. "I apologize, Shug. My fault."

Twice Shug looks over his shoulder and anxiously considers the empty backseat before turning the key.

"You lose something back there?"

Shug shakes his head.

"Good. Anyway," Henry explains, "the reason I'm late is I had an idea that I think might actually help a few people here in Galado who aren't beholden to the prince or the cultural preservationists or a corporation, and I wanted to ask Ms. Ellison what she thought about it." As they back out of the driveway, Henry rolls down his window, then says, "She actually kind of liked it. In fact, if you don't mind, Shug, I'd love to hear what *you* think of it."

Shug nods. It takes Henry about ten minutes to lay out a Shug-appropriate version of his proposal. If anything, he reasons, telling people such as Madison Ellison, Shug, Meredith, and even Norman is helping him hone his pitch, trim unnecessary details, and answer questions he hadn't anticipated. For instance, "How long would each straw last?" and "What happens when they run out and you have thousands of people who have grown dependent on them?" And "It is not our nature to accept charity without reciprocating. What do you propose for people to do to somehow return the favor?"

All of which leads Henry to believe that Shug may approve of it and, by association, him. From his brief and guarded answers, Henry is able to discern that he doesn't come from a river village but from a lowland town in the southern part of the country, where runoff pollution isn't a major issue but raw sewage seeping into groundwater and wells is. "Many die because of this," Shug says, with a weight that makes Henry think that included among the many was more than one of Shug's loved ones.

Neither speaks for the last five minutes of the drive. When the truck stops in front of the call center, Shug turns to Henry. "So this is what your company intends to do here in Galado? This . . . straw?"

Henry shakes his head. He notices several dark blue Toyota work vans and an old Mitsubishi bucket truck parked alongside the back wall of the building. Phones! "It's what I am going to try to *get* them to do," he finally answers. "There are, as Madison Ellison told me and I'm sure you can confirm, a lot of variables. But yeah, I'd like to make it—the straw, cleaning up the water somehow—part of the mission here."

Shug lifts his chin toward the building. "She gonna help you?"

"Maya?" Henry opens the door, gets out, and leans back inside. "I don't know. I hope so. I think so. I know that I'd like to help her."

Shug stares at the call center, as if looking intensely enough might summon her outside.

"Do you . . . do you think she's a good woman?" Henry asks.

The older man inhales deeply before almost imperceptibly nodding. "I know her people a long time," he answers. "Father, mother, brother, and nephew. They've been through a lot."

Henry taps the roof, closes the door, and walks away. As he

reaches the entrance of the call center, he hears the SUV's horn beep again. He turns: *What?*

Shug leans across the front seat and says through the open window, "No later than three p.m. We cannot be late for the prince."

After thinking about it for a moment, Henry turns and flashes his middle fingers at Shug, and to his surprise, the audacious bastard smiles.

Inside, Mahesh is talking to a group of three workers while the others are broken up into groups, earnestly going over, Henry presumes, his freshly amended and simplified scenarios. Mahesh looks up, waves, and smiles. Henry responds with an exaggerated salute.

In the back of the room a man in a gray suit is supervising three men in green jumpsuits who are threading long clumps of thin multicolored wires along the base of the wall. Outside, another worker feeds more wire through a recently drilled hole in the wall. Henry is fairly sure that the man in the suit with his back to him, bent over at the waist and barking orders in Galadonian to the tech guys, is the minister of future commerce.

He feels a tap on his shoulder. He turns, surprised that Maya is here this early, but he's not about to say so. "You had a busy night," she says, showing her copy of the deck.

"I was on fire."

She smiles and holds his gaze for a moment before tilting her head toward the bent-over man in the suit.

"The minister?"

"He says he got your e-mail in the middle of the night. He was here before we opened and has been looking for you all morning."

"Good."

"He said we should have service by the end of the day."

"Nice."

"What did you write to him?"

"Nothing, other than variations of 'My very good friend the prince, unnecessarily angry and extremely disappointed.'"

"'Mister Henry,' he calls you."

"I prefer Master Henry. Or the minister of all things aquatic, but fine." He points at the deck. "So what do you think?"

She waves him toward a corner table. "I think . . . it's a great start. But I have some thoughts."

Royal Playdate

"Where's the fish tank?"

"What fish tank?"

"There was a giant freaking fish tank right here the last time I visited."

The chaperone looks at Shug and Henry, then shakes his head. "You must be mistaken. No fish tank."

Shug dips an elbow into Henry's side. "We really should be moving along, Mister Tuhoe."

Henry doesn't move along. Instead he steps closer to the dark-paneled wall where the fish tank was the first time he visited the prince and runs his forefinger along the fade lines left by the missing tank. "Right here. Gally. The blind bottle-nosed Galadonian river-fish. Used sonar to catch smaller fish. The last known in existence. According to the prince, up until now it had survived for twenty million years without incident. Tell me," Henry presses, "when did Gally, um, pass?"

The chaperone shakes his head. "No Gally."

"I wonder how many years it took to kill it. Render it extinct."

"No Gally. No riverfish. No tank," the chaperone curtly says. "You must not speak of this with the prince. And technically, for a species to be functionally rendered extinct, decades must pass before a quorum of international scientific organizations can make it offi-cial."

Another royal aide appears and tells them that the prince is running late. "I presume you received the message that he would be unable to power-lift with you today because he is quite busy, and he may have torn a pectoral muscle."

"Yes," Henry answers. "I got the message this morning. Please tell him I'm sorry about the pec, and that if this is a bad time—"

"Oh, no," the aide interrupts. "The prince told me to implore you to stay. He very much wants to spend time with you."

Shug is taken in one direction by the chaperone and Henry is led by the aide down two long, marble-floored corridors and into another building entirely. They stop in a lounge, indigenously antique in structure yet incongruously modern in decor. Black leather couches beneath hand-carved coffered ceilings. Flat screens hang where, judging by the fade marks on the walls, royal portraits once hung. Aqua blue shag carpeting covers, presumably, centuries-old marble floors. IKEA meets *The King and I*, he thinks, dropping down onto a black leather easy chair. Or *The Prince and I*.

For more than an hour he sits, dividing his attention between CNN on one large screen and a Bollywood musical on another. The doorway, centered between the two video monitors, serves as a third screen, on which the real-life drama of a kingdom under siege plays out. In between images of beautiful Hindu women in sheer silk gowns singing and dancing on Mumbai-soundstage clouds and titans of American finance doing the perp walk in handcuffs, he takes in the living, 3-D images of frantic Galadonian ministers and aides, groups of monks and military officers. Every ten minutes or so one of them mistakenly enters the lounge and asks, "Is he here?" or "Have you seen him?" or "Can you tell me where the crisis center is?"

Several times a young woman in a *gho* enters and asks if he would like some more tea, even though he hasn't had any to begin with. Just before the prince enters the room, three security guards in Western suits appear. One asks Henry to rise and pats him down. One performs a cursory scan of the premises, looking under seat cushions, out the windows. And the third quickly walks the perimeter of the room, waving a long steel wand that crackles with varying degrees of intensity.

"Is he on his way?"

The man patting him down looks up from Henry's shoe tops but doesn't answer.

"Want to give me a sense of what kind of mood he's in?"

The man rolls his eyes and shakes his head before rising. Henry Tuhoe is clean.

"Well, well. If it isn't Henry Yo-Town Tuhoe. H_2O. Water impresario. Corporate titan. Esteemed friend of the state. And one baaaad muthafucka."

Henry turns and sees the prince standing at attention in the doorway. This time he's not wearing Lycra workout tights but the full dress uniform of the commander in chief of the Galadonian Armed Forces. Henry is not sure whether he should salute, bow, or exchange gang symbols from the hood.

Before he can attempt any of these, the prince is upon him and extending his left arm for a royal fist thump followed by a fragile hug.

"Heard about your pec," Henry says, stepping back. "Sorry about that."

"It wasn't the muscle," the prince tells him, touching his arm to make sure that he understands the distinction. "It was a ligament. The muscles grew so fast that the ligaments couldn't keep up. Can you imagine?"

Henry shakes his head. "Wow. I . . . I really can't."

"Come." The prince slaps Henry's back with his left hand. "I'm sorry for the change in schedule, but there is a great deal going on, and I hope you don't mind if I ask you to accompany me while I make the rounds."

As they walk through an arched doorway at the far end of the lounge and head down another hall, a group of six advisers and security people trails ten yards behind them.

"Tell me," the prince continues, "what was it like coming here?"

"Pardon?"

"The protesters. The demonstrators. The Alliance. Were the sides of the highway a sea of red?"

"There were demonstrators in red," Henry answers. "But not as many as I saw the other day on the road just north of here that runs along the river, during the official protest."

"Was it violent?"

"Today?"

The prince shrugs. Today. Yesterday. "I don't care about when you saw it as long as it's true." He jabs a thumb over his shoulder. "I can't count on them to tell me the truth anymore."

"Yesterday, not that I could notice. Wait—I did see some soldiers clubbing someone at a checkpoint. A young man at an intersection near the river. But other than that, nothing. And today, nothing."

"How about the monks? Any monk activity? Because they're telling me that if the monks join in, I am truly doomed, in this world and the next. If they commit to the Alliance, I will surely lose the military. Or enough of it to be toppled."

Henry shakes his head. "I don't recall seeing any monks."

"This is good. You know why all of this is happening, don't you?"

"People are uncomfortable with the speed of the changes you're proposing? They're afraid that their culture will be lost?"

The prince shakes his head and laughs. "Wall Street. Once Wall Street went in the toilet, foreign investment dried up, and when that happened my programs, the programs that so many of them had been clamoring for, became wildly unpopular."

"I did hear this too."

"They don't give a shit about their culture. If the markets had remained vital, companies like yours and much larger than yours would have continued to come in and we would have been able to implement the rest of our plan, which would have led to jobs, growth, and prosperity."

The prince stops at a window at the end of the hall. "Look," he says, pointing to a massive construction site a half-mile away, where a concrete horseshoe-shaped edifice rises thirty feet above grade. As far as Henry can detect, no living thing occupies the site. "This was to be our Olympic stadium. Designed by a dude who helped the dude who designed the Bird's Nest in Beijing."

"Is Galado petitioning to host an Olympics?"

The prince steps away from the window, stares at Henry, and decides to ignore the question. Instead of answering, he swings open one of the large oak doors in front of them. An intense blast of light from the other side momentarily blinds Henry. He rubs his eyes as he steps through the doorway. When he looks up, he sees at the far end of an otherwise empty room a half-dozen 750-watt halogen tri-lights positioned around a small stage rigged for a photographic shoot.

More than a dozen people are scrambling around the periphery. There is an upright industrial fan blowing toward the stage, a crafts services table, and makeup and wardrobe stations. House music thumps off the walls. "Boom Boom Pow" by the Black Eyed Peas.

Henry tries to glimpse what they are photographing, but there are too many bodies in the way. All that he can see is the residual flash of a camera. He looks at the prince for an explanation.

"State-of-the-art photographic studio and soundstage, bro. Designed by a major motion picture company head from Mumbai, with technical input from the people at Industrial Light and Magic."

Henry nods. Behind them, the door reopens and a young woman carrying a tennis racket and a double-barreled shotgun hurries inside. Upon recognizing the prince, she stops in her tracks and bows before hustling on toward the stage.

"Come," the prince tells him after the prop woman has moved on. "Let's take a closer look."

The stage is being dressed to look like a meadow. In the foreground a strip of high alfalfa grass stuck into foam blocks runs along the length of the floor. On stage right, two grips are attaching the severed branches of juniper trees to light stands. To the left, another is on a ladder, positioning a spotlight that will stand in for the sun. The rear wall is a royal blue screen that, Henry realizes, will later allow the photographer to substitute any background he or she wants behind the central image.

Soon a small middle-aged man whose yellow-and-blue-flowered Hawaiian shirt barely covers his large brown belly approaches. His black hair is pulled back in a long ponytail, and a large digital camera hangs from a strap around his neck. He looks Galadonian, but Henry can't be sure. He bends his entire upper body at a ninety-degree angle before the prince and Henry.

"This is Rodrigo Spatz," the prince says by way of introduction. "The greatest filmmaker in Nepal and for the last two years the official filmmaker to the Galadonian Crown and part-time photographer. Rodrigo, meet the American business mogul Henry Tuhoe."

Henry extends his hand, but before Rodrigo can grasp it the prince steps between them. "Please excuse us, Henry Tuhoe," the prince says, and then he guides Rodrigo Spatz away for a private conference.

Alone, Henry wanders along the edges of the set. In the back of the room, he sees the prince's staff gathered by the doorway, watching and fretting. At the crafts service table he grabs a handful of M&M's and begins popping them into his mouth as he continues on. He stops at an easel upon which rests a large white foam-core presentation board. Taped to the board are dozens of outtakes from the shoot. In the photos the same old and feeble man—eighty or ninety, Henry guesses—is wearing a series of costumes and uniforms, performing a variety of activities that seem to belie his age and physical condition. Saluting in a military uniform. Wearing a brown barn jacket and tossing a stick to two Irish wolfhounds. In a suit adorned with an orange royal sash, holding an infant in his stick-thin outstretched arms. And finally, in the least believable shot of the group, the man appears to be suspended in midair in a crash helmet and orange jumpsuit, clutching parachute cables. They can retouch and PhotoShop this all they want, Henry thinks—clouds, vapor trails, the curvature of the earth—and it will never look real. The only thing that appears real in this shot is the look of mortal terror in the old man's eyes.

"What do you think?" a woman asks from behind.

He turns. It's Madison Ellison. "Howdy, neighbor."

"How do you like our work?"

"What is it for, AARP Galado?"

"Clearly the lowest point in a career that seems to be reaching new depths by the day."

"Who is the old bastard?" Henry asks.

Madison Ellison steps forward and puts a finger to her lips. "Shhhhh." She looks around to see if anyone heard him. She mouths, "It's the king."

"Get out. I thought he was—"

She takes his arm and walks him away from the set. "Almost," she whispers, stopping beside a cart filled with props: bow and arrows, a cricket wicket, a saddle. "He's barely alive, which is why we're doing this."

"I don't follow."

She takes a deep breath before explaining. "With the . . . political situation being what it is, and the rising opposition to the prince claiming that he has been trying to kill the king, and rumors of the king's death abounding, the prince thought it best that we release some recent photos that show him vital and active."

"Enter Madison Ellison, PR queen."

"I don't want to piss him off. My home office says that if things deteriorate much more, they'll get me out of here in a week or so."

"I understand there's a blue screen involved, and they're unretouched," Henry says. "But with all due apologies to Mister Rodrigo Spatz, those are some of the most disturbing photographs I've ever seen."

"And you weren't even here when he dropped the baby."

"No."

She nods. "Well, you can't really blame Rodrigo," Madison Ellison replies. "Since he is a filmmaker by training, not a photographer, and he was kidnapped and everything."

"Excuse me?"

She takes a sip of what appears to be tea in a paper cup. "Kidnapped. About two years ago he was visiting from Nepal and apparently did some unauthorized filming. The prince had him arrested. Because his previous film had been highly critical of the government in Nepal, no one there fought on behalf of his release. In fact, some back in Kathmandu threatened to execute him if he returned. After a while the prince, who is, as you know, a huge movie fan, struck up a relationship with him, which is why, even though he is still officially being held against his will, he is recognized as the official filmmaker to the Crown, with no less than three biopics based on the prince's life in various stages of production."

Henry turns and looks at the set. The crew is breaking down the pseudo-meadow props and rigging a tennis net across the stage. Rodrigo Spatz and the prince are overseeing the proceedings.

"The prince's idea," Madison Ellison says. "They're afraid we might lose the king, literally, if he does too much. So he chose tennis over hiking for the final setup."

"What's with the film camera?"

"Oh. You know. Viral videos. State TV."

From a screened-off area behind the stage four people emerge, followed by a nurse pushing the king in a wheelchair. An IV tube is stuck into the king's right forearm and connected on the other end to a hanging drip bag on wheels. He's wearing tennis whites and sneakers and appears to be asleep.

"I have a question," Henry says.

"Shoot."

"If the purpose of this exercise is to let the people know that the king is far from dead—is indeed an extreme-sports-playing freak of nature—and if ninety-nine percent of the country has no television sets and the Internet for the most part is banned in Galado, how will anyone even know of the existence of these images?"

Madison Ellison stands beside Henry and watches two aides rouse the king and lift him to his feet. A photographer's assistant places a professional-quality, oversized Head titanium tennis racket into his right hand and a neon green Penn #3 tennis ball in his left. They reel out an extra ten feet of IV tubing to keep the drip stand out of frame. The king looks down at the objects and weighs them in his trembling hands as if they are artifacts from another universe.

"This is an excellent point, Henry Tuhoe. Very astute. And if by some chance you choose to share this with your royal friend, I will hunt you down and hang you from the highest prayer flag."

An assistant hands Rodrigo Spatz a camera, and he manages to squeeze off a half-dozen shots before the racket slips free and crashes the first time. The second time is when an aide briefly manages to raise the racket high above the king's head, giving him the appearance of preparing to serve a ball to, say, the Grim Reaper, or the late Althea Gibson, only to have the IV hookup tear free, causing ball, racket, and HRH the king of Galado to come tumbling down.

Without missing a beat, Rodrigo Spatz turns to the prince, nods, and says, "I think we nailed it."

"Ms. Ellison."

"Your Highness."

"I see you've already met Mister Tuhoe."

Henry steps forward. "We're, uh, neighbors."

"That's right. I forgot you left your suite at the spa."

"I did. I thought that moving to USAVille might set a precedent for other, um, corporate visitors."

The prince looks Henry over, and for a moment Henry is sure that the prince knows he is bullshitting. But if he does, he doesn't show it. "That's an admirable gesture. I only hope it's not too late."

Madison Ellison puts her hands together in front of her chest and leans forward. "I was just telling Mister Tuhoe about the Shangri-La Summit next week."

Henry widens his eyes at her as she continues. Shangri-La Summit?

"I think having a Happy Mountain Springs contingent at the summit and the hospitality—the river cruise after-party would be a real asset, especially, you know, if Mister . . . if Henry could be a sort of spokesperson for how the, um, process works when executed properly."

The prince turns to see what Henry thinks of Madison Ellison's proposal. Over the prince's shoulder Henry can see two men trying to reinsert the king's IV drip while the king sits slumped and semiconscious in his wheelchair.

"I'd be happy to attend," he answers. "In fact, the founders of Happy Mountain Springs are coming next week to celebrate our initiative. Perhaps they can attend as well."

Sitting back in the lounge he waited in earlier, sipping a mango protein smoothie and watching the prince play Wii Boxing against a digital opponent.

"I had such grand plans for this country," the prince explains to Henry while throwing punches with the controller like a drummer. "Not just industrial plans, but artistic and social. Did anyone show you the giant hares?"

"No. Not that I know of."

A right uppercut hits the prince's avatar, Wii King, knocking him to the animated canvas. He rises on six and continues to talk. "To deal with our food shortages, we have been treating ordinary hares with massive doses of steroids and hormones and in some instances have grown hares the size of a ten-year-old child."

"Wow. Amazing, Your Highness."

"My scientists also tell me they are on the verge of finding a use for the poisons and toxins in our rivers—a way to turn something so prevalent into a valuable natural resource."

Now the Wii King lands a knockdown punch. Henry sees one of the prince's handlers motioning to someone near the game console and—surprise—his opponent does not get back off the canvas.

As the prince begins an elaborate, in-your-face victory dance, Henry decides that this is a good time to tell him about his proposal for Happy Mountain Springs to help provide fresh water for rural villages with water shortages and pollution problems. When the dance ends and he has the prince's full attention, he folds the Happy Mountain Springs sustainability story into a version of Madison Ellison's larger story of how they can serve as an example for the way other companies can ride the momentum of the larger global sustainability movement to balance profit and goodwill in Galado.

When Henry is finished, the prince reboots the boxing game and gets ready for another match. Henry sits back, unsure if any of it sank in, and waits through three more rigged bouts until the prince says, without taking his eyes off the game, "What would you like from me, then?"

Henry decides to go for it. "Ideally, we could orchestrate things so that we could have a royal presence at our little ceremony before we go to the summit. And then, if it is to your liking, something akin to a royal endorsement."

"That sounds terrific, Henry Tuhoe. Whatever I can do to help."

Finally the prince puts down the controller, takes a sip of his smoothie, and squints at Henry. The gaggle of aides fidget on the other side of the door. Henry can see their shadows bouncing off the outer walls, and he can only imagine what horrors they have to report from outside the palace gates. "What you saw with my father today is not something I am proud of, but it was necessary. He was, in his time, extremely popular with our people. I have tried to lead as he would, to be loved as he was loved, but there was never a connection with me the way it was between my father and his people."

"Perhaps with time—" Henry begins, but the prince raises his good arm and shakes his head four times.

"There is no time. Circumstances have eliminated the courtesy of time. I must act swiftly and without remorse or I'll lose everything."

Henry puts his head down and sips his smoothie. He doesn't know what to say.

"Why? This is all that I can think of. Why is this not happening?"

"Maybe," Henry offers, "the country is like your wounded pec. Maybe the muscles developed so rapidly, so spectacularly, Your Highness, that the ligaments that hold the greater structure together haven't had a chance to catch up."

I Say Tomato

Henry contends that they are tomatoes, but Shug calls them something else, these soft red objects splattering against the windows of the SUV as they creep out of the palace drive. Several hundred red-clad protesters are chanting at the gates, thrusting red-painted signs into the air, throwing tomato-like objects, without a soldier in sight.

"This is a new development."

Shug lowers his head to see better through an unsplattered portion of the windshield bottom. "I've never seen them allowed so close to the palace. For some reason the military has chosen to look the other way."

When a group of five protesters surges up to the vehicle and begins pounding on the doors and windows, Shug holds up some kind of pass, written in red. One of them recognizes it and shouts something to the others, and one by one they back off enough to let the SUV crawl on.

"How far would they have gone if you hadn't gotten them to back off?"

"Hard to tell. A week ago I might have had an idea. But now it's impossible to know who is going to do what."

The scene outside reminds Henry of a story that Victor Chan once revealed to him on the way home from a neighborhood men's night gathering. Chan's wife had become so nervous about the world beyond her kitchen window that she had taken to clutching her cell phone in both hands during her daily two-mile walks along the community bike path, "repeatedly dialing nine-one, nine-one, waiting, almost hoping, to dial that final one, which would either signal that tragedy had befallen her or alert the people who would finally take her away." In the end, Henry recalls, as a stone clacks against the tailgate, Cindy Chan didn't dial the final 1 of the 911 call that would take her away. Victor did.

Galado, Henry thinks, is waiting to dial the final 1.

"I saw the king today."

Shug raises his eyebrows, skeptical. Five minutes later, away from the crowds, back on the road to USAVille, he asks, "When you saw him, was he alive?"

Henry scratches his chin. "That's a good question."

Home-Cooked

Maya sits at his kitchen table. Two places are set, but she sits at a third chair, tapping something out on her laptop and drinking a glass of *ara*. A butter lamp burns beside the open bottle, and on the gas stove a hidden meal simmers in a covered pan.

She gets up when he reaches the table and hands him a glass of wine. She is wearing a black cocktail dress and no shoes.

"What's this?"

"This," she says, raising her glass in a toast, "is the prelude to what will surely be a disaster."

He clinks his glass against hers. "To disaster." He drinks and smiles. He doesn't care. He cares more than ever. He sets the glass down, opens his laptop, and accesses his music library. The Shuffle gods serve up "I Will Survive," by Cake. He considers pointing this out, perhaps as an answer to her disaster comment, but decides against it. Nothing good ever comes from pointing out anything. Especially to the woman you think you love.

When they sit down, he tells her about his day and she tells him about hers. Looking at them, one would think they were an average couple in an average home, discussing quotidian, average matters. But the things they are discussing are far from average: angry monks and fading kings, droughts and coups, corporate dirt and Shangri-La.

By both accounts, it was a good day. Henry seems to have secured the scatological support of the prince. Phone service at the call center is up and running. And other than a brief politically incorrect slip when Mahesh lip-synched and crotch-grabbed his way through Madonna's "Like a Virgin," Maya says that he was a real asset, making significant progress training the customer service staff. Finally Maya says, "Meredith just called about an hour ago from New York to give us a heads-up."

"Us?"

"Yes. Us. Giffler heard that the marketing people at Happy Mountain Springs already took a look at your proposal and think the LifeStraw program is a potentially awesome idea."

"It's already awesome. The potentially part is their deal."

"They think it's very syn . . ."

"Synergistic." Henry puts down his wineglass. The thought occurs to him: "How did they find out about this so soon? I only sent you and Meredith the deck this morning."

Maya smiles. "Meredith and I had a nice talk after you left for the palace. Turns out we both had some minor suggestions to improve on your inspired piece. We spent the morning collaborating and tweaking the document online. In real time. She heard they were getting together today and we made the executive decision to release it without your final approval."

Henry sighs. Nods. Why not?

"She's quite a smart woman, you know."

"I know."

"And she thinks the world of you."

He nods. "We've known each other a long time. What does she think they'll want to do?"

Maya gets up and walks to the stove. She lowers the flame and responds as she spoons food onto their plates. "Well, she says they're going to want to be assured that we could pull the straw distribution program together in time for Pat and Audrey's visit. If so, they think it would make for some brilliant and much-needed PR. If not, according to Giffler, according to Meredith, they'll scrap it in a Happy Mountain heartbeat."

He smiles when she puts his plate in front of him. "Meat loaf?"

"Yes. And gravy. And mashed potatoes. Mashed taro, actually. But potatoes are hard to come by out here."

He breaks off a piece and takes a bite of the meat loaf. "Delicious. Where'd you learn to cook meat loaf?"

"Hah!" Maya laughs as she takes her seat. "I can't cook Galadonian food, let alone meat loaf. Mahesh made it for you. I asked him for an American recipe."

While they eat they talk about work, but what they are really discussing is possibility. The possibility of something good actually coming out of a corporate enterprise. Out of a tedious, thankless back-office job. Of something good happening because of them and between them.

The work talk, they both come to realize, is nothing less than a prelude to foreplay, which is nothing more than a prelude to disaster.

He cleans the table while she drinks wine and watches. "Women's Prison" by Loretta Lynn plays on the laptop. Headlights strobe through the kitchen window. Madison Ellison, back from a hard day's work of resuscitating a monarch, pulls into her driveway.

Wiping his hands on a dish towel, Henry tells Maya that he is going to go upstairs to shower, "to wash off the royal ick."

His eyes are closed and his head is tilted back under the steaming water when she joins him. He'd thought she might and hoped she would, and when he feels her fingers gliding up his arm, he tells her as much.

"With me being your boss and all," he says, "you realize that this constitutes a major breach of corporate policy."

She moves up against him from behind and presses her cheek between his shoulder blades.

"I mean, I could lose everything. No, wait, I already *have* lost everything." He turns and looks at her. She's laughing. He's shaking. Fear and exhilaration. It's been a long time.

"You have to promise to keep making me laugh," she says, taking his face in her hands. "Because I can't go through with what we're about to get into without laughing."

"This won't be a problem." He places his hands on her waist and waits a beat. "You're talking to a guy who faked his orgasms the only two times he had sex in the last four months."

Bedfellows

Maya sleeps upstairs while Henry sits at the kitchen table, exchanging predawn messages with Meredith, Giffler, and Madden.

According to them, via others, it's a go. Shockingly, he thinks. But then again, nothing in the corporate world should shock anyone anymore. Whatever you think will happen won't, and whatever you think doesn't have a chance will sneak up and kick you in the ass. And depending on anything from a man in a suit, he learned a long time ago, is a cruel mistake.

According to his in-box, Marketing and Sustainability have allocated him a combined initial budget of $25,000 to procure and distribute the LifeStraw to a sample group of Galado's parched and needy. A big enough sum to make a short-term statement, he notes, but small enough to allow them to cut and run if things change.

Still, according to the final e-mail, written by Meredith and titled "Pat and Audrey's Amazing Adventure!" Pat and Audrey will be in-country next Thursday, "with a three-person film crew, a personal chef, a same-sex marriage counselor, and a check the size of a long board for the photo op."

Thursday, he notes. The same day as the Shangri-La Summit.

For several minutes Henry stares at the bank of onscreen messages, all unequivocally good, the subject headings laden with emoticons and exclamation points. All regarding not some fool's promotion or quarterly earnings that exceeded expectations but a small yet potentially life-changing act of goodwill. Then he turns and looks toward the top of the stairs, where in what is more or less his room a beautiful woman sleeps in what is more or less his bed, and his stomach begins to turn.

It can't be.

Things can't possibly be going this well. After a lifetime of meticulously planned failures, can it be that he has found joy, if not bliss, through a series of random reckless and impulsive acts?

Can it last?

"How does it feel to be half of the most glamorous couple in all of USAVille?"

Maya accepts a cup of tea that he's brewed for her. She's not wearing the dress but a fresh set of casual clothes for work. Tight black pants, black boots, and a bright red sweater. "Special," she responds, leaning down to kiss him. "Living in an abandoned subdivision built to accommodate the absolute worst that corporate America has to offer is, for a local girl like me, a dream come true. So what have you been up to?"

He stands, already dressed in jeans, white T, and black cashmere sweater. He looks down at his laptop as if it is a person, a supposed acquaintance he doesn't yet understand or fully trust. He taps the back of the screen. "It's . . . crazy."

"How so?"

"Surprisingly crazy. I-don't-believe-it-in-a-good-way crazy."

"Clarify, please."

"They approved start-up money for the straw."

Maya smacks her free hand on the table. "Meredith was right!"

"It's not a lot. Not enough to last more than a few months, to sustain one or two locations at best. But it's a start."

"My goodness, Henry," Maya says, putting down her teacup and wrapping her arms around him. "Do you really think that this might happen?"

"For some reason," Henry answers, "I do."

"Then why do you look so unsettled?"

"Because I'm not used to the feeling that forces beyond my control are inexplicably conspiring on my behalf."

He sits back down and begins to type an e-mail to Madden. Then, thinking better of it, he stops and reaches for his sat-phone.

Over his shoulder Maya asks, "What are you doing?"

Pressing illuminated numbers on the tiny flip pad, he answers, "I'm trying to take care of one last minor detail: acquiring the actual straws."

"From whom?"

He waits for the ringing to commence. "Madden."

"Madden? I still don't understand his connection to water purifiers." Maya turns, walks to the kitchen sink, and then turns back to finish. "I know that he knows all about how to exploit the situation here for maximum personal profit, but I didn't know that he was at heart this passionate humanitarian."

"You want to go through this again? I know you're not a fan, but he guaranteed me that he knows the guy who has the distribution rights in Galado, who has a direct pipeline to the regional straw guy, and working under this time frame, I have no other choice."

"Guaranteed. Hah." She plays with the faucet, pivoting it left and right but not pulling it on. "It's just that this is such a good thing and . . . well, he's not."

Henry presses Stop and snaps the phone closed. As he watches Maya, he thinks of what Madden said on the night drive to his meeting with the timber people: *You have to know all the wrong people to get anything done in this country.*

"Listen," he says, "if you can put me in touch with someone else who can turn this around just as fast, that would be all right with me. I'll meet with them immediately, wherever and whenever they want. Otherwise, I don't know what to tell you."

When Maya doesn't reply, he continues: "All that the suits from Happy Mountain care about is handing over their token check and taking a few well-choreographed photos of their heroic, world-changing founders. They are all for it if it goes down without a hitch, but if we don't have this ready to roll out by the time they arrive, I can almost guarantee they'll shut it right down."

Maya places her cup in the sink, releases a splash of cold water into it, and comes back to the table. "Fine," she says. "But I don't want anything to do with him. I don't want to see him or hear him or hear what anyone else has to say about him."

Henry nods. Okay.

"And I don't want you to mention my name or discuss any aspect of me with him at all."

"Yeah, sure."

"I just want the damned straws."

"I understand, Maya."

"And you should be very careful, because he is a despicable, greedy, self-serving human being who cannot be trusted."

"Okay. Other than that, do you mind if I ask what he ever did to make you feel this strongly about him?"

Maya straightens her chair, sits down, and rubs her eyes with the palms of her hands. "Well," she says, blinking and laying her hands palms down on the table, "for starters, about a year ago we kind of slept together."

Angle of Deterioration

"So how's your lady friend, then?"

They're in Madden's Range Rover, heading toward the capital for a lunchtime meeting with the man who has the Galadonian distribution rights to the LifeStraw. How Madden got the Range Rover back after their mountain-road hijacking is a mystery to Henry. He thinks of asking but decides not to. He doesn't want to know. "What lady friend?"

"Playing coy, eh, mate?"

Henry stares at the smog-blurred mountains. It's not yet noon, and already the astonishing scale and clarity of the morning peaks are diminished, obscured, something that he can't be sure he ever saw to begin with. It's a malicious tease every dawn. Brilliant sun rising upon a day filled with beauty and possibility, only to disappear a little more each second behind massing clouds of natural and unnatural origin, all but disappearing before peak inclination.

"I know, Madden."

"Pardon?"

"Maya told me."

Madden makes a popping noise with his lips. "I didn't mean to do her any harm, mate. I tried to do right by her."

Henry sighs. According to Madden, a year earlier he met Maya when she was part of a committee representing local interests during the first phase of the prince's corporate revolution. Madden had promised her that a construction deal he was working on would

include housing and jobs for locals. During the process they began
sleeping with each other. No explicit promises of fidelity. When a
more lucrative and easily resolved situation presented itself, Madden reneged on his promise and abandoned Maya's interests. She
was outraged. Several days later, after discovering that he was also
having a relationship with a woman in a remote village in the southern part of the country, she abandoned him.

"But, of course," Henry replies, "you did do her harm and you
didn't do right by her. Plus, if I'm not mistaken, you were married."

"It's more complicated than she might lead you to believe,
Tuhoe. I tried to bring her plan to life, but it became more and more
unrealistic. It was purely business."

"I really don't care," Henry says. "Other than hating you more
than I think is healthy, she's over you. That's between you two and
this is between us."

Madden nods. "All right."

"Just don't accuse me of being coy when you're the one groping
around for information and pretending you barely know her."

"She deserved better than me."

"This is true. She deserves better than me too. The only question is whether I represent a step forward or back."

They meet in a Western-style steak house called Holy Cow a mile
outside the capital, in the shadows of the unfinished sports stadium:
Henry, Madden, and the regional distributor of the LifeStraw, a
man named Sirajh. They order drinks in the bar and then Madden
and Sirajh excuse themselves and leave Henry and his warm Chinese lager to consider the abundance of cow paraphernalia in the
lobby while they step outside to have a private conversation.

Upon returning ten minutes later, a smiling Sirajh places an
arm around Henry's shoulders and leads him through the large,
empty restaurant to a corner table that overlooks the abandoned
construction site. Sirajh explains that they may eventually be joined
by another guest, the Galadonian minister of health, "who, along
with the prince, offers his full support for this enterprise. But with
the situation in the capital, I cannot guarantee this."

Madden had warned Henry that it was impolite to discuss a business deal until after they have finished their meal, so he bides his time, gnawing on an overcooked rib eye the texture of cork and an oily plate of mixed vegetables while Sirajh describes a recent trip to textile factories in southwestern China. The growth. The productivity. The whores. "And unlike here," he whispers, pausing to sip from his glass of American rye, "the government knows how to put a fucking boot on the throat of dissenters."

Henry wonders how a person as crude and ruthless as Sirajh came to be the regional distributor of a product as pure and altruistic as the LifeStraw. Then, he figures, to Sirajh the LifeStraw is simply another product, another potential profit center, which then leads him to wonder if Sirajh even knows what it does.

But Sirajh surprises him. He reaches into a bag under his seat and tosses a ready-to-use LifeStraw into Henry's hands. "So," Sirajh says, addressing Henry in a less amiable, more direct tone as soon as their entrée plates are cleared. "There you have it. Twenty-nine centimeters long by twenty-nine millimeters in diameter. How many units are we talking about?"

In his left palm Henry weighs the straw, which isn't much more than a surprisingly light and portable white plastic tube. He clears his throat. "Well, we have an initial budget for twenty, twenty-five thousand U.S. dollars. So, however many—"

Sirajh interrupts. "Eighty-five hundred units of the personal LifeStraw. Each filters up to seven hundred liters and lasts about a year. The family straw, another option, which has a much larger filtering capacity, is considerably more expensive and also more difficult to procure."

Henry shakes off the family straw, takes a drink of warm beer, and hears himself say, "Is that the best you can do on the personal?"

Sirajh looks at Madden. Is this guy serious? "Okay," he responds, taking a sip of rye and seeming to run some numbers in his head. "Nine thousand units for twenty-five K. This is less than three dollars per, and you should know the markup on this humanitarian shit is a joke. Next to nothing. But since you know this son of a bitch and he speaks highly of you, I will do him, and as a result you, a favor."

Henry smiles at both men. "That sounds reasonable. I appreciate your consideration, Sirajh. How quickly can we get them?"

Sirajh fixes his eyes on a place in the distance and makes the cal-
culator face again. "Once the financial situation is settled, we can
have them packed, shipped, and ready to use in two weeks."

"Two weeks? Two weeks won't work for me. Madden said we
would be able to have them within two days. And the financial situation can be settled now if you'd like. I can arrange a transfer immediately."

Sirajh shrugs. Henry turns to Madden. What now?

"The thing is, mate," Madden explains to Sirajh, in a tone that
bears no trace of joviality, "Henry here has corporate types coming
within the next few days for a very important PR dog-and-pony
show. An event that is important not only to Henry but to his very
close mate the prince of Galado. And if you think you're gonna
exploit that situation, I guarantee that will be a decision you will
deeply regret."

Sirajh sighs and closes his eyes for a series of more complicated
calculations. "Do you need all nine thousand for this pony show?"

Henry shakes his head.

"What I can do is get you a box of one hundred, which is more
than enough to hold up to the cameras and hand out to the villagers.
I can even get you a few dozen empty boxes for props to give a more
impressive appearance."

"That would work for me," Henry says, nodding in gratitude.

"I will have them delivered to your place tomorrow, no money
down. And after the rest arrive, in a week or so, this is when you can
arrange payment."

Henry begins to pass the straw back to Sirajh, but he'll have
none of it. "Yours to keep," Sirajh says, waving him off. "Just don't
go drinking all seven hundred liters in the same place."

Outside, Henry and Madden hear chanting coming from the direction of a village *djong* about a hundred yards away from the restaurant. Assuming it's a political demonstration, Henry listens alongside
Madden for a moment, then turns to walk in the opposite direction,

toward Madden's Range Rover. Madden touches his arm before his next footstep lands. "Let's take a quick look, all right?"

Henry rolls his eyes, but as soon as Madden begins walking toward the *djong,* he sticks the LifeStraw into his back pocket and follows. Before they headed inside for lunch the area was almost empty, but now the street is buzzing with pedestrians. They walk past groups of young people in celebratory *ghos* gathered in small groups, singing and laughing, old street vendors with dark, creased faces selling chile snacks and drinks and brightly colored beads and scarves. Unlike Maya's village near the river, the village near the call center, and most of the rural towns Henry has driven through, this one is well taken care of. The paved main street is lined with clothing and electronics and food shops with whitewashed fronts and colorful hand-painted signs. At a large carved mahogany archway to the monastery, a block-long structure of brilliant white stucco capped with a series of terracotta-tiled pyramid hip roofs, Madden turns to Henry.

"We've stumbled upon a *tsechu.* At different times of the year, almost every large village has one for up to five days, always near the tenth day of the lunar calendar, to celebrate the deeds of Padmasambhava, the bloke who introduced Buddhism to Galado in the eighth century. People used to walk for days to get to them, but they say they're not as popular with the young people as they used to be."

Inside the courtyard they stand against a wall and watch four monks in brilliant gold and orange and purple costumes performing a dramatic dance, accompanied by two drummers and a dranyen player. As Henry watches the monks sway and reach and flow as if in a sort of underwater dream ballet, he thinks of the song Maya left on his computer. "It's beautiful," Henry whispers, more to himself than to Madden.

Madden raises his chin toward the dancers. "This whole country is so caught up in the bloody process of trying to preserve its culture, but really, if an aspect of a culture is worth a damn, it'll preserve itself, right?"

Henry doesn't agree. Madden has a way of doing that, answering his own hypotheses for you, but Henry's fairly sure that Madden, who moments earlier told him that the *tsechu* is a fading tradition, doesn't agree either and is merely rationalizing, coming to terms with a flawed aspect of himself.

Across the courtyard, Henry notices two boys, perhaps twelve, watching a slightly older boy play a handheld video game, all oblivious of the ceremony. When Henry sees that Madden has noticed them as well, the two contrasting forces at the heart of the country's future—the spiritual and the commercial—in the same line of vision, he sees no reason to reply.

After the music stops and the monks bow and disappear through a side door, there is a lull. Two four-year-old girls in maroon *ghos* sneak out into the center of the courtyard where the monks just performed and begin an impromptu dance of their own. While Henry watches the girls, transfixed, the courtyard begins to fill with a parade of new visitors coming in off the street, all wearing some form of red. Shirts, bandannas, *ghos*. Madden has stepped away and is in deep conversation with an acquaintance who owns a local taxi company.

At once a dozen bass drums begin to sound. The little girls end their dance and scatter as the first line of more than a hundred red-clad men and women carrying red-painted signs begin chanting in a tone that is much more aggressive than a sutra. The newly formed crowd responds with a cheer before joining the chanting with an intensity and anger that is such a contrast to the dreamily dancing monks and children that it disorients Henry. He turns to Madden for an explanation, but Madden is gone.

A door opens behind him and a scrum of angry men pours out into the reddening courtyard. On the lower edges of the terracotta rooftops are perched dozens of chanting people pounding their open hands on the limestone gutters, legs thrashing in the air. Henry tries to move to his right but is confronted by another group of young men in red bandannas, rushing the other way. One slows and, making the flash decision that Henry is an ideological enemy, shoves a raised forearm against his throat, knocking his head against an iron wall sconce. When he regains his balance, he wipes his forefinger against his brow and sees that it is smeared with blood.

Another face appears in front of his, twisted into a hateful smile.

He begins to lift his hands in a gesture of peace, or cease-fire, or submission, but they barely move before the man shoves him, sending him stumbling backward into the courtyard. Two others in red T-shirts and bandannas pursue, steering him with small shoves toward the center of what minutes earlier had been an artistic stage. One spits at him and another condemns him. Henry doesn't understand but assumes that the words have to do with money and commerce and the destruction of their culture. And something about him too. Something that he lacks.

"Friend!" he half shouts, finally getting his hands up in front of him, but they don't understand or don't want to. Another double-handed shove to the chest pitches him backward onto the courtyard's dry earth floor. He rises, thinking, What else can I say? Future LifeStraw provider? Friend of Maya? Sustainability expert? Approaching from his left he sees a muscular young man with fists cocked at his sides, but instead of shouting any of the above, Henry twists his hips and lunges upward from a crouch and uncoils a tight, fierce right uppercut that crashes into the man's lower jaw, lifts his bare feet a half-inch into the air, and sends him careening onto the ground in a burst of dust.

For a moment Henry's violent response stuns the other two, but then it just makes them angrier. As they rush toward him, Henry spreads his legs and half squats for balance. But instead of bracing for their impact, he reaches into his back pocket, pulls out the LifeStraw, and charges them. They freeze. He bashes the LifeStraw tube against one man's temple, then pounces on him and thrashes his head and face with the hard plastic life-saving device. When the third man moves forward to rescue his stunned companion, Henry raises the LifeStraw behind his ear with two hands as if it is a broadsword, and the man freezes.

A hand grips his shoulder. He spins, the now bloody LifeStraw still cocked high and ready to strike. "Easy, mate!"

It takes Henry a moment before bringing down his hands and beginning to see Madden with the slightest glint of recognition. Madden jerks his head toward the entrance gate some twenty yards away. "Come on," he implores, clenching his fists and preparing to make a dash. "Let's get out of this fuckshop."

———

In the Range Rover, Henry presses a wet napkin against the gash on the right side of his forehead. "What the hell was that?" he asks, checking to see how much blood the napkin has sopped up.

"That," Madden says, "was an impassioned plea for the preservation of art and culture."

Henry stares at the napkin and decides, based on the size of the blood spot, that the cut, other than being a festering ground for any one of a half-dozen indigenous and potentially fatal infections, isn't serious.

"So howzit feel, mate?"

"How does *what* feel?"

"Bashing a bloke in the face like you just did. Like a bloody man, I imagine."

"I beat a Buddhist with a life-saving water purifier endorsed by UNICEF."

"When's the last time you knocked a bloke on his arse like that?"

Henry stares out the window. They're on the road back toward the call center, USAVille, and Maya. "I don't know. Fifth, sixth grade. I don't think we should play together anymore."

"You should be proud of yourself, Henry Tuhoe. You negotiated a damned nice deal to get your bloody water thingamajigs in time for your little event. You stood your ground against an angry mob. And you brought down two men with your bare hands."

"And a LifeStraw."

Madden smiles, and after a while Henry does as well.

For the next five minutes they drive without speaking. Madden breaks the silence when he says, "She's a good woman, mate."

"We've already covered that territory, mate."

"Truth. But you know, I never lied to her. Never told her I was gonna marry her or be true to her. Shit, she knew I still had a wife back in 'stralia."

"Forget it."

"I can be a cutthroat motherfucker, Tuhoe. But I'm no liar."

"That's fine, but you should know"—Henry stares at Madden until Madden decides to look back—"in those rare instances that I truly care about something or someone, I can be as cutthroat a motherfucker as anybody."

Madden nods and returns his gaze to the road. At the bottom of the next hill they can see the newly shingled roof of the call center. Madden stops the Range Rover some seventy-five yards from the building and says, "Why push it, right?"

Henry shrugs. He holds out his hand, and Madden accepts it. "Getting these straws is huge, Mister Madden."

"I'm glad to help and glad for you."

"And that's it? No strings attached?"

"Oh, there are strings."

"Shoot."

"Well, for starters, I'd like an invite to this fancy conference for the corporate titans at the palace. Much opportunity to be harvested there."

"Shouldn't be a problem. That it?"

Madden shakes his head and squeezes Henry's hand harder. "I want you to promise me you'll keep at it, Tuhoe. You may not ever get to it. You may fall on your arse and fail. You may die. But the key is to never stop. I stopped a long time ago in just about every conceivable way, and as much as I may lead people to believe otherwise, the state I'm in, I'm fucking done, mate. But for you, I can tell, it's not too late."

IV

Rehearsing the Lie

They do not rehearse reality.

Instead they concentrate on depicting a short-term facsimile of it. Just enough to make Pat and Audrey believe. And the dignitaries. And the cameras.

"If we're not convincing enough to make people believe that this thing is going to work," Henry is telling Maya and Mahesh, out of earshot of the others in the call center, "we at least want to prevent them from dwelling on the fact that it's doomed."

"But it's not doomed," Maya says.

He smiles. "You're right. It isn't. But it will be if we try to do too much and reveal the true situation here. If those phones were to start ringing tomorrow, for real, we'd be ruined. We have little time left to properly rehearse. For now, for the next few days, we just have to be able to *demonstrate* competence. Not *be* competent. Okay?"

Maya nods. Mahesh twists two thumbs up and says, "You're the boss."

Behind them the operators are rehearsing. To avoid overloading them, Henry split them into three groups of four and had each group memorize two basic customer service scenarios. Maya spent the morning decorating the interior walls with Happy Mountain Springs posters. A four-foot-by-four-foot logo banner hangs from the ceiling behind the worktables: the first thing a visitor will see upon entering. Outside, workers are raking the scrub lawn and setting up a small stage for tomorrow morning's ceremony. A man on a stepladder is nailing another banner along the edge of the fence behind the stage. It reads, *Happy Mountain Springs: The Purity Runs Through Us All.*

There was anxiety about the LifeStraws until they arrived, early. There's still anxiety about whether the prince will attend, but that's beyond their control, and they've been assured that someone from the palace will attend if the prince is indisposed, "not to be confused with predeposed," Henry said to the person on the line. This was met with silence.

Just before lunch a van drives through the gate. It's driven by Maya's cousin, the restaurant owner. With Madden's help and without Maya's knowledge, Henry contacted him and arranged for him to cater tomorrow's event as well as this surprise luncheon for the employees.

"Was this okayed in the budget?" Maya asks.

He shakes his head. "I made an executive decision."

They gather to eat lunch under bright sunshine at a group of folding tables set beneath a row of cypress trees. Mahesh has set up a boom box playing what he's calling an "American party mix" CD. Maya's cousin is busy cooking over two flaming, wood-fired, halved fifty-gallon drums and two long serving tables covered with hot trays containing a half-dozen different local delicacies.

After filling their plates, Henry and Maya sit at a table with Mahesh and three women. Maya speaks to them in Galadonian and then translates their replies for Henry. How many kids do they have. Where do they live. While they are talking a female operator named Teara approaches, lays a white lily beside his plate, then kisses him on the cheek. A few moments later Henry excuses himself, not because he isn't interested in their stories but because he doesn't want them to feel as if they have to perform for his benefit. He wants them to enjoy their lunch as much as those at the other tables without having to suck up to their flaky American boss.

———

Alone inside the call center, he walks to the lone network-connected desktop computer and stoops to check his messages. Meredith wrote to him this morning with the latest itinerary for Pat and Audrey, from takeoff at JFK to tomorrow's call center ceremonies, the audience at the palace, and perhaps even the hospitality cruise on the river before they catch the first flight out the following morning. Also from Meredith, under the subject heading "No shit," is a confidential document for his eyes only titled "Audrey and Pat's Etiquette Manifesto," a six-page missive detailing special dietary requirements (organic, hormone-free meats, filtered, distilled water served in sterilized Happy Mountain Springs bottles) and procedural dos (nothing smaller than a town car, stick to the corporate bio when introducing them), don'ts (ask for autographs, look them in the eye), and nevers (ask personal questions, touch them, call them Ms. or Ma'am).

He's still laughing as he moves on to the next e-mail, from Gerard back home, of all people. Inside is a group picture from the Son of Meat Night, a Cajun feast in Marcus LeBlanc's backyard. They're all there—Marcus, Gerard, Victor, and the brothers Osborne, each toasting him with what were no doubt meticulously prepared hurricanes. The note at the bottom reads: "To Tyler Durden, aka the Kid, aka H_2O, we miss your belligerent spirit! Cheers, from Sub-Bourbon Street!"

He smiles, but only for a moment. Sentimentality is soon replaced by regret. For the way he treated them, despite the way they treated him. And for never writing that note of apology. Who did he think he was? Staring at the life he left behind, the life he rejected and disparaged and in many ways ran from, he feels like crying.

As he reaches to click offline, a new message flashes up. Another note from Meredith, sent seconds ago, but not from her work account. It's from Eva @ landofeeee.com and titled "EEEEnormously Entertaining New Content." Because it's not work-related and he should be getting back outside—it sounds like Mahesh has them doing some kind of group dance—he almost decides to ignore it. But because it's not simply from Meredith but from Eva, who hasn't updated her content in months, he doesn't. And immediately upon opening it he sees that it has nothing to do with new content, or Eva, or entertainment.

It's this:

Erase this as soon as you read it. I did as soon as I sent it. There's something you should know. Something I'd suspected for a week and overheard today while having drinks with a certain high-level executive one of whose brands is Happy Mountain Springs. The short story (unless you want to know the long one about this guy's three ex-wives and Viagra dependency issues) is that the big company, perhaps as soon as tomorrow, is going to fold HMS into a larger bottled water brand. Glacial something. The one from Greenland with an umlaut. By folding it into a larger brand they mean to eliminate anything associated with HMS. Including, in a corporate, not homicidal, sense, Pat and Audrey, who know nothing about this. Also including Giffler and you and the call center and your seemingly admirable LifeStraws project. Of course you can't tell a soul, especially Pat and Audrey, who, incidentally, are somewhere over the Pacific as you read this. Why did I tell you this? Certainly not to bum you out. I did it to give you a heads-up in hopes that it might in some way help you. Sorry about this, Henry. Be strong and stay safe.

                                                                —M (EEEE)

PS: Don't bother checking the site for content. I'm actually shutting it down soon; will explain later.

After deleting the message and clearing his digital history, he walks to the doorway. Outside, backed by the boom box, Mahesh is teaching three rows of orange-robed women the steps for what appears to be the Cha-Cha Slide. Maya and her cousin and several other nonparticipants laugh and clap as they watch from the side. It almost would have been better, he thinks, if this had been a disaster from the start. Last night in his bed they told each other again and again that it couldn't work. That they couldn't work. They should be happy that they found each other at this moment and they should enjoy it while it lasts. But as they made love and talked and watched each other with astonishment as the night went on, the sentiment transformed from a joke to a warning to a plea and finally, near dawn, to a sort of sentence. They went from saying they couldn't last but not meaning it and pretending they didn't care to knowing that they wouldn't and understanding it and caring more than either thought possible.

Watching the Galadonians, almost as a punishment for indulging in the vices of hope and expectation, he is filled with, for the first time in a long time, guilt. Against his better, fatalistic judgment, he had gotten these people to depend on and, it appears, to believe in him. Even worse, he had gotten himself to believe in himself.

He steps halfway into daylight before stopping, straddling the doorway, and wondering where to step next. Wondering what to do and what to say. What do you say to these people? What do you tell Maya?

"Hey there, hero." Maya, out of nowhere, alongside him.

"Excuse me?"

"Don't be coy." She grabs hold of his right arm by the triceps and begins to escort him toward the others. "Look at how happy they are."

He looks, thinking, The happier they are, the harder they will crash. The worse things will be. And by all signs they are pretty damned happy. Mahesh and the group have moved on to the intricate choreography of the Chicken Dance. A cappella.

"Like this! *Na-na-nenenene-neh! Na-na-nenenene-neh!*"

He feels horrible about the recent turn of events, and it is about to get worse. Mahesh and the twelve giggling Galadonians are waving him out to join them.

"Hey now! Well, well!" Mahesh yells, stopping midflap, already walking toward Henry and away from the dancers. "He's back! Everybody!" From three sides they begin to converge on Henry, enveloping him with thanks for a gift not yet delivered. When Mahesh begins to clap, they clap too. When Mahesh wraps his arm around Henry and begins to chant "Speech!" they do too. And when someone grabs a bench for Henry to stand on, to tease the promise of tomorrow, he begins rehearsing an all-new version of the lie in his head.

If Sex Is Involved,
Altruism Is Not

If the benefits gained from an altruistic act exceed the cost of the act itself, it ceases to be altruistic. Well-intentioned, win-win PR, at best, Henry thinks. But more likely it plays out as some form of sleazy opportunism rather than the selfless helping of others. Add deception to the equation, and the fact that the so-called altruistic act may never be consummated, or that the person in charge of said act at least originally thought of it to win the attention of a woman, and it becomes criminal. At least in a karmic sense.

They are in Maya's truck, returning from an after-lunch visit to her old river village. She's driving. It is almost dark, and for the second time this week a rare post-monsoon rain falls on the empty highway and pounds the hard-chalk earth on both sides of the road. Henry is in the passenger's seat, with his head tilted back and eyes half closed, and four children, including Maya's nephew, are singing a song that he has never heard in the back row and hatch area. They headed for the river right after the party this afternoon; to ensure that her village would be included in the LifeStraw program, Maya was determined to have it represented at tomorrow's ceremonies.

He didn't think it possible, but seeing the river and the base of the mountains and the kids again, exchanging high fives with her admiring nephew, makes him feel even worse. At one point on the ride over he considered telling Maya about Meredith's note, but she was so happy, so exhilarated, he didn't have the heart. Or the balls.

Near the end of the return trip from the river, Maya asks, "Every-thing okay?"

After a moment during which he reconsiders and again rejects the idea of coming clean to her, he answers, "Yeah. I'm fine. Just a little exhausted."

"Well," Maya says, resting a hand on his thigh, "you have every right to be. You've been amazing."

They don't speak again until they pull into his driveway in USAVille. She drops him off first because his place is the first they come upon. The plan is for Maya to leave the children to spend the night at her cousin's home, and after running some errands she'll be back, around nine, for the night. He stands in the black drizzle, watching her taillights disappear, then heads up the walk to Madison Ellison's house. Maybe she can help. He rings the bell. Knocks. Walks around her darkened house. No one's home.

Shuffle gives him "All the Wine" by the National.

Big wet bottle in my fist, big wet rose in my teeth

Over the kitchen sink is a death threat on a Post-it note. A cartoon figure of a man hanging from a prayer flag. Hardly welcome, he thinks, taking it down. But using the Post-it note as a medium somehow diminishes the threat.

. . . I'm a festival, I'm a parade

Upstairs, papers are scattered on the office floor. Torn, shredded, and apparently pissed upon. The desk is flipped up on its side, and the top of the laser printer has been smashed into a mosaic of gray plastic shards. He doesn't pick any of it up. Just shuts the light and heads back downstairs.

He calls Shug on his sat-phone and asks if he would be interested in spending the night at the call center, for double salary, watching out for vandals.

Shug agrees, then says, "Have you heard the news?"

Henry thinks. Shug couldn't know about the pending sale of an American bottled water company. Then again, who knows what Shug knows. "No, Shug. I don't think I have."

"The . . . king . . . ," Shug says with difficulty, then pauses. Henry's fairly sure he hears sniffling on the other end. "The king has died."

And all the wine is all for me . . .

He wonders if the old man was dead when he saw him being handled like a mannequin during the photo shoot. He wonders if this is good or bad for the prince and his plans, and for Happy Mountain Springs and its plans.

He calls Sirajh, thinking that if he can get him to agree to a transfer of the money from the HMS account into Sirajh's, the deal would be considered complete, and then, for a year at least, they could help several thousand rather than a hundred Galadonians for a month. But Sirajh doesn't pick up, doesn't even give him the opportunity to leave a message.

He checks e-mail. Nothing from Meredith, or Giffler. He visits Eva's Web site, only to find an announcement saying that it has been shut down. He keeps thinking of Madden's tenet: *To get anything done around here, you need to know all the wrong people.* Madden's phone rings and rings. Henry puts his phone on speaker and lays it on the table, still ringing, as he begins to tap out a message on his laptop. When he's done, he presses Send, rises, and pours himself a tall glass of *ara.*

Maya doesn't return until after ten. He gets up from an uneasy sleep on the couch.

"Sorry I'm late, but I had to stop at the spa."

"My spa?"

She nods as she reaches back to undo the red scrunchie that holds her hair in a ponytail. "Our friends have arrived."

"They weren't due until much later."

Maya shakes her head. "Apparently they were able to catch a flight to Seoul on the corporate jet."

Good luck catching one back, he thinks. "Is everything okay? Were they looking for me?"

"They were too busy fighting with each other to look for anyone. I spoke under condition of anonymity with their same-sex-marriage counselor. Separate rooms. Separate buildings."

"The purity runs through us all."

She smiles. "I told them we'd meet for breakfast in the morning and go to the event together."

Henry pours them each a glass of wine. "Have you heard about the king?"

She accepts the *ara,* sips it, and squints one eye. "How did you find out?"

"Shug."

"I don't even think they've officially announced it. Some say they never will. At one time this is exactly what the prince wanted, but with the way things are now . . ."

"What do you think is gonna happen?"

Maya thinks about this, takes another drink of wine, then steps forward and leans against him. She rests her head against his neck and whispers, "I don't know." Then she steps back, takes his hand, and begins to pull him toward the stairs. "Let's just go to bed, okay?"

This time the sex is different. More velocity and aggression. Less cuddling and tentative exploration. This time everything is physical and nothing is spoken. Whenever it feels as if he is taking charge, claiming more of the moment, she pushes him into a different place, and then another, her eyes fierce and distant, her body telling his what it's doing right and wrong until he reasserts himself and the struggle becomes the thing, until the smashup of their conflicted spirits becomes everything. At times he is convinced that they're

fused as one, but then seconds later they are strangers off in separate, self-made worlds, grasping for the unattainable and running
from the unavoidable.

This time there is no joy, only the fatalistic thrum in the loins
that comes from a shared sense of urgency and desperation, a tick-
ing detonator clock, and the solitary knowledge of a thing that if
revealed would destroy the spirit of the other.

For Henry, the last proves too much. The secret. Not a lie, but
an avoidance of the truth. When they started, it was the last thing on
his mind, but as he goes along, it is all that he can think of.

When she is done he rolls to the side and stares at the wall,
sweat-covered and panting, playing out the part. She doesn't ask
him when he turns over to face her, but he can see the question in
her eyes. Did you? He touches her face, pushes wet hair away from
her eyes, and kisses her.

Of course he didn't.

He couldn't.

He did what he swore he'd never do again.

He faked. To cover up a secret.

Only this time he doesn't feel as if he's gotten away with anything.

Bullet Points

"Pat won't be joining us."

Henry smiles at Jules, who is Pat and Audrey's same-sex-marriage counselor and personal assistant, and says, "I see. What about Audrey?"

"Audrey should be here," Jules explains. They are sitting at a table on the garden veranda at Ayurved Djong and Spa, sipping jasmine tea: Henry, Jules, and Maya. It is 10 minutes after their nine o'clock Pat and Audrey breakfast was to start and 110 minutes before the ceremony at the call center. "But," Jules continues, "go ahead and order if we have a schedule. The way things have been going, I can't guarantee anything."

Maya puts down her menu. "Will Pat be joining us at the call center, or the conference, or the hospitality cruise?"

Jules laughs. "I. Have. No. Idea." And then, changing her tone, sitting up and smiling brightly, "Well, well." Maya and Henry turn. Pat is coming after all.

Pat ignores Henry and Maya and speaks directly to Jules. "Where's Fatso?"

Jules looks down at her menu. "Audrey should be here. Won't you join us?"

Henry stands and introduces himself and Maya, but Pat, a tall, athletic, handsome woman, doesn't acknowledge his extended hand or say a word. She gives them each a curt nod. He wonders if he's already broken one of the rules of engagement regarding Pat and

Audrey—thou shalt not shaketh the executive hand—but then remembers that it doesn't matter because they no longer matter and he no longer gives a shit.

"No," Pat answers. "I will not be joining you. Just let me know when we're leaving for whatever the fuck we're doing here. I'll be in the garden talking to my new best friend, Lacy."

A minute later Audrey materializes. Demure, contrite, apologetic, Audrey, looking considerably larger than she had in the creation myth video. Her face is swollen from crying. Her mascara is already smudged in a raccoon oval around her watery brown eyes. After an introduction that actually includes eye contact and the shaking of hands, she looks around and asks, "Where . . . where's Pat?"

Jules goes out of her way to look into Audrey's eyes before saying, as if addressing a child, "Audrey, Pat won't be joining us for breakfast this morning, okay?"

Audrey nods and sits. From a basket in the center of the table she takes a banana walnut muffin, a blueberry scone. Jules looks at her plate disapprovingly, but Audrey doesn't care. She takes a bite of the muffin and doesn't stop to speak until it and the scone have disappeared. Maya attempts to take Audrey through the agenda for the day and the deck she and Henry have prepared, but when she sees how distracted Audrey is, she distills it to the three most salient bullet points:

- Thank the prince or whatever dignitaries happen to be in attendance.
- Tell the people of Galado how honored you are to have the Happy Mountain Springs brand represented in their beautiful country.
- And talk about Happy Mountain Springs' mission statement of providing pure water to the world before handing out the ceremonial check and the first LifeStraw.

When Maya is finished, Audrey turns to Jules. "Did Pat say anything about me—about us—before she left?"

Jules clears her throat and takes a breath. Henry glances at Maya and is relieved when his phone buzzes in his pants pocket. "Excuse me," he says, rising, considering the incoming number. "I have to take this."

He answers as he rounds a corner, stopping next to a meditation fountain. "Tuhoe."

It's the minister of future commerce. "I'm calling to inform you that because of pressing affairs of state, the prince will be unable to make it to your ceremony this morning."

"I understand. Does this have anything to do with the passing of the king?"

This is met with several seconds of silence, then: "I do not know what you are alluding to, Mister Tuhoe."

As Henry thinks of what to say next, he notices Pat out of the corner of his eye, stroking Lacy's thigh on a granite bench on the other side of the fountain. "Okay, then, will anyone from the palace be attending today?" Henry asks.

"This I cannot confirm. But the king hopes that you and your colleagues will still be able to attend the conference-opening hospitality cruise this evening."

"You mean the prince."

"Yes, of course. The prince."

After hanging up, Henry walks away from the fountain. He tries not to pay attention to Pat and Lacy, who are snickering at him, while he attempts to make sense of what is going on: The prince will not be attending the ceremony for the opening of a call center for a company that is soon to die, if not already dead, during which an equally doomed humanitarian effort will be launched and celebrated. Afterward, he is to take the leaders of his possibly defunct company on a river cruise to kick off a business conference for a nation on the verge of collapse, hosted by the prince, who refuses to acknowledge his father's death. He leans against a whitewashed wall and closes his eyes. Then he makes a flurry of calls: to Meredith, Madden, Giffler. When he finishes his last message, he sees a text note from Sirajh. He has cashed the check. So at least there's that, he thinks, a year's worth of LifeStraws for a few thousand people.

Maya is alone at the table when he gets back. At the other end of
the terrace, Jules is standing with her hands on Audrey's trembling
shoulders, trying without success to console her. Placing his hands
on the back of Maya's chair, he says, "What happened? You made
her cry?"

"Not funny. Apparently Pat is something of a bullying slut.
Audrey, the poor thing, is a mess."

Henry looks at Jules and Audrey, then down at Maya.

"What?" Maya says.

He motions for her to get up and follow him. They stop near a
bench in a meditation garden. Neither sits.

"Okay," she demands, squaring off in front of him. "What?"

First, for no apparent reason other than that he thinks it might
be best to ease her into it, he tells her about the call he just received
from the palace. No one will be attending. Okay, she nods, unfortunate, but under the circumstances that makes sense. Next he decides
to tell her about his most recent message, the one about the check
from Sirajh. "This is significant," he says.

Maya tilts her head to the side. She's not following.

"Cashing the check," he explains, "completes the transaction,
and at the very least we have three thousand LifeStraws."

"O-kaaay . . . Was there a concern that this might happen?
That Happy Mountain Springs would renege?"

"Well," he says, "originally, no. But now the problem isn't so
much about Happy Mountain Springs reneging. It's whether they'll
continue to exist by, say, eleven this morning."

Maya looks left and right, then closes the gap between them
until their chests touch. Her eyes—to Henry, they look like the eyes
of a person he's never met. "I want you to tell me everything," she
whispers, but with a fierce, threatening edge. And he does.

"And you knew this when?"

"Yesterday . . . I was . . ."

"You knew during our drive, you knew last night?"

"I'm trying to fix it."

She smacks him. "Fix what? I believed in you, and in your
ridiculous company, and you . . . and they . . . betrayed me."

"They betrayed all of us, Maya."

"But you chose not to tell me. Rather than being honest, you chose to hide it. My brother is right. I shouldn't have trusted any of you. You're all liars. There's only one way to fix this."

He puts his hands on the outside of her shoulders, but she wriggles free, pushes him away, and rushes toward the lobby.

He doesn't follow her, doesn't move as he watches her round a corner and disappear. Even if you caught up to her, he thinks, what could you possibly say?

As he picks up his phone to check for messages, he hears footsteps on the stone floor. When he looks up, he sees Jules, Audrey, Pat, and Lacy gathered where Maya just stood. "Whenever you're ready," Jules says, "we're good to go. Isn't that right, ladies?"

Make-Believe Water

He executes the lie without assistance.

He delivers the opening remarks. He reads the note of congratulations from the prince (which is met, not surprisingly, with silence). There is a tense moment during the demonstration inside the call center when Pat stops Mahesh and the operators mid-fake-call performance, but it passes when she enthusiastically applauds them and holds up Mahesh's hand as if he has just won a prizefight.

Outside, Pat and Audrey, once introduced, perform their face-of-the-company functions with grace and professionalism. Audrey, despite the ongoing turmoil in her personal life, is quite eloquent and seems to have absorbed enough of Maya's preparatory bullet points to sound informed and sincere. For her part, Pat is all smiles and unbridled, sustainability-based energy as she addresses the gathering. She even throws in a bonus Galadonian toast, some kind of good-luck prayer that someone—Lacy?—must have shared with her, before handing out the surfboard-sized check, before calling the children from Maya's old village onstage to give them their very own LifeStraws while the corporate videographer gets every second of it.

As the children put their mouths to the plastic tubes, inhaling make-believe water as celebratory music blasts through speakers stacked alongside the stage, Henry looks among them for Maya's nephew, but he is nowhere to be found.

The whole thing takes about thirty minutes. Because few dignitaries of note are present, there isn't a lot of glad-handing afterward. As refreshments are served, Pat checks her wristwatch and pretends to sip a glass of root tea while Audrey sneaks off to check her messages under the shade of a juniper tree. First her mouth drops open, then she gasps. Drawing the device closer to her eyes to make sure she got it right, she says, loud enough for Henry and Jules and several employees to hear, "Oh. My. God!"

Meredith had the announcement timed almost to the minute, Henry thinks, as he watches the founders of Happy Mountain Springs briefly reunite to stare at a two-by-three-inch LED screen that is telling them that their company no longer exists, that the goodwill program they just flew halfway around the world to launch technically never happened. Not that either of them gives a shit about goodwill at this point.

Audrey seems to be looking for some kind of sentimental gesture from Pat, hands ready to rise to accept a hug. But Pat's only response is to begin to laugh. Henry hears her say, "What does it matter to us? We got our money. If anything, it gets us out of having to do this phony back-slappy bullshit."

"But," Audrey implores, laying her fingers on Pat's wrist, "what about our . . . our legacy?"

Pat shakes free and laughs at Audrey. "Our legacy?" She puts her arm around Lacy and squeezes her close. "If by 'our legacy' you mean our names being friggin' conjoined as if we were one, as if we were the thing that marketing made us and others expected from us, well, *that,* finally, thankfully, is over."

Audrey stares at her soon-to-be ex-wife and business partner. She wobbles, then tips back in a sort of premeditated faint into the arms of Jules, who seems to have been on the receiving end of this more than once. This only makes Pat laugh more.

"Come on," Pat says, pulling Lacy toward the car. "Let's go have some water-free fun."

Terminated

While checking for messages from Maya or Madden, he sees that he's been fired.

"Because of the closing of Happy Mountain Springs Water Company," begins the note from a person he's never met, someone in, for some reason, Toledo, Ohio, "your position has been terminated." Not outsourced or reassigned or transferred. Fired. He reads this in the lot outside the call center as Pat drives away in a limo with Lacy and Audrey sits on a bench sobbing while Jules pats her trembling back.

"What now, boss?" It's Mahesh. As soon as he gets to a computer, he'll find out too. Henry reaches into his pocket and pulls out his corporate credit card. He hands over the card and two hundred American dollars. "Nothing left to do here, Mahesh. Your next assignment is to take everyone into town for celebratory food and drinks."

Mahesh grabs the card and cash and wraps his arms around Henry. "You're coming, right?"

"I've got some stuff to do, Mahesh, but keep me posted and I'll try to stop by." He turns to leave, only to bump into Shug. "Can you get me out of here?"

Shug shrugs.

"Technically," Henry says, "you don't have to do this if you don't want to." They are driving toward the capital, the palace, the Shangri-La Zone.

Shug answers, "I know."

"The call center, the whole company, just blew up."

"I said I know."

Henry looks out the window. Of course he knows. Everyone knows everything except me. And the little I do know, the little I keep to myself, I get in trouble for not sharing in a timely fashion.

"So where to?"

This is a good question. USAVille? Corporate HQ in Manhattan? The about-to-be-foreclosed-on suburban McMansion? On the one hand he has no home or job or really anything beyond a laptop and two suitcases filled with clothes he never wants to wear again. Uniforms of conformity. Two modest suits and a depressing assortment of khaki slacks and polo shirts, representing a phrase he has come to detest, to think of as an oxymoron, an impossibility: business casual.

On the other hand he has six months' severance pay, a valid U.S. passport, and nothing to stop him from going anywhere.

Except the will to do it.

He's not sure what's worse, being paralyzed by the lifestyle you've chosen or by the freedom to start over.

"How did you already know?"

"This is a small country. You know this. You are a person of interest. Connected to the prince."

"Completely by accident."

"And a friend of a controversial businessman."

"Madden?" Henry laughs. First the boys from Meat Night were his supposed friends, and now Madden.

"He has many enemies."

"He's also responsible for securing that truckload of LifeStraws. And maybe something more."

Shug nods. "Hmmmm."

Perhaps, Henry thinks, he's finally found something Shug wasn't aware of. "The funny thing is," he says, "there's really nothing about me worth bothering to know."

Shug doesn't answer, and Henry interprets the silence as an indictment of his attempt at self-pity.

Near the entrance to USAVille, Shug glances across the front seat. Without looking back, Henry shakes his head, waves him on. "I've got my documents. Maybe I should just go straight to the airport."

Shug clicks his tongue. "Not today. Today a bad day to fly." They drive on toward the palace, the early evening Shangri-La cruise on the river.

"You know," Henry says as the blurred shapes of royal towers appear like black ghosts in the filthy sky, "when I got here, I didn't care much about the job, the so-called mission, certainly not the fate of the people of Galado. But I changed. Once I got to know her, I did. I tried. And not just because of her. Because of the way she changed me. I did want to help."

Even though they are on the highway, Shug slows the Range Rover almost to a stop. He doesn't speak until Henry caves and looks at him. "You still can help, you know."

Fahrenheit 212

Here are 193 people gathered on the banks of a poisoned river affixing laminated name tags, waiting for permission to revel.

Hello! My name is Greed.

Hello! My name is Excess.

Hello! My name is the Opposite of Shangri-Fucking-La.

Here's a plastic flute of Moët & Chandon for the preboarding toast and a reminder to pick up your royal swag bag when the cruise is over.

Here's Henry, signing in, concerned that perhaps they've already found out about the fate of his mission here and crossed him off the list. But there's his name. Here's his tag and complimentary bubbly. If the people at the welcome desk know his secret, they don't seem to care. As he says good-bye to Shug and approaches the gangway, he thinks it is hard not to notice this about his hosts and fellow capitalists, about this event: there is a pervasive, collective, and absolute vibe of not giving a shit.

Hello! My name is Fuck It!

He takes stock of the surrounding guests. Mostly corporate refugees whose home offices have ignored their pleas for permission to return home, their warnings that this country is on the verge of disaster, that the seed money is gone, that the business opportunity has evaporated, that the king is dying if not already dead, and that the prince's grasp of reality diminishes with every tick of the Shangri-La clock. These are the first to ask for refills.

Henry recognizes a first-term congressman from Idaho last seen
shouting down a bank official on CNBC and is surprised at how
small and powerless he now seems, leaning against the starboard
rail, alternately staring at his BlackBerry and glaring at the sub-
stantially larger fuss being made over the head of the Walmart delegation, who for some reason has decided to ride this thing out to
the end.

Henry takes a breath of low-tide river air and steps on board.
The boat is a double-decker, tricked-out ferry. White lights laced
along the rails of both tiers shine in the graying dusk. A string quartet is playing jazz in the back of the boat, so he heads toward the
front, where he recognizes and tries to avoid eye contact with two
American beer distributors and a guy who claims to be an advance
textile scout from the Gap.

Hello! My name is Francis.

"I didn't know you had a first name."

Madden tries to smile, but it comes off more as a grimace. He's
not wearing a suit or anything close to business casual. He's in camouflage cargo pants and a sleeveless wrinkled white T-shirt stained
with sweat and a spray pattern of blood. He raises an unlikely flute
of champagne and taps glasses with Henry. "Thanks for getting me
in on this. I was running out of places to hide."

After Madden guzzles his champagne, Henry hands over his
glass as if it were expected and Madden drinks that as well. "What's
going on?"

"What's going on," Madden replies, "is I'm done here. I took
some calculated risks that didn't quite work out, and right now
some people are fixing to bring me down. Did you come through
the capital?"

Henry shakes his head. "We came from the country. Why?"

"Fucking chaos in the streets. Smashing storefronts. Banging on
the palace gates. I heard demonstrators took over the airport today."

Henry thinks of Shug's warning about flying today. A horn blows
twice and the boat begins to drift away from its slip. "You all right?"

For the first time in the conversation Madden makes eye contact
with him. "I lost everything, mate. I've got nothing."

A waitress with a tray of champagne approaches and they each grab a flute. Near the far rail Henry thinks that he sees . . . yes, it's Audrey. For some reason she's decided to fulfill her obligation to represent the same nonexistent company as he does. She smiles wanly at Henry and raises her glass. He asks Madden, "Why'd you come to this thing, then?" '

"A few days ago I thought I could do some business here, try to change my fortunes, but now it's flat-out asylum. My half-assed ties with the prince are pretty much all I've got, and those're dwindling by the second."

"I heard the king died."

Madden looks right and left as he thinks about this. His hands are trembling as they touch his cheek, his eyes. Finally he lights a cigarette and says, after exhaling, "That makes sense. That explains a lot."

"I imagine this is why he's not here."

Madden laughs. "Here? I'd be surprised if the little bugger is still in the country."

"What will happen to him?"

"They're Buddhists. If he loses the military and there is a coup, they will ask him to leave peacefully. And if he doesn't do that or hasn't already fled, I imagine they'll bloody well kill him."

Henry looks out at the river. As the sun drops behind the western peaks, the purple smog cluster in the surrounding sky deepens like a bruise. "I got fired a few hours ago."

"Congratulations. That makes your presence here more confounding than mine. Where's Maya?"

"Gone," Henry answers. "She deserves better than me."

Madden stares at him. "I spoke to some people about your plan with the straws. UNICEF. Soda people. There might be something there for you."

"Thanks. What about you, then? Is there still something here for you?"

Madden looks at him, then, before heading inside for another drink, he shakes his head and says, "I did some things, my friend."

On a video monitor mounted beneath the overhang for the second deck, a message from the prince and king begins to play. While the prince offers greetings in French, English, German, Spanish, and Galadonian, the first in a series of explosions sounds on shore, from the direction of the capital. Fireballs rise in the southern sky, and small-arms tracers arc through the darkness closer to shore.

"It is a royal fireworks display," explains one of the organizing hosts, even though no one asked for an explanation. Now the king is onscreen, seemingly talking to camera, seemingly holding a tennis racket, seemingly alive. But Henry knows better. They all know better. The more the host talks, it seems, the more the group drinks. Someone—is it the Walmart guy?—has begun to pass around a hashish pipe.

Now the host is saying something to Henry's group about the king, something about his extraordinary vitality and athletic ability. But no one is listening. They are all looking at a bend in the water upstream, where the river is burning down. Or is it up? More than a hundred feet up.

The host is talking faster, making less sense with every word, as they're drawn closer to the flames. The engines ease and the boat slows as it approaches a village illuminated by great waterborne tongues of fire.

It should come as a surprise when a man in a red hood rounds the corner from the starboard side and smashes the host in the back of the head with the blunt face of a machete, toppling him, mid-lie. But it doesn't.

Hello! My name is Potentially Bloody Insurrection!

Before the man hits the deck, Henry looks back at the monitor. The familiar montage of the deceptively active king is playing. The flash of a bomb strobes against the base of the mountains upstream. Before the sound registers, Henry raises his champagne flute, drains it, and lets it drop onto the deck. Three more men in red bandannas appear, holding machetes. One turns and smashes the TV monitor with the blade, bringing to an early close the dead king's fabricated hunting trip.

The quartet, for some reason, continues to play, *Titanic*-like.

The boat briefly slows and then reverses the engines. New captain, Henry thinks. New itinerary.

They are herded into a group at the front of the boat. A separate group that presumably includes Madden and Audrey is contained on the stern. One of their captors tells them that no one will get hurt as long as they cooperate. "There is a coup going on in the capital. The king has been dead, perhaps for days, and the prince, who chose to withhold this information from his people—well, he is gone. Seeking asylum in a land of excess."

The congressman steps forward. "What are you going to do with us? Do you know who is on this boat?"

"We know exactly who is on this boat. Corporate criminals. Enemies of culture. And a minor politician who needed a runoff to win his election and whom no one would miss should tragedy befall him on this river."

They begin to circle in a slow-motion holding pattern between the flames and the river village. Two men with machetes stand in front of them, saying nothing, letting them drink and smoke and talk among themselves. Henry separates himself from the others as much as his captors will allow and watches the burning river and the agitated villagers.

The flaming water reminds him of the flawed chemistry of his former backyard pool. Maybe some things need to be set on fire before they can be made right. He wonders if setting the pool on fire would have gotten Rachel's attention. Or his.

"I'm not gonna stand for this!" It's the Walmart guy. Drunk. Stoned. Used to getting his way. "I want to talk to your manager immediately." After they strike the Walmart guy with the blunt side of a machete, Henry is fairly certain they are going to kill them all, but then again, if that were the case, they probably would have used the blade.

His phone vibrates. Service on a flaming river in a third world country during a coup. Someone should make a commercial. It's Giffler. No shit. "Are you all right?"

Henry watches two men drag the Walmart guy into the cabin. Along the river's edge flames lap at the interior upholstery of a late-model Toyota Prius. "Oh, I'm doing just fine, Giff. Why do you ask?"

"Hey, it was not my call. But you know, you should have seen the writing on the wall."

"You are right. I should have seen the writing on the wall of my nonexistent office."

"What you need is a nice tour of Bangkok's red-light district before coming home. I'll make sure T&E pushes it through."

"Thanks, Giff."

"And if, you know, you need any references or anything moving forward, you know I'll always be here for you."

"That is so good to know. Thank you again, Giff."

Out of curiosity, as they continue to circle the flaming river, he checks his messages. Why not? Rachel heard about the fate of Happy Mountain Springs on the business news and wants to know what kind of package he got, how this will affect his standing in the profit-sharing plan. Warren in Bangalore sends his professional condolences and urges Henry to visit him in Mumbai before going home "to find yourself."

Then, from Meredith, the announcement that she is using her severance to go to India to have breast reduction surgery, because it's much more affordable there and because, well, Warren is there, and he is really happy, and they are going to give it a go. Fucking Warren, Henry thinks, looking for stars through the thickening smoke. Warren with his fulfilling job and his unflappable ideals and now the company of a T. S. Eliot–quoting one-time big-boob web mistress who might be the most authentic person he has ever met. Good for him. Good for them.

The last message is a day-old video attachment from Norman that Henry never got around to watching. Titled *The Weight of Make-Believe Water,* it opens on a group of malnourished, impoverished kids straight out of a Save the Children commercial squatting on a sunbaked desert floor somewhere in Darfur. But as the camera pulls back we see superimposed just beyond them two impeccably dressed Western businessmen and a businesswoman laughing and standing around a five-gallon Happy Mountain Springs water-cooler. Just as one of the children turns to look at them, they flicker and vanish, cooler and all. The next vignette shows a battered well bucket being raised on a rope in a dusty African village. But when the bucket appears, it isn't filled with well water, it's filled with a half-dozen superimposed icy cold one-liter bottles of Happy Mountain Springs water, all of which flicker and disappear just before a desperate mother's hand can grasp them. The same appearing/disappearing sequence plays out as fifty-foot bottles of Happy Mountain Springs water and HMS coolers and logos flicker on desert floors, in crowded refugee camps, at the edge of a foaming, chemically fouled river not unlike the one on which Henry is precariously floating. The sound track is Massive Attack's instrumental "Two Rocks and a Cup of Water." After the final sequence, which culminates with the powerful and sentimental propaganda of a match dissolve from a drop of HMS cooler water to the teardrop in a parched child's eye, Henry closes the screen and stares at his captors. He raises a finger and gets the attention of the leader. The young man waves him forward.

"Really, what are you going to do with us?"

"Hold you captive until we get our way."

"And if you don't?"

The man shrugs, looks at his machete.

Henry stares at him for a moment and smiles.

"What?"

"I have an idea. Are you the leader?"

He begins to nod yes, then says, "No."

Upstairs in the pilothouse, the view is even more dramatic, because it provides a 360-degree panorama of the pyrotechnics. His suggestion for the three men gathered is simple:

"If you kill us, you will turn the world against you and no one will want to do business with you, let alone give you an ounce of aid. If you make an example of us by showing us the door, by escorting us out of your country for excessive greed, for an assault on your culture, your purity, the world will listen. Kick our asses out and make a show of it—film the fucking thing. Tell us to come back with a more humane and culturally sensitive business plan. If you do that . . . well, besides the fact that I would remain alive, it would be a lot better."

He watches them look at each other. He feels good, relieved even, because it seems to have registered to some degree. One of the men, presumably the leader, glances at one of the guards and gestures toward the door. As the guard steps forward, Henry realizes that he has seen him before. It is Maya's friend. Her brother. Small world. Smaller country. As he nears, Henry smiles and begins to raise a hand to say hello, perhaps to shake, but his once and former girlfriend's brother swings the butt end of his machete handle against Henry's temple.

Last Drop

An hour and a half later, two rust-pocked school buses appear at the boat slip at the edge of the village. A dozen men in red bandannas lead the fallen front men and women of industry down the gangway and onto the idling vehicles. Henry takes a window seat in the back of the first bus and looks out the window. The river is still burning, but with less intensity. He hasn't seen the flash of explosives or tracers for a while. Some of the villagers are shouting and banging on the side of their buses, but most are more intent on boarding and looting the royal ferry. He watches Madison Ellison and then Audrey stumble past, both sobbing, both, thankfully, headed toward the other bus. And there is Madden, his face bruised and matted with blood that wasn't there when he came on board. Two men hold him by the arms and a third walks behind him with a half-cocked riot stick. Madden looks up at Henry's somber face as he passes, and winks.

On the black empty road to wherever they're taking them, he closes his eyes, thinks of a song, "Step Right Up" by Tom Waits, and sleeps.

Bright lights, a film crew, and several thousand angry Galadonians greet the buses at the airport. As he walks a gauntlet of red-clad guards, he is shoved and tripped and spat upon. Lying on the

concrete sidewalk, waiting to crawl into the terminal, he is frightened yet exhilarated. Certain that this is all for and because of him.
The spectacle. The sparing of questionable lives. The public ban-
ishment of the greedy interlopers, chronicled for posterity.

Inside the airport it is silent. The demonstrators are kept outside, and only a few dozen rebels stand guard as the soon-to-be-
released hostages shuffle toward the terminal's lone gate. They stop
and form a line, waiting to be processed at a makeshift customs
desk. He notices Maya's brother standing guard several spots ahead
of him.

"Excuse me."

Her brother looks to see who is watching, then approaches him.
"What?"

"What happened to the Australian?"

"Madden?"

Henry smiles, nods. "Yes. He's leaving too, right?"

The young man stares at Henry but doesn't answer.

"You know," Henry says, "he did some good here too. He wasn't
all bad."

The man smiles. "No, he wasn't. I imagine no one is. But apparently he was bad enough."

The line moves slowly. Henry's mind drifts. At one point a man taps
his shoulder. He says he represents the largest Coca-Cola distributor
in Asia. "A friend of yours pointed you out to me earlier, before . . .
well, you know, before this. Big Aussie."

"Madden?"

"That's it. He told me that you had some admirable ideas."

Henry stares at the man. "He was a good soul."

The man smiles. "If by 'good' you mean full of life, then you are
correct. Anyway, here." He hands Henry a business card. "Call me
when and if your life regains a bit of normalcy."

A few minutes later, he's tapped on the shoulder by Maya's brother.
"Follow me."

Henry sighs and follows him across the terminal to the entrance to a small office. Outside the office stands Shug, who nods and jerks his head for Henry to go inside.

When she sees him, Maya hugs him and touches her hand to the most recent rising bruise on his temple. "I'm sorry this happened."

"I'm sorry too. But for the best, right?"

She looks through the doorway at the line of foreigners. "My brother said this was your idea."

"Sometimes they actually work out."

She smiles. "The other thing, the way it turns out, it wouldn't have mattered."

"I thought everything mattered. Every gesture. Even my presence in this room."

"You're right. It does. It did. They won't let you stay, you know. Legally. I tried."

He nods.

"But perhaps someday you can come back."

He nods again, hugs her, and says, "I'd like that."

She doesn't walk with him back to the line. They won't allow it. At the desk a small man who reminds Henry of the prince looks at his papers and asks him what his final destination will be.

He touches the bruise on his temple and answers with another question. "What are my choices?"

Acknowledgments

Thanks to everyone who told me their vasectomy stories and tolerated my graphic and inappropriate follow-up questions. Thanks to Jonathan Swift for the Grand Academy of Lagado, upon which my magical mountain kingdom of Galado was partially based. Thanks to the new and constant friends who help, inform, assist, and provide life to my work in so many ways, including the families Othmer, Spallina, Sobieski, Wollman, Gagnon, Holiday, and Griffith; to Kleber Menezes, Lisa Goore, Tracy Spinney, Corey Rakowski, John McNally, Jonathan Evison, Rick Webb, Eva McCloskey, Benjamin Palmer, Steve Wax, Matt Comito, Richard Nash, Mark D'Arcy, David Sable, Rick Boyko, Mark Fenske, and the amazing Cindy Gallop of ifwerantheworld.com; to Susan Ellingwood of the *New York Times*, Jonah Bloom of *Advertising Age, Knock* magazine, Dave Daley at fivechapters.com, Elizabeth Eaves at Forbes.com, the four guys at threeguysonebook.com, my Fiction Files pals at Goodreads.com, Ron Hogan at Galleycat.com, my friends at the Mahopac Public Library, and all of my bookseller, bookblogger, and booklover friends on Twitter; to Sylvie Rabineau at Rabineau Wachter, Mark Johnson and Tom Williams at Gran Via Productions; to Zach Miller at Reason Pictures; to David Gernert, Erika Storella, and Matt Williams at the Gernert Company; to Bill Thomas, Melissa Ann Danaczko, John Pitts, Alison Rich, and Rachel Lapal at Doubleday; and

finally, thanks to the many people at charitable organizations working around the world to provide clean water to everyone, and
who need our continued support, including Tapproject.org and
Charitywater.org.